THE LIE

HELEN DUNMORE

ISIS
LARGE PRINT
Oxford

First published in Great Britain 2014
by
Hutchinson
one of the publishers in The Random House Group Ltd.

Published in Large Print 2014 by ISIS Publishing Ltd.,
7 Centremead, Osney Mead, Oxford OX2 0ES
by arrangement with
The Random House Group Ltd.

CIP data is available for this title from the British Library

ISBN 978–0–7531–5376–5 (hb)
ISBN 978–0–7531–5377–2 (pb)

Printed and bound in Great Britain by
T. J. International Ltd., Padstow, Cornwall

If any question why we died
Tell them, because our fathers lied.
Rudyard Kipling

CHAPTER
ONE

The use of veils and coats of a colour to match the background is useful. If near sandbags, an empty sandbag worn over the head is a good disguise. Against an earth background a brown gauze veil, against grass a green one are both difficult to detect. Grass, weeds, wood or branches may give concealment.

He comes to me, clagged in mud from head to foot. A mud statue, but a breathing one. The breath whistles in and out of him. He stands at my bed-end. Even when the wind is banging over the roof that I've bodged with corrugated iron, it's very quiet. He doesn't speak. Sometimes I wish that he would break the silence, but then I'm afraid of what he might say. I can smell the mud. You never forget the reek of it. Thick, almost oily, full of shit and rotten flesh, cordite and chloride of lime. He has got himself coated all over with it. He's camouflaged. He might be anything, but I know who he is.

I light my candle and get out of bed, because I know I won't sleep again. The wind bangs, and behind it I hear the sea booming at the base of the cliffs. It's night, but I can still work. I light my lantern and get out needle and thread from the sewing box Mary Pascoe left to me. My trousers want patching. They are good, heavy corduroy, worn thin at the knees. I may not be nimble at sewing, but I can get the job done. They want leather patches but I haven't got leather, so I use cloth from inside the pockets. I sew the patches all around, as firm and as neat as may be. I look at my work and then I go round again until I am sure that the patches will hold.

When I look up out of the dazzle of stitches, he's gone. At the foot of my bed there's nothing but the heavy pine box with Mary Pascoe's initials burned into it. The box was black with smoke, but I've scoured it.

I think about how he comes. Does he displace the box? Is he in it, or is it in him? I shouldn't think of it. It makes my mind dazzle, like my eyes.

Tomorrow I'll plant main-crop potatoes. I've prepared the ground. In October, soon after I came here, I dug the earth deeply and then covered it with rotted seaweed from the pile that Mary Pascoe carried up from the shore, when she was still able. She said that seaweed made the potatoes grow clean of disease. My seed potatoes lie ready in their trays, sprouting. The sprouts are strong.

Frederick. I can say his name aloud now, without danger. He won't come again tonight. I *have* thought that if he ever came by day, I'd take him to the horse-trough in the next field and wash him until white flesh appeared. Or he could stand by the stream while I poured water over him, bucket after bucket. It would be like taking new potatoes out of the soil. But I know that he'd be back again the next night, with the mud still on him. It never dries or forms a crust. It is always wet and shining, like the eyes of a rat in the back of a dugout.

2

He's been out there in the wind and rain, rain sluicing over him, turning the land to mud that can drown you.

A man stuck in the mud can't free himself. He needs two men to help him. You lay a piece of wood down on either side of him. You work him out, one boot at a time. It's a slow job. Often there isn't time and you have to leave him. Usually it's not that the mud is so deep. It doesn't come above his knees but he can't free himself, and if he loses his balance and tips forward, he will drown. You hear the cries of men caught like that. But that was later. Frederick died before the worst of the mud.

I have a calendar on my wall and I mark off the days. I keep records of how many rows I've planted: early potatoes, turnips, carrots, beetroot, spring cabbages and all the rest. This mild spring has made the earth soft and ready. I've planted gooseberry bushes, because they'll stand the wind. Mary Pascoe made hedging around her vegetable patch. She didn't look after her cottage: she stuffed her windows with rags and let birds nest in the chimney, but she always knew how to make her bit of land feed her. She left me the cottage and the land around it, which maybe never belonged to her at all, but which she'd made her own. *Why shouldn't she have her bit of land,* my mother used to say, *when there's others that own half the county?* Mary Pascoe left me her goat and her chickens. She used to keep a pig, she said, but I don't remember that.

I knew her more than the other children did, because of my mother's friendship for her. I'd see her striding into town, with a basket of eggs on a strap. Sometimes,

Frederick and I met her on the shore, picking mussels, when we were walking out to Senara or beyond. Me and Frederick, side by side, swinging out. We had bread and cheese in our pockets, and he might have brought chocolate, or a handful of plums. He shared between us so easily that you couldn't tell what was his and what was mine. I never met anyone else who had that gift, until I was in the army. We had poetry books, or rather Frederick brought them from his father's library, and I read them. Frederick was going to be a lawyer. He'd stayed on at school, gone upcountry to Truro for his education, and then farther still to boarding school.

I left school when I was eleven, a year before I ought to have done, but in the circumstances a blind eye was turned. My mother needed my wages. She had no other family to provide for her. For years, when I was a child, she went out to clean in the big houses: Lezard House, four or five of the houses along The Row, Carrick House in the summer season, when the family that owned it were down from London. When I was ten she had rheumatic fever, and after that she hadn't the strength for cleaning. She was soon out of breath walking uphill, no matter how slowly she went. Sometimes she had to lean on me. I hated it. I'd like to think I gave her my arm willingly, but the truth is that her weakness frightened me, and made me ashamed of us, the two of us, when I wanted to be proud. Bolts of shame would go through me as we struggled up the hill, like flies in milk.

I remember how I knelt on the bare boards of the bedroom, on the night my mother was so ill that she didn't know I was in the room. I'd never known her not to come to me at the lightest sound, if I woke from a bad dream. But now she didn't know me. Her eyes went beyond me. She was talking all the time, in a low quick mutter, but not to me. I heard my father's name and my grandmother's. She cried out for them once, her voice rusty and tearing, and she tried to heave herself off the pillow, but Mrs Jelbert held her. I sank down to the floor, and pressed my face into the quilt. All the prayers I'd ever been taught jumbled in my mouth.

"You go on downstairs, boy," said Mrs Jelbert, but I couldn't. "Don't you fear, my chiel. We'll slock 'er round." I was beyond believing her. A black wind of terror blew through me and I prayed for my mother until sweat trickled down my back. No one answered me, nothing spoke.

Mrs Jelbert sent a boy for Dr Sanders. He came that night, and stayed until morning. He refused to let her die, even though it was clear that she had left us in her mind. She was with those other ones, those ghosts I'd barely known but who called her more strongly than my own voice could call her. But Dr Sanders wouldn't let her stay with them. He bent over her, hauling her back, hurting her I thought from the way she cried out.

I'm not sure that my mother ever came back again, truly, but she was good at pretending. She got better. All through, Dr Sanders treated her for nothing, and afterwards he bestirred himself to find work for me, and settled it with school that I was to leave early. I was

5

taken on as gardener's boy at Mulla House, two miles' walk from the town.

"You're the man of the house now, Daniel," Dr Sanders said to me.

The doctor called me Daniel in deference to my mother's wish, although most people called me Dan. She always said, "Daniel is his christened name." It may seem strange that a doctor whose house my mother cleaned should show her this respect, but it was a fact. My mother was always someone you wanted to please. She was dark-eyed and dark-haired and her face was made so that you had to turn and look at it again, to see what it was that had struck you so. Even I felt it, and I was her son. It was anguish to me when other people looked at her. One of the artists who came to the town wanted to paint her, but she wouldn't even answer him. I can see her now, drawing her shawl around her face, turning away. She was a widow. What she had left was her good name. The artist wouldn't take no for an answer, and annoyed her more by saying that she had "the most spiritual regard he had ever seen, outside Italy". Spiritual! She was hungry. We were both hungry, in the years after my father died.

I was three years old when he was killed. He was leading Brittan's cart on a steep downhill, with a brake on the wheel. The brake slipped and gave way, the cart came down on the horse which stumbled and plunged so that my father was flung sideways against a wall. Even then it wouldn't have been serious, but a protrusion of granite caught his temple. He was

6

twenty-two, barely a year older than I am now. My mother was twenty. There was no insurance.

Soon it will be light. Nothing visits me in the daylight. There's only the wind soughing, the wrinkling of the sea even on the quietest days. I dig, and mend the chicken wire. The cottage and the land are mine now. Mary Pascoe's nanny goat, her ten chickens, the midden, the little stream that barely grows wider than a child could step over, the clean, difficult land, full of stones. She grew too old to tend them. Her eyes were milky and had lost the wildness that scared us when we were children, but she still knew me when I came along the path with my pack. She said, "Is that you, Daniel Branwell?" and I said yes. Then she said, "Come in, my chiel."

That was the first time I ever heard of anyone going inside Mary Pascoe's cottage. It was full of smoke, and the walls were black with it. The house and everything in it was kippered. I coughed until my eyes watered, but she seemed untroubled. There were other smells, of age and sickness and the two cats that she used to keep, which twined around her legs and gave her the reputation of a witch. I'd always known that she was no such thing. The cats are dead now. My mother used to visit her, taking a bunch of yellow roses from our yard, the flowers no bigger than buttons but sweet-smelling. They talked on the threshold, never inside the house. I was jealous of those visits.

Mary Pascoe gave me a cup of sage tea. She knew that I'd been in France but she asked nothing about it. "Where are you living now, Daniel?" she asked me. She also knew that our cottage had gone back to the landlord, because there was no one to pay the rent.

"Here and there," I said. I asked her if I might make a shelter from corrugated iron and canvas, on the edge of her land. She nodded. She told me where the spring was, and that I should dig myself a latrine. She had no doubt I'd know how to do it, having been in the army. Neither had she any hesitation in mentioning such things.

"Come in when you want a warm," she said. She'd made the sage tea in her black kettle, and even that tasted of smoke. She moved surely, feeling for things. I wondered how much sight she had left.

"I went to see your mother before she died," she said. I started as if electricity had gone through me. By the time I'd come home, my mother was already in the grave we'd visited together every Sunday throughout my childhood: my father's grave. The wind used to pucker up the grass, and the sun shone on her hair as she knelt to tidy and tend. Below us, the sea glittered. I never remember it raining: perhaps she only took me there on fine days. She would talk about him sometimes. That's how I learned most of what I know about my father.

When I came back, the grave was narrower than I remembered it. I couldn't see how there would be space for me there, as well as them. I wanted to know what my mother had said and how she'd looked before she died, but no one would tell me. The doctor said she died peacefully. I didn't believe a word of it.

8

"I found some buds on that rose of hers, and put them in her hand," said Mary Pascoe. She said nothing more on the subject, then or ever. She stirred the sage tea and said that it could do with sweetening. Even with her milky eyes she still seemed more like a bird than a woman. We used to call her a buzzard when her cloak flapped in the wind. Now she was hunched and silent. I was glad that the humanness in her seemed to have been parched away, so that she was light enough to fly.

That was five months ago. She never ventured as far as my shelter. I dug myself a latrine pit, and boiled water from the stream. I knew it was pure enough, but I had army habits now. I dug a trench around the back of my shelter, to carry away the winter rains. I had money. My mother had saved as much as she could from the pay I sent her. She put it away in the tobacco tin that belonged to my father. If she hadn't saved it, she would have been warmer and better fed, but the doctor said it would have made no difference. The valves of her heart were damaged by the rheumatic fever she had when I was a boy, and it was her heart that killed her.

I never went into town. I would walk to Tremellan, or Senara. On market days I walked as far as Simonstown, to be there when prices dropped at the end of the day. I fed Mary Pascoe's hens for her and soon I was taking care of them entirely. She said I should have the eggs, because she couldn't stomach them now. She still drank the goat's milk, but there was plenty of that for both of us. I remember when she used to make goat's cheeses, wrap them in nettles and sell them, but such things

9

were beyond her now. All the time, I was thinking about how the land could be used. She had been famous for her vegetables once. The sweetest and earliest potatoes came from Mary Pascoe's patch. She grew white lilies and sold them in the church square. But now, the hill was taking her land back to itself. Much of her hedging had disappeared. The fencing around the chicken run was in poor condition. Bracken, furze and briars were swallowing her land, and stones were breeding in it like rabbits. I began to clear it. Of course I knew that I would be observed. This is my country. I know how many eyes it has.

On the afternoon of January the fourteenth I heard her calling to me, her voice high and wild. She was like a curlew, I thought, because I was still trying to put a name to the kind of bird she was. I ducked my head and went into the black cottage.

She lay in her nest of rags. She looked up at me, but her eyes were now skeined over with milk, and completely sightless. She wanted water, so I fetched her a cup and held it while she drank. She was hot. I took her wrist and felt her pulse, which was rapid but light as a thread. I'd seen the doctor do this with my mother.

"Shall I fetch the doctor?" I asked, but she moved her head from side to side: no. I saw that she was gathering her strength to speak. I gave her more water and told her I'd mended the fence of the chicken run. I was glad, really, that she didn't want the doctor. He would come, and then more people would come after him. She was gathering herself for an immense effort. She took more water, coughed, and then said, "I want to lie here, not under a stone in the town. You'll do that for me, Daniel."

When I say that she said this, I mean that she brought it out between deep, harsh breaths, and twice a coughing fit stopped her. I was afraid she would die saying it. There was sweat all over her face.

"You'll stay here after me, Daniel," she said. I nodded, then remembered that she couldn't see me, and said: "I will." It was enough for me, to hear her say that. After this she was exhausted and slept for a while. I stayed with her because I was afraid that if I went back to my work she might be too weak to call me. The fire was nearly out, so I put more wood on it. Smoke was better for her than cold. Outside, the light was going, and it began to rain. I thought of the pliers I'd left outside, at the chicken run, but they would still be there tomorrow and I could oil them before they had a chance to rust. She opened her eyes and looked about blindly. I thought she wanted more water and I held the cup to her lips, but she moved her head away.

"Is it Daniel?" she asked. I nodded, then remembered she couldn't see me and said, "Yes, it's Daniel." It seemed as if she were searching my face, and then looking to my side and beyond me. I knew that she could see nothing. She said, "Who have you brought with you?"

CHAPTER
TWO

Dead, disposal of: Bodies of dead men will be taken right away from the trenches to be buried.

It will frequently happen that substantial buildings are found close to the selected line of defence. The question then arises whether to occupy them or to demolish them.

I buried her at the very edge of her land, at its highest point. I knew what she wanted, and there was no sense in waiting. If my mother had been alive, I would have gone to tell her, but I couldn't think of anyone else in the town who would want to come to Mary Pascoe's burial. Or would have any right to come. I dug down, always expecting to strike a shelf of granite, but the soil was deep enough. I dug her a decent grave, and lined it with dry brown bracken and branches of the rosemary bush that grew close to her door. I wrapped her in a piece of the army canvas that I hadn't needed for my shelter. The smell of her was bad when I lifted her, like a bird that you find crawling with lice and maggots after it has gone away to die in the foot of a hedge. But I didn't mind it. I had worked all day on her grave and I was sweating in spite of the cold. After the burial and the infilling of her grave, I stamped the earth down to settle it. I rolled a granite boulder to the head of the grave. I knew how quickly green would cover the turned earth.

The stream was running full after the heavy rains we'd had. I filled a bucket, took it to the outhouse where the goat was tethered, and stripped off my clothes. I thought that every pore of my body would be black with dirt, but my skin was white where my clothes had covered it. My hands and wrists, neck and face still held the tan of exposure. I washed myself with household soap, and when I was finished I sluiced the bucket over my head and over my entire body, until I was shaking with cold. I had one full change of clothes, and I put them on. That was when it came to me that I wouldn't sleep in my shelter that night. I would sleep in the cottage.

I told no one about Mary Pascoe's death. At first I didn't know who to tell. She never went near church or chapel. The people who used to visit her to buy vegetables, eggs or goat's milk had fallen away. My mother was her friend, perhaps, but I couldn't think of another. If I told the doctor, he'd say that I should have called him. He would have come, I'm sure, because he was known for treating those who couldn't afford to pay him, while he took his guineas from the big houses. There was nothing he could have done to help her. Mary didn't want him anyway. She wanted to die under her own hedge. She'd have feared the workhouse most, because it's said that if you die there, your body is taken for dissection. I don't think Dr Sanders would have sent her to the workhouse, but some busybody in the parish might have thought it a duty to have her conveyed to the infirmary.

After a few days it was too late to tell anyone. She had lived indoors for long enough that she wouldn't be missed. I couldn't remember the last time she had walked into town.

The cottage was my first task. I had to get the smell out of it. I opened the door wide, but the two windows that fronted the cottage had cracked or broken panes, and their wooden frames were rotten. I pulled out the rags with which Mary Pascoe had stuffed the broken panes, and examined the glass and wood carefully. I could bodge the sills. In time I could buy new panes of glass, and putty. For now I replaced the rags, and left the windows as they were.

The chimney wanted sweeping. I would do this first, so that the soot could fall and be cleaned away with the rest of the dirt. I had Mary Pascoe's broom, and an old ladder with rungs that didn't look rotten. The ground at the back of the cottage was higher than at the front. I scythed and trampled down the brambles that hooked from the hillside to the cottage wall, set down the ladder and tested it. I was well hidden. I grasped the side of the ladder with my right hand, and the broom in my left, and mounted the rungs to the top. First I cleared the guttering, which was packed with moss and rubbish. I needed to get higher, on to the roof itself. The slates had fallen away in parts and the roof had been patched with corrugated iron, rusted now. I would patch it further.

14

I tested the guttering with my hand and it held firm. Besides, it wasn't so far to fall. From the top of the ladder I could push myself up, twist sideways and get my foot into the guttering, but I had to be sure that, having climbed, I could get down again. I thought that I could.

It was easier than it looked. The guttering cupped my foot as I spreadeagled myself on the roof, and pushed upwards. The corrugated iron gave me another foothold, and then I was there, grasping the ridge piece, and in another moment I was astride. I was strong, I knew it, with the life I'd had, two years of it, and then the miles I walked each day and the ground I dug. The chimney was squat. I grasped it and looked out.

I seemed many miles higher, rather than the fifteen feet or so that I had climbed. I gripped the roof between my thighs as if I were riding a horse. There was the brown, bare, sinewy land running down to the cliffs. There were the Garracks, and Giant's Cap, and the Island. There was the swell, like a muscle under the sea, moving in long, slow pulses to Porthgwyn. I looked west and saw rainclouds, damson-coloured and making a bloom of shadow on the sea. It was a cold, still day and eastward the land humped and widened from the lighthouse to St Anne's Head.

I looked towards the grey huddle of the town. My eyes began to hurt, and I turned away. I must sweep the chimney. I didn't want anyone who might be working on the land or walking the paths to see me up on the roof. I got hold of my broom, awkwardly because of the angle, then gripped it lower down the shaft and plunged it into the chimney.

It wouldn't go down cleanly. I poked and prodded. I twisted the handle round so that the broom would drill itself down into the darkness. The rain was coming closer and I didn't want to clamber down from the roof when the slates were slippery with wet. I felt the broom grating, grinding almost, as if against something more solid than a bird's nest.

It broke through. The broom brushed against the sides and then dabbed into the void. It was as much as I could do, and my arm ached with the effort of raising the broom and plunging it up and down. I lifted it for the last time, black and thick with muck, and threw it down the roof, clear of the gutter to the ground. I cursed myself for not having thought of chicken wire. I could have brought some up with me, and covered the chimney top to keep birds out.

It was raining hard by the time I'd climbed down and put away the ladder. I went into the cottage, thinking of shelter, but the filth drove me outside again. It seemed impossible that so much dirt had come down one chimney. I took breaths of the rainy air, then forced myself back inside.

Crushed and broken birds' nests lay in the fireplace, some of them caught on the chain where the kettle hung. On the grate lay a mess of white bones and feathers. Soot was caked and lumped all around, and a finer, sticky coating covered floor, furniture, walls. She must have burned coal for years, in the days when she was strong enough to push her handcart down to town.

Later, she'd burned wood and furze and anything that came to hand.

I touched the table and my hand came away black. I couldn't think where to begin. For the first time I thought of leaving the cottage, dismantling my shelter, packing up the canvas and making my way to another place. I didn't know where.

I needed hot water to scrub away the filth, but until I could light a fire there would be no hot water. I didn't want to make a fire outside. It's the kind of thing that draws attention.

Very well then. I took the broom and washed it in the stream, until the water ran black. I brought it in, wet as it was, and began to sweep out the wide, craggy granite fireplace. Time after time I washed the broom, swept, washed the broom again. I was wet with sweat, and glad of the coolness each time I went out into the rain. It fell so thick now that it had blurred into a mist, wiping out coast and town.

The tethered goat was noisy in the outhouse. I had forgotten to milk her. I washed my hands again, up to the elbows, and went in to her. She was agitated, rolling her yellow eyes at me and kicking out, but I knew how to deal with her and she was used to me now. She ought to have been pegged out at the far end of the land, but I had left her in all day. I milked her and drank some of the milk. There was a tang of wild garlic in it, from the bundle of greenstuff I'd brought in to her that morning. I couldn't remember why it was that I hadn't pegged her out. She was calmer now.

I lit the fire. The chimney drew the flames straight up, pulling them like ropes. The wood was blackthorn and the fire burned clear, after the first smokiness of damp. I sat back on my heels and opened my body to the heat, then after a minute I remembered what I had to do and why I had lit the fire. The kettle was dirty, so I washed it inside and out, filled it from the stream, hooked it to the chain and swung it over the hottest part of the fire. I would fill the kettle over and over, and scrub the floors, the walls and even the ceiling until they were clean. I would scrub down the deal table, the two chairs, the bedstead and the box. The bedding I had already buried, and I would drag the mattress out into the air to purify it. I had my own blanket to sleep in.

It took all the rest of the day, and most of the night. I worked by candlelight because I had no oil for the lamp. I thought that people might see the warm light flickering in the windows, so I drew the curtains across. I had beaten the dirt out of them, and would wash them on a warmer day. My nose and mouth were full of the acrid reek of soot, but I didn't mind. The scrubbing brush was worn down almost to the wood by the time I had finished. I couldn't sleep on that mattress, so I rolled myself in my blanket in front of the fire, and slept, slept until the birds woke me.

In the light of day, it was another matter. I hadn't cleaned the house as well as I thought, and there was more to do. I found washing soda, packed hard, under the stone sink, and remembered how my mother dissolved it in hot water and scrubbed with her red, raw hands. The washing soda cleaned much better than the household soap had done. The rain had been followed by strong wind and clouds that chased the sun, and I dragged out the mattress and humped it over the barrow. There were stains on the ticking but I scrubbed them away. I would leave it out all day and night, if there was no rain.

I forgot to eat all that day, but I remembered the goat and pegged her out, and when I milked her I drank the milk again.

By nightfall everything was clean. The wind had dropped and it was cold, with the stars swimming above the sea. Venus was so bright she seemed to dance around the moon. I made myself tea with the last pinch I had in my pack, and drank it so thick and black that it made my heart jump. I was very tired. I stood in the doorway of the cottage with the cleanness of it behind me, and the fire still burning, and looked down at the sea. There was almost no moonlight, because the moon was the thinnest crescent, but there was enough starlight to see the black shapes of the rocks. Tomorrow I would clean out the earth closet. I would need to walk to Simonstown anyway, to buy tea and seed, and I would buy Jeyes Fluid there.

At last I went back inside the cottage and closed the door. I had only one candle burning, but it was enough. The kettle sang on the fire. I would wash myself in warm water tonight, at the sink.

I wrapped myself in my blanket, and lay down by the fire. The floor was hard but I was used to sleeping on earth. I thought of the mattress, with the cold night air washing over it. I wrapped my arms around my body and tucked my head down, ready to sleep.

That was when the smell came to me. It was not the old smell of the cottage, not dirty rags or sickness, not soot or the muck I had scraped off the floor. That had all gone. This was a new smell, and an old one too, so familiar that as it touched my throat I gagged.

It was the smell of earth. Not clean earth, turned up by the spade or the fork, to be sunned and watered. This earth had nothing to do with growth. It was raw and slimy, blown apart in great clods, churned to greasy, liquid mud that sucked down men or horses. It was earth that should have stayed deep and hidden, but was exposed in all its filth, corrosive, eating away at the bodies that had to live in it. It breathed into me from its wet mouth.

I rolled myself into a ball. I put my hands over my face, the hands that I'd washed in warm water and soap, but still they stank of earth.

CHAPTER
THREE

There is an insidious tendency to lapse into a passive
and lethargic attitude, against which officers of all ranks
have to be on their guard, and the fostering of the
offensive spirit, under such unfavourable conditions,
calls for incessant attention.

Today the sun shone as if it were June and not the
end of March. I mended the chicken run, sowed
beetroot seed and planted the onion sets. I laid
broken eggshells around the young lettuces to keep
off the slugs. I have put in three rows of carrots,
two of turnips. There is a bristle of green over the
black earth. Everything is orderly. I hoed out
the weeds, and opened and turned the compost
heap.

I have some money left. I feel the weight of the
tin where I keep my coins. I know there are florins,
some sixpences, a few joeys and a heap of copper. I
saw a woman selling bunches of primroses in Turk
Street, and it came to me that I could do the
same. There are more violets in the hedge-banks this
year than I ever remember. You have to set them off
with leaves, fasten them with a wrap of thread, then
douse their heads upside down in cold water so
that they are fresh for morning. There I'd be in Turk
Street, with violets spread in a wooden tray covered

with damp moss. You could sell a bunch for threepence I'm sure.

There'd be people I knew among the market-day crowds. I'd have to speak to them.

The best thing I've bought with my money, apart from vegetable seeds, is the fishing line I use to catch mackerel off the rocks. The fish come in close, nosing for rot. I let down the baited line stealthily, and if the water's clear enough I glimpse the iridescence of the mackerel, twitching under the rocks before they rush for the hooks. Mackerel is a strong fish. Its colour changes quickly in death, and it never tastes as good as when it's first out of the sea. I split the fish down the belly, gut them and cook them within the hour, so that their flesh is white and clean. I keep a few strips back to use as bait. Mackerel are like crabs, which will scramble over themselves to eat their own kind.

I drink milk at midday, and eat the heel of a loaf. The sea shines like pewter. I squat down out of the wind, and smell the wild garlic. I know everything that can be eaten, for five square miles around. Mussels on the rocks, samphire growing around the estuary in season, spider crabs and wild strawberries, blackberries, elderberries, bread and cheese from the hawthorn, new dandelion leaves for salad, chervil, nettles for soup in spring. But it would be a lie to say there was ever enough to do more than blunt our hunger, or flavour the soup my mother made from a handful of bones, potatoes, a parsnip or two, a couple of carrots. Every child in the parish was out after the blackberries, and although I knew the best places, we didn't always have enough sugar to preserve them.

Once Frederick and I milked a cow, secretly, in one of the small fields set with loggans, up beyond Senara towards Bass Head. It was one of those wild little cows they keep there, and it backed off from us, lowering its head and digging its front hooves into the pasture. But slowly, with the two of us chirruping and gentling, we came on, one from each side. Frederick flashed me a triumphant smile as the cow stood still at last, trembling, and let us touch her. I knew how to milk, well enough, and we filled our cupped hands and gulped it down, warm and frothy in our mouths. The farmer would have tanned the hide off us. Frederick said it was a pity we hadn't a pail. We drank and drank, and then we heard a yell and two big lads erupted over the gate. They must have been the farmer's sons. We ran like hell until they stopped chasing us, then we flopped down by a stream. I saw that there was brooklime growing, which Frederick had never tasted. He said it was bitter, and spat it out.

"Why do you eat that muck?"

"It cleans the blood."

He rolled on his back, laughing. Frederick ate meat every day, once if not twice or three times. They had eggs and bacon for breakfast every morning, and kidneys in a dish. His father ate chops, with Worcester sauce, but no one else was allowed them. His father was a mining engineer who had gone out to Australia, not as thousands of other poor men went, in search of work, but to introduce a new type of winding gear. Mr

Dennis took his payment in shares in the mines he worked on. Frederick explained to me how that was better than money. Sometimes he drew a blank, but even so he sailed home three or four times richer than he'd been before. Or richer still, maybe; no one ever knew. He married, and then he built a square granite house surrounded by a high granite wall. It wasn't beautiful, but it would stand for ever. Frederick was going to be educated at the Cathedral School in Truro. But when Frederick was four and his sister Felicia two, their mother became pregnant for the third time. She died of puerperal fever, and the baby died a fortnight after her.

This was how I came to know Frederick. My mother cleaned for the family, and Mrs Dennis had grown fond of her, as people did. After Frederick's mother died, and his father took to work as he might have taken to drink, my mother looked after the children more and more. I might have been jealous, but my mother always had me along with her. I learned the world of Albert House. There was Mrs Stevens who came in to cook, and there was Annie Noble who cleaned now that my mother was so taken up with the two little children. It was the best job my mother ever had, and it lasted three years. I ate at the Dennises' table with Frederick and Felicia, and I grew until I was the tallest boy in my infant class. If either Frederick or Felicia was ill, my mother would stay all night, and a little bed would be put up for me in the slip-room by the nursery.

I make it sound as if everything fitted together. My mother, me, Frederick, Felicia. Mr Dennis mostly a voice behind a closed door, or a pair of long black legs scissoring across the hall as we watched from the top of the stairs. But once he came close.

Felicia had cried all night with the toothache. My mother was to take her over to Simonstown, to the dentist. I had never been to a dentist and I wondered why Felicia cried harder at the news. She was bundled in her coat and hat with a scarf tied around her face, and they went off in the dog cart. Frederick had his handwriting to practise. It was a disgrace, now that he was almost seven. It was high time Frederick was taken in hand.

It was Mr Dennis who said that. His voice was loud through the study door. He had to stay up until the early hours of the morning, my mother said, because of his business. Other black legs, not only Mr Dennis's, scissored to and fro, and bundles of documents lay piled on the hall chest.

Frederick was in the schoolroom, on the first floor. I was there too, lying on my stomach on the rug. I was reading "The Fisherman and His Wife", out of Felicia's *Grimm's Fairy Tales*. The fisherman was stupid, and so was his wife, I thought. They didn't listen to what the sea was telling them. You had to do that. I finished the story and then kicked my heels in the air and thought about whether the whole world could be drowned, if the sea grew angry enough. Frederick wasn't doing his handwriting. He was singing to himself and drawing in the margins.

We both heard the heavy steps in the corridor. Loud, strong footsteps, meant to be heard. The door handle went round. The door opened and there was Mr Dennis, all of him, tall, whiskery, in black from head to foot. He wasn't looking at me, but at Frederick. I shuffled back on my knees, towards the curtain. I knew Mr Dennis mustn't notice me. He threw a glance around the room, unseeing, scorching. I felt it run over me without stopping and I was glad. Mr Dennis strode to the table and picked up Frederick's book. It was covered with little drawings: that was what Frederick always did.

"What's this?" he asked.

Frederick looked up at him. "It's my handwriting book," he said.

"How dare you answer me like that? What's this diabolical mess you've made in it?"

Frederick dropped his head, and said nothing.

"Answer me!"

"It's my handwriting book."

"Handwriting book!" Mr Dennis picked up the book and threw it across the room. "It looks like it. You're as stupid as you're idle. Now fetch it."

I was almost in the curtains now. I felt the cold trickle of winter coming through the glass behind me. I wriggled back. Frederick got up from the table, and went laggingly across to where the book lay on the floor. He glanced at his father before stooping to pick it up, as if he didn't want to turn his back on him.

"Bring it here," said Mr Dennis. Frederick held out the book to him, and Mr Dennis snatched it and hurled it again, hard, into the corner of the room.

"Fetch it!" he said, as if Frederick was a dog, and again, even more slowly, Frederick did so. A third time, Mr Dennis shied the battered book across the room. This time he said nothing, but jerked his head at the book, for Frederick to get it. But Frederick didn't move. Mr Dennis's glance went round the room again, and he saw me cowering in the curtains.

"Get out," he said. I didn't want to. I was afraid of what he'd do to Frederick if there was no one to see it, but I didn't dare defy Mr Dennis. It had been drummed into me to keep out of his way and never come to his notice. I let go of the curtains and began to edge out of the room. There was Frederick, standing still, not fetching the book, not looking at me.

I left the schoolroom, and hid myself behind the grandfather clock on the landing. I heard their voices, a slither of feet, a cry, then the door banged open and Frederick flew through it, skidded across the floor and fell. Mr Dennis was after him. He kicked Frederick with his boot and Frederick's face went forward and banged on the skirting board. Mr Dennis was shouting at him to get up like a man. Frederick scrambled up, on his hands and knees, and backed away from his father towards the stairs. I couldn't see him any more because Mr Dennis was over him, blotting him out. Frederick whimpered and wriggled across the floorboards.

"Get up those stairs!" shouted Mr Dennis in a thick voice as if he was drunk. "Get up those stairs and don't let me see you again." Frederick crawled upstairs with Mr Dennis behind him, kicking and beating him. Each time Frederick tried to get away, Mr Dennis was on him. Each time he left off, Frederick jerked like a fish.

A bell rang below: the front door. There were footsteps and a voice. A woman's voice. Not my mother, or anyone I knew. Mr Dennis stood still, as if he'd forgotten about Frederick. I willed Frederick to run, but he didn't move. Slowly, Mr Dennis settled his jacket. He put up his hands and smoothed his hair. His hands travelled down his face, over his whiskers, as if he was making sure of who he was. Without looking at Frederick, he turned and went away down the stairs.

I slipped out from behind the clock. I was frightened that if the man came back he would kill Frederick. "Frederick!" I whispered. He didn't stir. I went to him and huddled on the stair beside him. He shrank away. "Frederick, it's me." I heard him gulping for air, so loud that someone might hear it. I had to pull hard, jerking him, before he would move. I put my shoulder under his arm, the way I'd seen the big boys do when someone was hurt at a match, and we went down to the landing and along the corridor to the back stairs. We could get out of the house through the scullery door, without going through the hall. Frederick wasn't crying. There was blood on his forehead where he'd fallen against the stairs.

The garden wasn't safe enough. "We'll go down mine," I said. We slipped through the streets and I held Frederick's hand tight because I was scared of the way he looked. Rain was pouring, thicker than ever, and it hid us. No one was about. We went into ours through the yard, and into the house. It was dark and cold in the kitchen without my mother there. "Take off your boots," I said. We went upstairs, and I lifted down the big jug from my mother's washstand and put it on the floor. She kept clean rag in a basket, and I took a piece, soaked it and twisted it, and wiped Frederick's face. The cut wasn't so bad. I wiped off all the blood while Frederick sat there on my bed, not saying a word. He was shivering. I got the quilt from under him and pulled it over us both, and we lay down. Frederick was stiff and cold and I had to push him over to the wall to make room for me. I didn't know what to do. I was scared of the way he wasn't talking. I held on to him tight and after a bit he stopped shivering. I kept on holding him, as tight as I could. I could hear the rain rushing off the gutters and into the launders below. The window square was almost dark, although it was the middle of the day. I wished that Mr Dennis would die and Frederick would live with us for ever.

The rain was still rushing when I woke up, and my mother was there, standing over us with a candlestick. She put out her hand and touched Frederick's face. Already it was going dark with bruises. I knew her so well that I could see the thoughts moving in her. She was afraid.

When Frederick was seven and Felicia five, Mr Dennis remarried. Naturally the new wife didn't like the old order. Felicia made the mistake of clinging to my mother and screaming when her "new mother" tried to take possession of her. Soon we were down the hill again and my mother was back to cleaning. I'd forgotten how to be hungry but I quickly learned again. Even so, those three years of Dennis food set me on. When it came to my army medical at Bodmin Barracks, I was still the tallest in the line.

I've been squatting here too long. The cold has got into me, and my hands are shaking. I grip them tight. The brightness of the day was a deception. I say aloud the name: "Felicia." I daren't say Frederick's name aloud, even out here in the sunlight. I don't know what he'd say if he saw me here, scratching in Mary Pascoe's plot of earth. He wouldn't understand that I'm lucky. Ex-servicemen are selling matches, dusters and fretwork boxes all over London, door to door and on street corners.

I've seen them carted down the line through the muck, the lucky ones on their stretchers. I've joined in with the grunt of "Lucky bastard, he's got a Blighty one." Even a man with his leg hanging at the knee, we thought: He's well out of it, and pictured him going back and back, out of the line. We thought of the hospital ship we'd seen in harbour, on the way out. Now we knew why it was big enough to hold a townful of men.

I get up, and overbalance because my legs are cramped. My clumsiness disturbs something by the wheel of my barrow, where last night's rain has puddled. A toad. It hops, with heavy grace, into a patch of sunlight. I have never thought of a toad as liking sunlight. It hunkers, its legs packed away again, its body pulsing. We used to say there was a jewel in the head of a toad. I remember Jimmy Kitto got hold of one and dug into its forehead to see where the jewel was, but he found nothing. Only blood, and some whitish stuff which might have been its brain.

A jewel. The toad looks at me and I look back. Its eyes might be the jewels. They are hooded and ancient. They are the kind of eyes that believe in nothing but what they see in front of them, and maybe not always that. The toad is so close that I can see the snake-like scaling between its eyes, and the dabs of cream and greenish-brown beneath its chin. Its mouth is a thin line.

For Christ's sake, it's only a toad. I never saw many in France, although often the shell-holes were full of frogs. There are enough slugs here to feed twenty toads. It's waiting for me to go, so that it can slip back into the shade. I put my hand towards it. Into my head there comes a picture of my own hand lifting a piece of granite, smashing it down on the toad. I see the forelegs sticking out from the mash of the body.

These pictures frighten me. They are too sharp and too bright, much brighter than the day around me. They flash on to my mind like the flash of a shell-burst, and they mark it. I put my hand down flat on the earth and press hard, keeping it still. The toad stretches itself and hops leisurely out of the sunlight, and back to its puddle. In the shadow of the barrow, it's almost invisible.

It's good to have toads in a garden. They rid it of pests, and besides, they are company. The hens pother about, picking grubs and insects, but a toad works seriously, all day long.

I'm very tired. I ought not to have let myself think about Frederick. It seems safe enough to do so in the daylight, but there's an afterlife to every thought. I stretch myself, like the toad, to ease my back. From here, I can see the footpath to Senara, although I can't be seen. If anyone walks by, I keep still. They might glance across and notice that Mary Pascoe's land has been dug and planted, as it was years ago. What I fear most is the sight of children. Those terrible pictures rise up in me. I see a child hurled off a cliff, with its petticoats blowing. I see a child on the ground, bloody and broken.

I am afraid to go into crowds. In Turk Street it seems to me that every creature is in disguise. Their skin is a veil to hide the intestines and the raw, slimy flesh within. I see how their bones would split and separate. I see a jagged edge protrude through a thigh or an elbow. I see bodies picked up, torn to pieces, flung on to the ground.

As I ease my back, the sun slides out from the clouds. I look towards the bay and the sea comes out in patches of turquoise, where the white sand lies beneath the water. There's a lugger bucking its way around the Island, where the swell is high. The harbour, of course, is hidden.

The Ancient Mariner is a strange choice of poem for children, you might think. We learned reams of it, the year I was ten, before I went to work, and it stayed in my head during the long days at Mulla House. There was Mr Roscorla, the gardener, and another boy, older than me, but we were always set to work apart so that we couldn't waste time. I liked the work but it was lonely. All the hymns and poems I'd learned at school came alive inside my head. Even when I was in company, the rhythms wouldn't leave me alone.

I would chant verses aloud to Frederick, as we sat propped against the harbour wall. It was his summer holiday. I worked Saturday mornings until one, but not the afternoons. He brought sandwiches, and so did I. His were beef, thickly sliced, black-edged and pink inside. It came from a sirloin joint, larded with its own fat. He would bring gingerbread in waxed paper, and cherries. I had bread and cheese and a slice of heavy cake. I don't know which was the more delicious. I'd given my wages to my mother and she had given me back a penny. I was hard-working and learned quickly. Mr Roscorla, who was a fair man, let me plant a potato patch behind the greenhouses. I paid for seed potatoes against my wages, and took home eight stone of potatoes the first year.

> Oh! dream of joy! is this indeed
> The light-house top I see?
> Is this the hill? is this the kirk?
> Is this mine own countree?

I made the hill and the lighthouse and the church into our own, inside my head, as I am sure we all did. The classroom hummed with our repetitions. In my mind the ship full of dead men sailed by the Garracks and

Giant's Cap, past the Island and into harbour. Every plot of land in the town and the country round about belonged to others, yet it was all mine, every roof and furze bush, every grain of sand. The sun soaked us through as we lay propped against the harbour wall, and we were utterly content.

I'd told Frederick that he must read *The Ancient Mariner*, and he'd found a Coleridge in the library of books that his father had bought, rows of them, all in the same livery. It lay on the sand beside us, and after we'd finished eating, he picked it up and began to read. He came to the lines I could hardly bear, even as badly as Frederick read them:

> Like one, that on a lonesome road
> Doth walk in fear and dread,
> And having once turned round walks on,
> And turns no more his head;
> Because he knows, a frightful fiend
> Doth close behind him tread . . .

I reached over, snatched the book away from him and shut it up.

"You don't really believe there's any such thing as a fiend?" Frederick demanded, with the lazy scorn he was beginning to learn at his school. "It's all superstition."

"It's in the Bible," I countered, though it wasn't the Bible that made me shudder. "Besides, what do *you* know? I'd like to see you walk back alone from Mulla House across the moor on a winter evening, when the light's almost gone. You get lugged about everywhere by pony and trap, with a lantern."

My words stung Frederick satisfactorily.

"I can beat you in a race any day, you ass!" he said, but it was feeble. I had won. He might bamboozle me with the rules of a queer game called Fives, but I was the hardened venturer, alone on the road in the dark. I couldn't get the words of the poem out of my head. After Frederick and I had parted that evening, they drummed in me all night, and for weeks afterwards. I didn't dare turn on the road, even when it was white with summer dust and the sun was high.

I must not let my mind jump from point to point. It's time to go inside, fill the pot with water and make soup with potatoes, a handful of barley and chives. Mary Pascoe's block of salt is almost finished. That's another thing to be bought. I haven't done well today. I've idled since midday, although there's a job to be done wherever I look. Tomorrow will be different. Better. And then, just as I turn, I see a figure on the path, far away, coming from the town and working its way uphill. I freeze. It will pass by on the coast path, which doesn't come close to the cottage. I keep on watching. Now the figure is near to where the paths fork. The path to the cottage runs left, and up through high banks of furze. It is overgrown, and I haven't cleared it. I hold my breath, and for a second I no longer see a human figure. Instead, it takes on the sharp, pouncing gait I imagined when I was a child and did not dare look behind me on the road from

Mulla. And then my mind clears, just as the woman's shape vanishes between banks of furze. She has turned left, and is coming towards the cottage.

CHAPTER
FOUR

All parties must be kept closed up while moving to and from the trenches; the pace in front must be <u>very</u> slow. An officer should always be in rear. On dark nights it is often advisable for each man of the party to hold the bayonet scabbard of the man in front. Nothing causes confusion, unnecessary fatigue and loss of morale so much as men getting lost from their parties while moving up to the trenches.

The woman's shape dissolves into one I know. I see her head first, coming through high walls of furze and bramble. Her neat dark head, very round because her hair isn't loose any more, but coiled and pinned. She isn't wearing a hat. As she reaches the cleared ground, and halts, I see that her hat is swinging from her hand. I thought she'd be wearing black, but no. Her skirt is dark blue, and her coat, too, which is shabby and too short. Her wrists poke out from the sleeves. I know that coat. She wore it to school, when she was fourteen or fifteen. I remember the braid on the sleeves and hem. I touched that braid once, and it was knotty but also smooth. Felicia told me that it was called silk cord.

I can't believe that the Dennises have fallen on hard times, not with a war to make them rich. So why is she wearing that old coat?

Her step falters. "Daniel," she says.

I nod at her. My hands feel clumsy on the end of my arms, like a clown's. I can't think of a single word to say to her. Her face is so pared and pale. I used to think Felicia would be lovely when she grew up, but it hasn't happened.

"I heard that you were here."

"It's no secret, Felicia."

She pushes back from her forehead the hair that has come loose in the wind. "Why haven't you come to see me, Daniel?"

"I wasn't sure that you would be there."

"Where else would I be?" she demands.

We stand still, and a little farther apart than seems natural, as if there were a stream running between us.

"I haven't been into the town, except to take away my mother's things," I tell her.

There wasn't much to take. When my mother died I wrote to the neighbours who had looked after her and told them to have whatever they wanted, apart from a few things that I named. I couldn't come home for her funeral. All leave was stopped, even compassionate leave. I felt sick when I counted the money my mother had saved out of my army pay, and saw how she had pinched herself for my sake. I had an impulse to throw the money over the wall into the lane for whoever would take it, but of course I didn't. I counted it again, carefully, reckoning up how many days it would give me, added to what I had left of my final pay, the clothing allowance and the pound from my greatcoat.

"You haven't been back," says Felicia. Her face is hollowed almost into ugliness. She's much thinner than

I remember. As her lips move I see they are dry and chapped. She glances at the cottage door.

"Mary's ill," I say quickly. "She's sleeping."

"What's the matter with her?"

"She had — She's had a cough all winter, with fever. She's very weak. She hardly gets out of bed."

"She needs someone to take care of her," says Felicia, with the old Dennis decision.

"I am taking care of her."

Felicia looks me in the face, to see if this is true, and what she sees appears to satisfy her. "But you'll come and tell me if she gets any worse, won't you, Daniel? I can find a nurse for her. Do you think she'd like me to come in for a minute now?" She's eager to help, even flushing a little.

"I don't think so." I'm reckoning back. It's three years since I last saw Felicia, the day before I travelled up to Bodmin Barracks. Frederick had already gone, but I don't think she believed in his departure, not properly. She talked about the parcels she was going to order for him from the Army & Navy Stores. "They send them out, you know," and I told her he'd be in England for a while yet, training. She was like a child, round-faced and with her hair in a tangle down her back. She didn't look at me straight, just kept talking and talking in a way that made me realise that she was frightened of silence. It must have been very quiet in Albert House, without Frederick.

She'll be nineteen now. You'd never mistake this woman for a child. She's not the Felicia we teased and ran away from and picked up when she tumbled on the paths. How she used to bawl. And then the storm was over, shaken out of her, and she was running about again. I see her as clear as if she was in front of me now: Felicia cross-legged in her pinafore, very slowly easing up a scab from her knee to show the new pink shiny skin. Her quick triumphant up-glance. I felt it as if it was my own knee, and the brown crust of the scab was mine to chew.

Frederick and I were blood brothers. We did it with words from *The Jungle Book*, using his seven-bladed knife. *We be of one blood, thou and I.* No one else knew about it. Frederick called me BB, and that was our password.

"You heard about Jeannie," says Felicia.

"Yes."

Three months after Frederick and I left her, Felicia married Harry Fearne, the brother of her schoolfriend Eliza. Not that I knew him, or any of the Fearnes, except by name. My mother wrote to tell me the news, while we were still in Boxall Camp. No one knew there was anything between them, she said, until the engagement was put in the paper. The Dennises weren't best pleased, especially Mr Dennis. But perhaps I'd known? I hadn't. I sat hunched over the letter, hiding it with my body. It shocked me to the core, and I didn't know why. It was as if Felicia had stolen something away from me.

"You all right, Danny? Not bad news now, is it?" Mitch squatted on his haunches opposite me, fished two Woodbines out of his breast pocket and passed one to me. I lit it from the proffered match and sucked in the smoke.

"It's a girl at home. She's getting married."

Mitch smoked for a while, then said, "She's not worth your time thinking about. Let her get on with it. You'll be all right, Danny. Take it from me, there's plenty of girls'll be falling over themselves."

I nodded. I couldn't trust myself to speak, or explain that he'd got it wrong. Mitch was eight years older than me, and a married man. He didn't ask any more. Carefully, he extinguished the half-smoked Woodbine and put it back in his pocket. "Well, this won't buy the baby a new bonnet," he said, and was on his way.

Felicia was sixteen then, and seventeen when Harry was killed, a month before Frederick. By the time Jeannie was born, just before Christmas, she would have turned eighteen.

"Jeannie's fifteen months old now," says Felicia.

"I'd like to see her."

"She's not like us," says Felicia, catching my thought quickly and dashing it down. "She's a Fearne all through. My parents-in-law wanted to bring her up."

"But you didn't agree."

"Of course not. They think of me as a child, but I'm Jeannie's mother and her home is with me. They can see her whenever they like," adds Felicia, with a steeliness I haven't seen in her before.

"And do they like?"

"Of course they do. They spoil her. They wanted me to call her Harriet."

"But you didn't."

"Harry wouldn't have wanted it either." She blinks rapidly, making herself look ugly for a second. "Do you know, Daniel, I can't remember his face? I don't dare tell them that. I don't dare even think it, when I'm with them. I can't make out his features. But everyone says Jeannie is like him."

"That's lucky, then."

"My stepmother is having a child too," says Felicia. "They are hoping for a boy."

"They can't be."

"They can. They are."

Mr Dennis is over fifty, his wife forty at least. They've been married for years. No one ever thought there'd be a child.

"It's a shame," I say. I'm sorry for Felicia, because she has to live with it. Old people cooing into cradles. Harry Fearne never as much as set eyes on his baby. They've taken that from him, along with everything else. Felicia smiles, for the first time. She has a wide mouth and I watch it curl, and then her lips open and I see her teeth, which are the same as ever.

"That's what I think," she says, "but no one else seems to. It's a miracle, apparently."

A baby, a half-brother for Felicia, who will be younger than her own child. A child that they'll call Frederick's half-brother. He'll grow up in Frederick's place. The dead don't even get a few feet of the town's soil. We dug them graves and stuck in a wooden cross if we got the chance, then the graves were shelled and then we dug them again. If there was anything to put in the graves in the first place. If those graves had all been dug here in England, they'd have filled up so many fields the farmers might have put a stop to the war, out of pure self-interest.

There were girls and young men everywhere in London, laughing in the streets. There weren't any gaps in the crowds that I could see, in spite of all the dead. They were younger than us, and we'd thought we were young enough. They knew I wasn't one of them. My kind were selling matches outside the theatres. These girls with their bobbed hair and silk stockings might drop in a penny and say, "Poor things."

They are hoping for a boy. Who'd have thought Mrs Dennis would have it in her? Maybe they'll have more than one. A little Frederick, and then a little Felicia, and start all over again. With luck there won't be a war this time. *For unto every one that hath shall be given, and he shall have abundance: but from him that hath not shall be taken away even that which he hath.* My anger cools on me like sweat. Why shouldn't the Dennises have what they want? They always did.

Felicia's looking around, noticing the ground that I've cultivated and the shelter in the distance. That's Felicia's nature. She used to be always following me and Frederick when we were children, eager to know where we went and what we did. She knew how to discover things without asking questions.

"Tell Mary I was asking for her," she says. She guesses that I want her to leave. It's not that I don't want her here, it's just that I'm not used to people. I'm tired, that's what it is. But behind Felicia the sky is

43

darkening, where she doesn't see it. Soon there'll be a squall. Felicia will be caught in the open.

"You'd better take cover here for a while," I say to her. "There's rain coming."

I lead her up to my shelter, by the fence. We're on high enough ground here for her to see Mary Pascoe's grave, but it's only another patch of earth, with green already well advanced on it. The granite headstone looks like any other boulder that might be lodged in these little fields. Felicia gives no sign of noticing anything. The first hard spatter of rain hits us, mixed with hail. I lift the curtain of canvas from the shelter, and we sit in its doorway, protected, while rain rushes down so thick and white that the cottage vanishes. Felicia's boots and the hem of her skirt are wet. I tell her to draw back further into the shelter. She'll realise, if she looks closely, that I am not sleeping here, but she may take that as natural. If Mary Pascoe were as ill as all that, I wouldn't sleep out of hearing.

The thrash of rain on canvas and corrugated iron is so loud we have no need to make conversation. I am back in the earth, in the rain, waiting. Her profile, when I look sideways, is too familiar. In spite of the chill, I'm sweating, and I move slightly away, in case Felicia smells me and knows that I'm afraid. She sits very still, watching the curtain of rain as it moves around us. I clench my hands. I'm afraid that the pictures will come, but they don't. The turned earth smells sweet and sharp, as if it wants to grow things. The stench of mud is absent. I look at the stalks of the alexanders that crowd up to the shelter. They grow so thick and rank

44

that they half hide it. There's a dusty flock of sparrows that lives in the blackthorn hedge, chattering from branch to branch. They'll be deep in the hedge now, sheltering, dun and brown and bright-eyed. When the rain's this thick, they don't even cheep.

"What's that tune you're whistling?" asks Felicia.

"It's nothing. Just a habit."

I was brought up never to whistle at night. The fishermen would tan your hide if they heard you at it. But in France we had different superstitions.

"It's passing over," says Felicia. She clambers up awkwardly. Her skirt swings and I see her stout little well-made boots. I bet she doesn't know how short the girls in London wear their skirts. I wait until she's moved into the open, and then I follow her.

"You must get back quickly, before it comes again. They'll be wondering where you're to."

"It's all right. Dolly Quick has Jeannie."

"I meant your — Mr and Mrs Dennis."

"Oh no. They don't live here any more. They've gone up to Truro," says Felicia.

"I hadn't heard that."

"My stepmother said that she wanted a fresh start, with the baby coming."

"But they haven't sold Albert House?"

"It's not theirs to sell."

I wonder at this, but let it pass. "What about the books? Did he take the books?"

"They left most of them. My father would have taken more, but she wanted things new."

I think about the books. I wanted them from the moment I first saw them. Yards and yards of books, in dark red livery, with gold names printed into the spines. Later, I understood that they were bound like that for the look of it, and that Mr Dennis had made a library by writing a cheque. There were all the novels of Charles Dickens, with dark and dazzling illustrations. There were Sir Walter Scott, Robert Louis Stevenson, and *The Woman in White*. How I wished I could draw, like Walter Hartright, and become a great man. Someone had read *The Woman in White* before me, because there were marks on the pages. Most of the books had never been opened. There was poetry: Keats, Shelley, Tennyson, Mrs Hemans, Adelaide Anne Procter. There were the *Complete Works* of Shakespeare in seven tall handsome volumes, and *Palgrave's Golden Treasury*. There was Lord Byron on a high shelf.

Those were the books that I read like a wolf. I took them out of the house one by one, under my jersey, and devoured them on the beaches, or propped against the rocks at Giant's Cap. I read at work, whenever I could. Anywhere that I wouldn't be observed. Even Frederick didn't know how many I took. Once, the book I was reading slipped over the edge of the rocky shelf where I perched, a hundred feet above the sea. It was *Kidnapped*, and I was David Balfour fleeing the Redcoats, lying up, watchful, hidden. The sun had made me sleepy. I must have nodded off without knowing it, and loosened my grip. The book went down, turning, and vanished into the sea. In my terror I almost threw myself after it. For weeks I waited in dread for Mr Dennis to notice its absence, and for roaring rage to descend on me, but no one said a word.

I would read the dialogues aloud, throwing words into the wind. They held patterns and rhythms I had never heard before. I learned so easily that I could read a poem once and have it lodged in my mind for whenever I wanted it. Mr Dennis was no longer the owner of his books: I was. I would bring out their contents as I weeded long rows of carrots and onions, or wheeled horse-muck to spread around the roses. I changed my speech to match the sentences I read, although even to myself it sounded strange. I hoarded new words and brought them out like coins.

Now there is only Felicia to read the books.

"So you and Jeannie are on your own there," I say.

"Mrs Quick comes in every day."

I think of Felicia living there with the child, in the square house with the floors my mother used to polish. When I was in France that house seemed as far away as the courts of heaven, that we used to sing about when we were children. And now it's close, but I don't want to go there. Just as I am thinking this, pushing Felicia far away from me so that I'm safe from everything to do with the Dennis family, she rounds on me.

"No one speaks about Frederick!" she cries out.

When Felicia is out of sight, I go back into the cottage. It's cold, but too early to light the fire. For the first time since I arrived, and Mary Pascoe let me stay here, I have no idea what to do with myself. There doesn't seem to be any little job of work I could do. I could lie down, I'm tired enough, but I can't do that in daytime. I stand in the middle of the room, and let my thoughts carry me. I don't do that very often. I keep myself busy. But today, after seeing Felicia, my mind has new things to feed on. I stand there for a long time, with my head bowed and my thoughts coming and going. Maybe I'm not even quite awake. If I was a sentry, they'd shoot me. Sometimes when you're on duty the longing for sleep comes over you so strong you're sick with it. Your thoughts loll. The ground rocks and falls away, and then you catch yourself, sweating.

There's a shaft of light, with motes running up and down it. Little bit of dust, they are. And here I am too, Daniel Branwell. There's no one in the world now who can stop me. I'm swinging, that's what I am, swinging on the bell of sleep.

Now I'm lying in Mary Pascoe's bed, with my blanket wrapped around me. I listen to the shock and boom of the waves at the base of the cliffs. A while ago, I heard an owl hunting. They take voles. Some years there's such a plague of voles that the owls multiply along with them.

I could go out and walk down to the cliff edge, taking care not to stumble. This room wants to push me out, send me away. But I won't let it. I've been outside too long already, hunkered down through winter.

I see Frederick on the fire-step. He is about to order the stand-to. He looks back at me: at least, I think he looks back at me, but really he is looking back at us all, because he is responsible for us all. And there's something in me, mutinous, that doesn't want to respond. It won't agree that he is responsible for me.

Even as I'm thinking, I know that he is here. The blanket wraps me tight but I'm growing cold, and there's the faintest whistling, the same that goes on all day long only I can cover it in the daylight. We are the ones whistling. We've jerked and bumped for two hours from the sidings to where the railway track ends. They are not coaches, but trucks which usually transport animals. We sway this way and that, holding one another steady, jostled by our packs. We are going up the line. Everything is new to our eyes but we try not to show it. There is a dead horse, split and oozing, hauled to one side of the street so we can march past it. Someone behind me mutters, "Poor bugger." That shows how green we are. There are no people, only smashed buildings. The ground is smashed too, but the worst of the holes have been shovelled full of rubble. We move our eyes sideways, keeping our heads pointed forward. We pass a pile of empty ammunition boxes.

Frederick stands at the foot of the bed. This time his back is turned to me. He is looking away from me, into a distance that I can't see. There is the round shape of his head, his cap, his shoulders. He is higher up than he ought to be, if he were standing on the floor. He looks at the wall, or at least in the direction where the wall is. Words are skidding about inside me but I don't make a sound. The air around me is thick, like water that will drown you if you try to breathe it in.

CHAPTER
FIVE

The disease known as "trench feet" is caused by prolonged standing in cold water or mud and by the continual wearing of wet socks, boots and puttees. It is brought on much more rapidly when the blood circulation is interfered with by the use of tight boots, tight puttees, or the wearing of anything calculated to cause constriction of the lower limbs. It can be prevented by:-

a) Improvements to trenches leading to dry standing and warmth.

b) Regimental arrangements ensuring that the men's feet and legs are well rubbed with whale oil or anti-frostbite grease before entering the trenches, and that, so far as is possible, men reach the trenches with dry boots, socks, trousers, and puttees.

c) By taking every opportunity while in the trenches to have boots and socks taken off from time to time, the feet dried, well rubbed, and dry socks (of which each man should carry a pair) put on.

The top right-hand drawer of the kitchen dresser is full of brown paper bags, each containing seed. Mary Pascoe hasn't labelled them. I doubt that she knew how to read and write. Nor am I sure how long the seed has been saved here, but what I've sown from her bags so far has sprouted.

I sit at the scrubbed table and lay all the bags before me, to see how much seed is left. Some are close to empty. There's radish, each seed dinted as if a nail has scratched into it as it formed. Carrot seed, slim and fine. Here's scorzonera; who would have thought the old woman would have had that? We used to grow scorzonera at Mulla House, black-skinned and white-fleshed. I cut a root of it open once to see inside, but I never tasted it. The seeds are long and curved, blunt at the ends. Parsnip seed, round and striped. Tiny spearheads of lettuce seed. There are a few peas and beans left, and a pinch of spinach seed.

I go outside and look at the rows I've already planted. I walk right up to the top of the land. Maybe I am imagining it, but it seems to me that the earth over her grave is settling. It is dinting under its fur of green. She wanted to be here, not in a graveyard all chambered underground with corpses. Here the earth is sweet. It will rub her flesh off her bones with brisk hands, like a washerwoman.

I shade my eyes and look up the hill where the furze flares yellow. It is quiet but every inch of the land is known to someone, and any movement on it is seen. Ridge. Copse. Salient. There's a shattered cottage covered with ivy, but you can't see it from here.

I want to see Felicia. I turn my face away from the town and set off along the cliffs. There are so many violets that you can't help crushing them. Stitchwort, primroses, alexanders, campion. Swarms of flowers so that you have to rub your eyes to clear them. There is blackthorn, beaten low and sideways by the wind, but still in blossom. I notice everything and name it. I note every dip and hollow, as if my life depended on it. It's very tiring.

The fact is that I ought not to be here among these flowers. I wonder what the Ancient Mariner did once he came back to his home country, apart from the times when he was driven by his memories to capture a listener and pour his story into him? He must have been a young man when he set out on his voyage, but now he is ancient. How many years has he lived, I wonder? Perhaps he cannot die. That may be part of the curse on him.

He killed an albatross. It seems petty to me. But the albatross I suppose was not only an albatross. It was the thing without which you can continue to live, but no longer be human.

> Oh! dream of joy! is this indeed
> The light-house top I see?
> Is this the hill? is this the kirk?
> Is this mine own countree?

But how can it be? If you kill the albatross, you can never come back to your own country. You'll be happier if you stop hoping for it. Like a fool I turn and look back across the bay to the town. There is the lighthouse, standing sheer on its black rock. Nothing has changed. The white stub of it looks far from shore, but really it's quite close. When you climb up to Devil's

Mouth and look back, the channel that separates lighthouse from land is narrow. Beyond it the land folds and humps its way northward. The foam creeps around the lighthouse, beating up against it silently, retreating, climbing again. I watch it for a while, until my breathing steadies. My heart beats solidly again, in thick, slow strokes. There is the huddle of the town, where Felicia is.

> ". . . And turns no more his head;
> Because he knows, a frightful fiend
> Doth close behind him tread . . ."

There is nothing. No tread. Not a footfall within a mile. Only the wind sifting over the flowers, and a faint smell of coconut from the furze. A bumblebee has got itself in among the thorns and it dips and falls, feeling for a gap. Now it's in, and fumbling at the yellow mouth of the flower.

A movement catches my eye. I drop down a little, to the level of the bushes. Two figures have appeared, close to the horizon. As I watch they bend, rise and bend again. I think they are leasing stones. Do boys still lease stones, as I used to do? That was before Mulla House. I'd get a day's work, and miss school. I remember the smell of my hand after I gave the ninepence I'd earned to my mother. Dirty coppers, and a joey. I was proud of giving her every halfpenny and keeping nothing for myself.

I walk on a way. Beyond here the land rises, and the cliffs are sheer. I won't go that far. Just here there is turf, and then a rough scramble down rock and boulders to a promontory that's good for fishing. I let myself down backwards, feeling for footholds. There must have been a fall of rock since I was last here, because the familiar ledge has gone. But I wedge my right foot into a cleft and find a spur for my left foot, and then another. There's a rhythm I've almost forgotten, but it's there, waiting to be discovered. Frederick had it always. You climb best if you never pause long enough for your weight to test the strength of the foothold.

I am down. The sea sucks and drags, but the tide is on its way out. I make my way out on to the promontory, jumping from rock to rock, the sea on both sides now. I go to the very end. Pulses of swell travel in diagonally, hitting the rocks with a shock of spray. It is stupid to stand here. We always used to stand here as long as we dared. Every hundredth wave the swell would gather itself. You would see it coming from far off, a dark hump like a monster travelling underwater. It would wash right over the rock when it came, and would snatch you away. We would watch it, judging the last possible moment. We took turns to be the one who screamed out: *NOW!* and the cry freed us to scramble back to high ground where the swell could only lick our heels. But the one who ran before the other gave the word had lost.

Once Frederick left it too late to shout, and the wave went right over me. I clung to the rock like a monkey but it picked me off then threw me back again. Water rushed over my eyes and I choked but the second time

I dragged myself up and got away. Lucky it was calm. On a wilder day the sea would have had me. Frederick was there, reaching down, pulling me out. I was cut all over, and bruised, though I didn't feel it at once and didn't know it until I looked down on myself and saw blood.

We be of one blood, thou and I.

I stand for a long time, but there is no hundredth wave. They break regularly, some a little higher, some lower. The tide is farther out now, and a small apron of wet white sand has appeared at the base of the cliff rubble. I climb back over the rocks. The patches of sand were always shifting after winter storms. We brought wood down to make a fire, and once we roasted gulls' eggs.

I strip off my clothes, lay them on a dry rock and weigh them down with a stone. In the lee of the promontory the water is calm. There are rips all around this part of the coast, and even Frederick and I, foolhardy as we were, never swam into deep water. We would bathe close to the shore, where it was shallow.

The sand goes on under the water. I feel my way out, looking down, following the pale tongues of it in between the black rocks. When I'm thigh-deep the tug of the current grows strong. I give way to it and crouch down, gasping at the cold of it. It pulls at me but the sea isn't deep enough to take me with it. There is only sand and rock and water. No earth to turn to silt or mud. The salt scours me clean. I must be moving without knowing it, because when I look back my pile of clothes is yards from where it was. But the sea can't take me far. It's going out, sucking what it can with it. I move my arms and push myself backwards, towards deeper water, but it's still not deep enough. It refuses to take me. Even if it did, I would fight it. I would cling and scrabble, as I did before. My mouth and eyes would fill with blood and I would think of nothing but myself.

Slowly, shuddering, I clamber out of the sea.

If I had not been so cold I would have noticed him earlier. I dry myself on my shirt then knuckle myself stiffly into my clothes, not seeing. But when I do turn and look up, he's there on the cliff path, watching me, one hand on the head of a collie bitch who is also pointing her nose at me. I nod, thinking he'll walk on, but he doesn't. He waits while I climb the rubble of rock and the low cliff, and heave myself over the lip of turf again. I brush myself down as if I'm alone. I'm damned if I'll speak first. I know him.

"Heard you were back, Dan."

"It's no secret."

"Living at Mary Pascoe's."

I nod. His dad had Venton Awen farm. A finger of their land points down to touch Mary Pascoe's, but it's poor land, steep and stony, and they've never cultivated it. He went before the Tribunal, the year before I was called up, and he got exemption. It seemed the farm couldn't get on without him.

His look flickers over me. "I'm sorry for your mother's death."

"Are you?" I mutter, three-quarters to myself.

Anger, or maybe some other emotion, fills his face. It must have gone down into the hand that held the collie bitch, for she whines and shivers. "You haven't changed," he says.

He was a year older than me in school. Geoff Paddick. I liked him then. He had one of those faces you want to please. A farmer's son, tramping in with his cold bacon sandwiches and a bottle of sweet tea. He had too many sandwiches once, and gave me one. Their bacon was cured with brown sugar and treacle. He was the only son and the farm would be his; he knew where he was.

"My mother and the girls went to her funeral," he says.

I've lost my judgement of people. They were there and I was not: that's the fact of it. Geoff Paddick may well mean no harm by telling me. I want to ask him everything. How my mother's coffin was carried in. What Mrs Paddick saw when she turned her head to watch it. Who was sitting in every pew. But the thought stings me that the people from Venton Awen went to the funeral only because my mother worked there long ago, when she first came to the town. She was fourteen, a poor girl from the other side of Camborne, away from home for the first time to cook and clean and help old Mrs Paddick, Geoff's grandmother. My mother used to tell me about the orchard at Venton Awen, and its low, twisted little trees, with their sweet fruit. I also think: If *you'd* been in France, Geoff Paddick, then maybe I'd have been at home, at my mother's side. There's no logic in such thoughts, but they burn in me just the same. I see him at Bodmin Barracks, not me, naked, canted over for the doctor to peer up his arse.

"I hear Mulla House is closed up," he says. He hears a lot, that's clear: all the whispers that come trickling along the stone hedges.

"It's to be sold in the autumn."

"And your job along with it."

I shrug. I was sorry about the garden at Mulla and that was all. By the time I was called up, I'd risen to under-gardener, in charge of the kitchen garden and hothouses. But that was in another life. I would never have gone back there, even if the job had been waiting for me.

"The Dennises have gone too," he says. "Except for Mrs Fearne." For a moment I don't know who he's talking about, then I realise it's Felicia. "And the baby."

"Harry Fearne's daughter," I say slowly, deliberately.

"That's right. You'd a known all of it, I dessay, before any of us."

I say nothing. Frederick did write to me, not long after my mother had given me the news. A letter full of jokes and scribble, with caricatures in the margin, and a PS. "Our Felicia has become a Fearne. What do you think of that, my dear BB?"

Our Felicia. *What's mine is thine and what's thine is mine*. That was another thing we swore. Frederick said it was from the Bible. It worked very well with chocolate and Woodbines.

Geoff was looking at the rise that hid the cottage. "Haven't seen the old woman for months," he says.

"She has a chest complaint. Keeps herself indoors most of the time, or else she starts coughing." I hear myself explaining too much, in the way of guilty men. Geoff nods, as if satisfied.

"You better get those cuts seen to, boy," he says, in the old tone of friendship.

I put up my hand slowly, to the side of my head, where for a while there's been the sensation of insects crawling down my scalp. There's stickiness. I say nothing, as if he hasn't surprised me.

"I thought the sea was going to have you there," he says.

But he stayed on the path, with the collie bitch. Either he didn't truly think I was in trouble, or he hadn't wanted to bestir himself. I don't blame him. I know how far away such things can seem. You don't think of all that's happening to the left or the right of you. You think of whether you'll get your fag to light with a wet match, and the bit of bad news in Blanco's letter, about his baby that's got croup. We thought of ourselves. Our company. Our platoon. Holding a candle flame to the seams of our shirts to get the lice. The time we spent, getting lice. Chatting, we called it. They'd be all over you like fire until you wanted to tear your skin off. Lice go black when they're full of blood. No matter how many you get, there's always more. Our boots, our letters. Our Mr Tremough, until the sniper got him. Fags and rumours. Cake out of parcels. The state of our feet. I see Blanco kneel at little Ollie Curnow's feet, rubbing whale oil into them and then bandaging them, tender as any woman. If you had a parcel you shared it out until it was all gone.

The fact is we had nothing left. Not to spare, not to go beyond us.

I look down at my hands. They are scraped and raw, as if from clinging to the rocks to save myself. I'm beginning to feel cuts and bruises all over my body. I'm cold, and very tired.

"I must get back," I say. I can think of nothing else now. I'll let myself down on to the bed, sink into it, go away on a tide of darkness where no one follows me. I'll sleep the rest of the day and maybe all night too.

The sun breaks out for a moment and there is too much glitter everywhere. A cold, jostling glitter, without a trace of warmth in it. Geoff says again, "You want to tend those cuts," and looks at me, and I'm startled, because for a moment I don't see hostility, or even indifference. He's uncertain. He wants a word from me. Company on the path, even though he's heading his way and I'm going the other. He's on his own, as I am, and a hand on the head of a collie bitch is no sort of comfort. But as I part my lips to speak I hear the slabby masses of the sea rushing together, green and pewter, as cold as icebergs, and I'm in the middle of them, climbing, struggling for a life I don't even want. They could crush me as your boot crushes an ant. They'd know nor care no more than the boot.

He's gone. He whistles to the bitch who hangs back behind him, mopping and mowing for my attention, because I've made no gesture to her, not a look, a touch or a word. "Get on with you then," I say, to release her, and she nearly dances as she runs to heel.

When I get back, I don't go to bed as I intended. I go to the foot of Mary Pascoe's grave and tell her what I've done that day. I start off standing but by the time I've finished I'm on my knees in the new, wet green that covers her. I tell her about the rocks and the sea; things she knows already. I wonder if she ever walked into the sea, in some confusion of her heart, before she became the old woman who had lived up here for ever, keeping her hens and her goat, hardened by the wind and not talkative, but the vegetables she grew were second to none. I don't ask her. Instead, I tell her about Ollie Curnow's feet.

CHAPTER
SIX

Good strong wire entanglements, of the pattern in fig 14, fixed to well-driven posts, should be constructed wherever it is possible. With proper training, infantry should be able to make entanglements of this nature as close as 100 yards from the enemy on a dark night. The iron posts now issued, which screw into the ground, can be placed in position without noise and strengthen the entanglement.

The maintenance of the wire obstacle calls for constant care. It must be inspected every night, and a few men should be told off in each company as a permanent wiring party for the repair and improvement of the obstacle.

I pack the last of two dozen eggs into the straw. When Mary Pascoe grew too old to walk into town with her eggs and vegetables, she came to an arrangement with a smallholder a couple of miles away. He took her produce to Simonstown market along with his own, and she got a better price there than selling through a shop in the town. He walked down to the cottage with his hand-cart to fetch her produce. She packed the eggs so well that never once did a single one crack, let alone break, or so she told me.

I didn't want him coming to the cottage, but knew that he'd think it strange if she stopped selling her eggs.

Besides, I needed the money. I told him that I would bring the eggs up to him, and vegetables too when they were ready. I could pack the eggs, layered with straw, and they would come to no harm.

He seems to see nothing unusual in it. Maybe he thinks there's some family connection between me and Mary Pascoe, and that is why I've come to take care of her. He doesn't ask after her. He nodded when I told him that she was ill and keeping indoors, and that was all. He's fifty at least, with a long straggle of beard and matted hair. He has a couple of half-savage dogs, and I take a stick when I visit the smallholding. They snarl from a distance, and he cuffs them back as he opens the gate. He barely speaks and never looks at me directly. I give him the eggs and he counts out the money from the previous week. His hands are hard and his nails broken. Before accepting the eggs, he turns each of them over to examine it for cracks or weaknesses in the shell. Sometimes he'll hold one up to the light and squint at it mistrustfully. When he's satisfied, he fumbles inside his clothes and brings out his pouch purse. There are never many coins in it, and I wonder where he keeps the rest of his money, given that he has the eggs from more than fifty hens to sell. He has never told me his name, but Mary Pascoe called him Enoch. The smell of him catches my throat as he leans towards me to hand over the money. His glance slips sideways, waiting for me to be gone.

This week there is one egg as dark as a chestnut. I pick it up and weigh it in my hand, then curve my fingers around it. I increase the pressure on it. The egg doesn't crack. I press a little harder, and then harder again until the shell crushes in on itself and slime oozes through my fingers. My skin crawls. I shake my hand to free it, but the egg clings, dripping from my fingers. I tear up a tuft of grass and scour myself furiously with it. The egg has gone. I am clean. I clench my fists to calm myself, but the panic inside me is too strong now and I lay the wooden tray of eggs on the ground and stamp into them, crushing them. I stamp and stamp, sweating, until the shells are mashed into the straw.

There are no eggs now. I have nothing to take up to Enoch's. Very slowly, trembling and looking away, I empty the mess into the bushes, scrape the tray, wash it in the stream and put it to dry. The hens peck up and down their run, unconcerned. The chicken wire is strong and good where I've repaired it. I wash the slime off my boots, and then everything is as it was before.

I am afraid that I will end up like Enoch. I want to see Felicia, but I'll wait until dark so that no one sees me go into the town. I'd like to take her something but I can't think of anything that she'd like, until a memory comes to me of the Gethsemane gardens we used to make at school, at Easter time. There was fierce competition, among the boys as well as the girls. We would lash twigs together to make the three little crosses, and girls would bring in flowers wrapped in wet moss. Tiny wild daffodils, herb Robert, primroses, violets with their smooth leaves. If a girl liked a boy, she'd bring in flowers for his garden. We shaped the hill of Golgotha, and to one side of it the tomb with the stone rolled away from the entrance. I remember one girl brought in a piece of broken mirror and made a pond in hers, with flowers all around. We were envious of her and wished we'd thought of it first. The gardens were laid out on a long table to be judged.

Felicia always liked flowers. She had her own patch in the garden, full of nasturtiums, cornflowers, candytuft and sweet williams. The kind of easy flowers that children grow. She used to make posies of them. She gave me a posy of marigolds and love-in-a-mist, but I dropped it as soon as she was out of sight. I hope she didn't find it wilted on the ground. I'll take her a bunch of violets wrapped in wet moss, as the girls used to bring them in for the Gethsemane gardens.

I wash myself and comb my hair. I have a clean shirt and my old Sunday trousers, which I haven't worn since before I went away. They were in the bundle that the neighbours kept for me. I must have grown while I was away, because the trousers are too short, but not so that it matters. I clean my nails carefully, and pare them with my knife. Around seven o'clock, towards sunset, I set out for the town. I walk quicker than I mean to, and it's not dark enough by the time I reach Giant's Cap. I sit there, waiting, while the sea thuds in beneath me. Frederick and I used to say that there were lions living in the sea caves under Giant's Cap. Slowly, the line of surf grows dim. In the windows a few lights show, like buds. The tide is out and I climb down awkwardly, because of the violets, and make my way along the rocky shore to the sand. When I reach Venton Wenna, I dip the flowers head-down in the overspilling water.

65

I'll go uphill, skirt the town and make my way secretly to the Dennises' house. This is what we always called it, although it had a grand name: Albert House, named after the Albert Memorial in London.

Because of the way the land folds here, this is one of the few places in the town from which the sea is invisible. Even from the attic windows you can't see it. There are sycamores around the house, which have grown taller since I was last here. They bend over it, inside the high granite walls. Mr Dennis wanted his own gates, and a short sweep of drive. When the house was new and raw, he bought land around it so that no other houses would swim up the slope to touch his. He planted two monkey puzzles in the front garden, but they are slow-growing things and still unimpressive.

The gates are shut, but not locked. I trace the name of the house, carved into the granite side-pillars. Albert House. And now I've seen the Albert Memorial too. It's an ugly thing. I'd never name a house after it myself. I open the small side-gate and go inside. The gravel is weedy, but the camellias are in flower, big white ones that show up in the dusk and go brown when the rain beats on them. I remember those camellias too. There is a light on in the bottom right-hand window. Mr Dennis had the ambition of generating his own electrical supply, using water power, but it came to nothing. They lived by gaslight and candles, like the rest of us.

The curtain to the window is not drawn. It's Mrs Dennis's old sitting room, empty, but there's a small fire burning in the grate. One wing chair is set close to it. I go round to the front door and pull down the bell chain. Deep inside the house, I hear it ring. Only one person can possibly answer it. All those others have gone.

Even though the door is thick, I'm sure I hear Felicia's light, firm footsteps, and then the drawing back of the bolt. A moment later the lock turns. She opens the door, and light spills out of the hall behind her.

"Oh!" she says, seeing me. "I thought it was Dolly Quick come back for something."

"You ought not to be so trusting. I could have been anyone."

"But you were you." Her voice has lightened, but she makes no move to welcome me inside.

I take my hand from behind my back. "I brought you these violets. I remember how much you liked flowers."

She looks puzzled, almost wondering. I hold the flowers towards her and she touches them lightly. "They're wet, Daniel."

"You hold them upside down like this, dip their heads into water and shake it off. They'll keep for five days then."

"Oh, I see."

Her voice strays into the night, like a child's voice. I keep on talking about violets, but she wants me to go. She touches the flowers again, and half turns. The line of her body makes a shallow curve against the light. My breath goes out of me. I look down at the violets, which she still hasn't taken.

"Goodnight, Felicia."

"Won't you come in for a minute," she says quickly, "after your walk? Jeannie's asleep."

I hesitate. Now that I'm at the threshold, I'm not sure that I want to cross it. Until I enter the house, I can remember it as it was. I've always thought that there was very little resemblance between Frederick and Felicia, given that they were brother and sister, but now I'm not so sure. Her face has grown thinner and the cheekbones shape it now, as they shaped his.

We are in the hall. The big pewter plate that used to stand on the black oak dresser has gone. There are no flowers. The house has lost its confident smell of roast beef gravy and floor polish, and there are pale patches on the walls where pictures and photographs used to hang.

Felicia says, "I was in the kitchen. I'll make some tea if you'd like it."

The Felicia of the old days would not have known where to find the kettle. In the kitchen, she goes to a small gas ring fed by a rubber pipe, lights it and sets the kettle on it. Beside the ring, the slab gleams coldly. The table is scrubbed white, but the long run of it is empty apart from the plate from which Felicia must have been eating. The kitchen is as chill as the rest of the house, and there's no smell of cooking. I notice Felicia's teeth-marks in her bread and butter, before she comes round the table and picks up her plate, as if she wants it out of sight.

"You should finish that," I tell her. "Don't mind me."

"I'm not hungry." Then she sees me looking at the food and says, "I'll cut some more bread, and there's plenty of cheese. I'm sure there must be chutney somewhere."

I am suddenly so hungry that my mouth floods with saliva. I watch as she takes the loaf, holds it in the crook of her arm and cuts inexpert slices. She fetches a crock of butter, unwraps the cheese from its muslin and lays it on another plate. The chutney jar, when she finds it, is still sealed.

"Do you think it's still all right?" she asks, showing me the label. *Apple & Walnut Chutney, 1916, DQ.* Four years old.

"I should think so."

"There are all kinds of jars in the larder. Jam, and marmalade, even eggs in isinglass."

"You should throw the eggs away. But jam and marmalade will be all right. You should eat those."

Felicia shrugs slightly. "No," she says, "I can't be bothered."

We are both looking at the date on the label. 1916. In 1916 we had never seen France. I think of Dolly chopping the apples and walnuts with her black-handled knife. That blade used to flash so quick. There wasn't an atom of motion wasted. Chop chop chop and the white apples were in equal pieces, plunged into water with a squeeze of lemon to stop them turning brown. It's a fact: this jar of chutney has outlived Frederick.

"Get rid of the eggs before they explode, like the rhubarb wine," I say heartily.

Felicia smiles a little. "Oh yes, I remember."

The rhubarb wine was bottled too soon, or too late perhaps. Anyway it continued to ferment inside the bottles until they exploded, one by one, in the middle of the night. It made a great story in its time.

"Have you a spare jar, to put the violets in?" I ask her, and she fetches an empty fish-paste pot. I fill it with water, and place the violets in the middle of the table.

The chutney is good. As soon as I taste the food, greed flares in me and I have to stop myself shovelling it in. It's fresh household bread, and the cheese is sharp and salty. I force myself to chew it slowly. It tastes so good, better than anything I've eaten since I came back. Felicia makes the tea, and then sits opposite me. She eats a little, chewing effortfully, then pushes her plate aside.

"It's very nice," I say.

"How do you live, out there? How do you get bread? You don't come into town."

"I do well enough." There must be a roughness in my voice, although I didn't intend it, because she looks down and busies herself with the teapot. I am sorry for it. She looks tired, and pinched, maybe with cold. There's a damp chill in the house which is more obvious now that we've sat here for a while. It was always a warm house. When he built it Mr Dennis installed a system that no other house in the county could equal for efficiency. Or so he said. There was a furnace deep under the house, in the cellars, and a warren of pipes and passages leading from it to every room. Pipes ran up behind the walls, carrying heat to the bedrooms. There were ducts in the floors, with grilles through which the warm air rose. The same furnace heated water, which was piped to the bathrooms and the bedrooms upstairs. When I told my friends at school about it, they didn't believe me. It sounded like magic, that you could open a tap at any time and hot water would gush out. Mr Dennis was in a position to care nothing for the price of coke or coal.

For this reason the house was built with only one downstairs fireplace, in the small square room at the front, which used to be Mrs Dennis's sitting room. She liked a fire, and he humoured her. All that big cold house, and only one room where Felicia could sit in comfort.

"Why don't you light the range?" I ask her.

"Are you cold?"

"I would be, if I lived here."

She sighs. "It'll be lit again tomorrow. Dolly let it go out so she could clean it properly, and blacklead it. I've got the gas ring. The house is warm, usually, but there's something wrong with the furnace. I need to get someone to look at it, but no one here understands the system." Again that small shrug, an indifference deeper than her words.

"Who used to look after it?"

"Bert Rosewall, but he was called up a few months after you. My father showed Josh how to manage it, but now it keeps going out every time he lights it."

"I could look at it for you."

"Could you?"

"Bodging's a speciality in the army. They train us to be handy."

She looks down. "Of course. I didn't mean I thought you couldn't, Dan—"

It's the first time she's called me Dan.

"Is the house warm enough for the baby?" I ask her.

"Oh yes. She sleeps with me, and there's a fire lit in my bedroom. She's warm enough."

The damp and cold didn't bother me. Square-bashing didn't bother me. The food was better than I was used to, although I kept that quiet when I heard the others grumbling and comparing it to what their mums cooked. I carried on, bulling my boots and belt, marching, jabbing my bayonet into a straw figure while it jounced and shuddered. All the while there was the war, that Sergeant Mills knew about and we didn't. What it was like to kill a man, or come under enemy fire that was meant to kill you. I didn't think about it too much. Each day was enough in itself, and Boxall Camp made a separate world between Mulla House and the war. I thought I'd be all right, even when they started us on gas drill. I was green as grass. And then there was first aid drill, which was like no first aid I ever saw in France. We had a dummy which kept still and didn't scream, bleed, or stink of shit because its insides were falling out. They taught us to tie a tourniquet, and apply field dressings, and that gas lies in pockets close to the ground long after you think it's cleared.

My eyesight is more than perfect. My aim too. When we got out on the rifle range, I was on the target time

72

after time. I knew my rifle, knew what it could do, knew what to do if it was firing high. I could have set my sights on a sniper detachment, but I didn't want to stick my neck out. It seemed then that if we all kept together, it couldn't be so bad. We were taught to look after that Lee-Enfield like a baby: oil it, clean it with metal gauze that we didn't yet know you could hardly get in the trenches, clean it with boiling water when it was fouled. You don't separate yourself from your weapon, any more than you separate yourself from your arms or legs.

I knew it wasn't so much that I had a better aim, but that I could see better. Or faster. Perhaps it comes to the same thing. Frederick's eyesight was perfect too, he always said, but it was never as good as mine. He used to argue about that when we were children, and I glimpsed a shoal of mackerel or a seal's muzzle, always a second ahead of him.

Frederick dropped out of my life like a stone. He was an officer cadet, because he'd been in the OTC at his school. Off he went to officer training school. In my ignorance, I'd thought it would be me and Frederick together, and we'd set sail for France in the same boat. I didn't realise that the training for a man who was going to be commissioned would be quite separate, although I should have done. Once I was in camp, I knew almost at once how mistaken I'd been, and what the distance was between an officer and a man. They were creatures from another world. But Frederick wrote to me, in his crabbed handwriting:

This is a very, very rum do indeed, isn't it, BB? I wonder if it's any rummer here than where you are. Rain pours through our huts like a river, and I am to referee the men's boxing match on Sunday. Mrs Dennis (*he never spoke of his stepmother in any other way*) writes that my room is to be repapered. She has chosen a nice light pattern which will do very well for nursery wallpaper. Her sister and family are coming to stay for several months, and Mrs Dennis thinks that my room will be best for the children. She knows that I will be quite comfortable in the Blue Room, since I shall be home so seldom. (Or at all, my dear BB? What do you think? How far shall I oblige her?) Mrs Dennis is having a most troublesome time over the nursery furniture. She supposes that she must blame this wretched war, which seems to have turned everything upside down. However, she is glad to know that I am doing my duty.

Felicia has knitted me a scarf which would wind around a baby's finger at one end, and the whole of the regiment at the other. She says they knit comforts for soldiers at school, while Miss Tringham reads aloud from *The Wide, Wide World*. Thank God, Felicia has not yet attempted socks. Was ever a girl so unhandy as my sister? I have no gift for words, my dear BB, but I speak truth. Please notify degree of rumness your end.

In the margin was a sketch of Frederick, flat on his back in the middle of the boxing ring while Mrs Dennis waved her paste-brush in triumph and a sergeant with ferocious moustaches counted him out.

When we first got to Boxall, there were no places in the huts. There were too many of us. It was winter, and our tents filled with rain and blew down in the wind. We slept crammed together, moaning in our sleep, farting, easing our stinky, blistered feet out of our boots at the end of the day. There wasn't any poetry here, except what was in my head. You were never alone and you were raw with being pulled out of everything you knew, and turned into something else.

I was pig-ignorant. I didn't know that at first, but camp soon taught me. Pig-ignorant, green as grass, a walking disaster in khaki. What I knew after the first week's basic training was to keep my head down and my nose clean.

Care of weapons soothed me. Stripping down, cleaning, oiling, reassembling. Sergeant Mills spoke to me about being on the Lewis guns, and about sniper detachments. He told me there were army schools in France now, where I could get specialist training. *You could make something of yourself out there, boy.* I thought about it that night, and the next day my aim wasn't so good. It was too soon to get picked out, before I knew what that might mean, even though it meant extra pay. I'd wait. What I hadn't reckoned with then was that the war was patient too. It had time for everyone. I learned that. I was fool enough to think that a human being could be cleverer than a war. You might keep your head down, or you might work your guts out to get a commission, but the war didn't care either way. It had room for everyone.

One of the last courses we did was wiring. There was a song in my head all that time:

> You can't get over it
> You can't get under it
> You can't get above it
> You can't get around it —

That was wire. When you put in a post for wire, you don't hammer it, you screw it in. I was too pig-ignorant even to know why. It was so you wouldn't draw fire, banging away at the posts by night. We learned so many things, all of them given equal weight, and it wasn't until later that we worked out which ones might keep us alive. I'd see faces go blank, because they couldn't take in any more, and what they couldn't take in might be the one thing that they needed to know. Such as not drawing on a lit Woodbine at night. You wouldn't believe how far off that little red core is visible. Such as making gooseberries out of wire, and throwing them in to thicken the tangle.

Felicia is speaking. "I'd be very grateful if you would look at the furnace for me," she says formally. I think she thinks that she's offended me. I've been quiet a long time, I know that. It happens. I go back in my mind. It's not the same thing as remembering, because it has colour and smell and taste. "But not tonight," she goes on, "it's late. You must be tired."

76

I agree. I'm not tired, as it happens. I'm lit up, in spite of the cold. But it's good about the furnace, because it gives me a reason to come back to the house. Besides, I have a hankering to get at that big cold mechanism and make it come to life. Felicia smiles. "You must have a drink before you leave," she says, and goes off to find a bottle of elderberry wine. Her father has taken the port wine and the spirits. A strange thing, to take the bottles and leave furniture behind.

The bottle is encrusted, but when I draw the cork the wine pours out a clear dark ruby. It smells strong, not sweet. She has brought two little glasses, and I fill them both to just below the brim.

The glass is so fine that I fear breaking it with my lips. The liquid slides down my gullet, warming me but making thoughts leap up that have been lying still. Felicia's thin face takes on a little colour. She rests her elbows on the table and sips from the glass she holds in both hands.

"What do you do, Felicia?" I ask her.

"I take care of Jeannie, of course, unless Mrs Quick can watch her for a while. In the evenings, when she's in bed, I study mathematics."

I nod. I was always the best at school, but when she begins to talk I realise that I know nothing of what Felicia means by mathematics. She's been reading the bulletin of a French mathematical society, she says. Fortunately, all those years of French at school have turned out to be good for something, because it means she can read the journals in the original. There's a man called Fatou — Felicia's hands grip the glass. Her eyes shine. Maybe it's because I'm jealous of that sudden life in her that I say, "I didn't think girls were interested in mathematics."

But I wish that I hadn't, because her face hardens. She puts her glass down on the table.

"In 1890, Philippa Fawcett scored thirteen per cent higher than the Senior Wrangler in the Cambridge Mathematical Tripos," she says.

Why it should be so fine to be a Senior Wrangler, I have no idea. Usually I'd have bluffed it out.

"What's the Senior Wrangler?"

"The person who gets the highest score in the examination."

"But you said that hers was higher."

"Yes. But because she was a woman, they couldn't let her be the Senior Wrangler."

Wrangling, to me, means arguing. Clearly it does in Cambridge too.

"Maybe they couldn't let her be, but she was, and that's a fact. There's no arguing with thirteen per cent." I half mean it, half want to please Felicia. There's something that I can't bear in the thought of her evenings in that cold house, reading cold bulletins in French. A house with a baby ought not to be like that.

"I know they wouldn't accept me as an undergraduate, not with the baby," says Felicia. "I don't think you can even go if you're married. But there are open lectures, and you can get a tutor. They're very poor, some of them, and they need to earn extra money."

"Why don't you do it, then?"

"What would I do with Jeannie?"

"There'd be women to look after her in Cambridge, same as there are here, if you can pay them." Which she can, I know.

"It wouldn't work."

"I should think it would." I don't know why I'm trying to persuade her, since I don't want her to leave. Maybe because deep down I know that she's right, and they won't have her, even at the open lectures. Not a woman who's been married and got a baby, when there are so many men wanting work.

"Anyway, I can't leave here."

"Why not?"

Her eyes fill with tears as I watch. It's uncanny. The wetness brims over the surface of her eye and gathers in the corner. The drop quivers but just doesn't fall. I wish she would stop doing it.

"If I go away from here," she says, "I won't be in a place where Frederick has ever been."

I move back, and can't help a sharp breath coming out of me, almost like a groan. If I'd known she was going to say that—

"They say that the dead aren't tied to one place," I say quickly, to stop her, and then I can't help myself, a shiver runs all over me, so violently that my whole body shudders with it. It's an awful ecstasy, and it feels like the first true thing that has happened this evening.

Felicia looks at me intently. "Do you believe that?"

I don't answer. I think of the graveyard we dug at St Agathe, that grew bigger by the day. They would bring the bodies and lay them on the ground, each with a wooden cross on top of it, if there were crosses to be had. But often there was no time for that. We'd stick a piece of wood with a man's name and number on it into the burial mound, if we knew them. But the Germans brought up their heavy artillery and shelled the graveyard to bits. So either the dead were killed twice, or they rose up, as the Bible says, in a shower of earth and flesh.

"I didn't thank you for your letter," says Felicia.

I'd forgotten about that. I can't even remember what I wrote. I wish she would stop looking at me like that, as if she's looking into me, in search of something that I've seen and she hasn't.

"It was true, what you wrote, wasn't it?"

"It was true."

She means the letter I sent her, when Frederick died. Full of lies. I addressed it only to her, not to the Dennises. They would have the official notification, and then an official letter, also full of lies. But the lies I wrote were better. They'd have convinced me, if I'd been Felicia.

The camellias still show white as I go down the drive. There's no moon but there is starlight. I decide it's late enough and dark enough for me to go through the town without having to speak to anyone. The streets are mostly dark, but in one or two windows a light shows. A dog yaps and someone comes to the door and looks out. Ellen Tehidy. I stand back in the shadows. I can't see her face, but I remember it exactly. Pale blue eyes, the kind that don't carry expression. High red colour. I used to run past her door for fear of her. She had six children, and washed the little ones under the pump, even in winter. You'd hear them whimpering because they didn't dare cry aloud. They knew what they'd get if they did. There she stands with the light behind her. A perfect outline: a sniper's dream. You wouldn't think there'd be such a thing in the world as a baby that's taught itself not to cry.

I'm on the cliff path, picking my way steadily, when I hear a sound behind me. I stop, and it stops too, then starts again. A stealthy scrabbling on the loose stones behind me, as if something — someone — is following. It's some way off, and maybe I'm confusing it with all the noises of the hillside at night, above the sea. It could be a fox, crossing the path. I hear it again, coming closer. I stand rigid, willing the night to cover me. I am cold but sweating. Even my heart inside me seems to be sweating out terror, pouring it into my blood. I don't turn. The noise scatters and scrabbles, like bones. It's close.

They say that the dead aren't tied to one place.
Do you believe that?

I step backwards, very slowly, trying to keep my bearings in case I blunder over the cliff edge. The mariners worked the ship even though they were dead. That's how much they wanted to come home.

There's a rush out of the dark and a thing buffets me, hot and hard, making me stagger. I kick out, roaring, and there's a yelp. It's a dog. It whines and bumps itself against me again, begging me to know it.

It's the collie bitch from Venton Awen. Lost, I suppose; out of her territory by night. Or perhaps she is

81

a wanderer. I put my hand down to her and she licks it. I am grateful for the hot fleshiness of her, the smell and roughness of her coat, but I don't want her following me home. I don't want anyone to come looking for her. She doesn't understand this, but sidles in close to me. I can't kick her away in cold blood. The path runs very near the edge of the cliff here, and even on a quiet night the sea sounds louder than it does by day. My foot slips in a rattle of small stones and she pushes forward, between me and the edge, butting me away from the drop. She can see it all far better than I can, I suppose. For a second I yield. It feels good to give way and let her be my lookout. But it's only for a second, before I catch myself.

I will let her come home with me, then in the morning I'll take her up to Venton Awen and tell them to keep her tied up at nights, or they'll lose her over the cliffs.

We walk on, and the noise of her claws on the rough ground covers any other sound that might be following us.

CHAPTER
SEVEN

Hand grenades are held firmly in the hand behind the thrower, the arm is brought quickly upward with a sweeping movement (the arm straight all the time), the grenade will be let go when the hand is above the thrower's head, and should describe a semicircle in its flight.

Trench storming parties should kill or drive back the hostile occupants of a trench as quickly as possible, clear as much of the enemy trench as has been ordered, and then hold the portion cleared with as small loss as possible to themselves. It must be remembered that in trench clearing, and especially in deep and narrow trenches, only the head of the attacking party can directly kill, and seldom more than one man can throw at a time. Therefore it is essential that a constant supply of grenades reaches the thrower and that the places of casualties are automatically filled by reinforcements. Men must be trained until they can do this either by day or at night time.

I have no food for a dog, but she doesn't seem hungry. I light a candle as she turns herself round and round on the rag rug, digging herself in. She seems quite at ease. I put down a bowl of water and she laps it with her eyes on me. I watch her tongue paddling in the water. She's thirsty but she is also playing, liking the touch of the water on her.

She'll have to go in the morning. I hold out my hand to her and she licks it thoroughly, back and palm, with her wet, rough tongue. I close my eyes. I am tired and I have the feeling that tonight I'll sleep deeply. The wind is rising. Whoever built this cottage chose the site well, for the wind passes over the top of the roof rather than striking the building with its full force. Often, here, you might think you were halfway out to sea. I don't like to be closed in. When you open the cottage door you see the hollowing curves of the land, like waves themselves, and beyond them the sea. Nothing stops your eye until the horizon, and often that is hidden by mist or rain, as if sea and sky are one thing. When the mist is down, you see nothing but what is at hand. The noise of the sea grows bigger, like a muffled drum.

Tomorrow morning I'll light the fire early, boil water and shave myself. I should visit the barber in Simonstown. I've tried to trim my hair, but it doesn't look right. I don't want a barber touching my head, moving it around.

I get up, pour water from the jug into the basin and wash my face and hands. I go to the door and hurl the contents of the basin into the darkness, then I blow out the candle and wrap myself in my blanket. The dog settles as close to the bed as she can be, and shuffles herself into a sleeping position. She's a farm collie and she won't sleep deeply. She'll have one ear cocked for danger all night.

We sleep. I drop down, like a diver who has learned the secret of breathing underwater. Whatever surrounds me, air or water, it tastes sweet. In my dream someone gives me a bunch of marigolds. I take them and hold them to my nose. They are spicy and acrid. I hold them to my nose because if you have flowers then you won't smell anything else especially sharp flowers flowers like lavender roses won't do it and lilies smell of rot you need hundreds and thousands of marigolds or more millions even you could bury yourself in them but still the smell would come through—

It's the dog whining that wakes me. I am fighting my way up through petals which have grown as big as dinner plates. She's scrabbling at the bed, trying to get up. The blanket is tight around me, trapping me. That's why I dreamed. I'm sweating. The dog's whining is frenzied now. She is jumping at the bed, trying to get to me, and in a rush she succeeds and she is all over me, palpitating, terrified.

I get a hold of her. "Steady," I say, "steady there," as if she's a horse turned crazy by a bombardment. She's so frantic I fear she'll bite me as she burrows into the blankets. I need to light the candle but I can't get at the matches.

The whining stops. She starts to growl deep in her throat, as she backs away from the foot of the bed. I put my hand on her collar and feel the hairs rising, bristling. On my own neck the hair stirs. I've got to light the light.

I shove her aside and swing myself off the bed. The candle and matches are on the deal table. I blunder, banging myself on the bedpost, the table legs, the chair, then my hands find the long smooth surface and I bat them this way and that until I find the box of matches. My fingers shake but I get the box open, pull a match out, strike it with all the control I can find so it won't break. Light spurts into the room. I see the candle in its holder, and feed the flame to the wick. Light settles and spreads into the room. I'm still holding the match and it's not until it scorches my fingers that I drop it on to the table.

I stare at the light, only at the light. The collie has jumped off my bed and is pressed against me. In a moment I am going to turn. I have got to turn or I will never be able to sleep here again. I am a coward. I have proved that. But I am going to turn.

The box is at the foot of the bed. From this angle I see it plainly, a sharp, solid thing that no one could mistake. The collie cringes into me.

"Frederick?" I say. No one answers. "Frederick, are you there?"

Again silence. Only the wind, the dog's quick breathing and mine. The candle flame quivers. It streams sideways as if someone is blowing it. It flattens, then rises again, straight. I know he is there. He won't show himself, not to me. Tonight he will show himself to a stray collie bitch, but not to me. Now I know that what I've seen before was only a shadow, the fruit of my imagination. This is real.

"Good girl," I say, "good girl now, it's all right, good girl." Her ears are flattened against her head and her teeth show where her lips are drawn back. But it's fading, I know that. He is going and as my terror weakens I am pulled after him. I make a step towards the end of the bed, but there's nothing there that I can see or feel or touch. Only a plain box with initials burned into it.

I don't expect to sleep again, but I do, and the sun is up and bright before I wake. The collie bitch is sleeping peacefully by the hearth. I light the fire, boil water and shave myself as I planned the night before, leaning into the scrap of mirror on the wall. I go careful around the angle of my jaw. My face is thinner than it used to be. The bones have come out in it. Maybe that's the war, or maybe it's what would have happened anyway. I scrub my fingernails and comb through my hair with water so that it lies down. There. I look respectable now. All at once I'm hungry. I break eggs into a pan with a bit of fat, and when they're cooked I share them with the collie bitch. She drops her muzzle and snuffles delicately into the food before wolfing it down. When she's finished, she shakes herself all over and walks stiff-legged back to the hearth, curls up and falls asleep. I'll take her up to Venton Awen in a while.

Tonight, I promise myself, I'll mend the furnace. There'll be no shortage of fuel, in the cellars at Albert House. I'll get it going and feed it until it roars. The heat will come up through the veins of the house, as it used to do, and Felicia will be warm. When she opens the taps, hot water will gush out.

The collie bitch is still sleeping. I go to her, crouch down beside her and begin to stroke her rough, warm coat. She quivers. I know she's awake, but she doesn't stir. I stroke her in long sweeps, from neck to flank, and she stretches languidly, for pleasure. Sunlight pours on to the flagstones through the door I've opened. Her head is smooth, pointed, intelligent. How fine she is. She lies flat, as if spilled there on the floor, yielding to my touch.

"You use too many words," Frederick said to me once.

We'd have been fifteen then or thereabouts. I was hardened by work and I always had a book tucked inside my jacket. I read by system at first, through the alphabet of the authors on Mr Dennis's shelves, but as I grew more confident I began to choose among them. In the potting sheds, when the rain was heavy, I would sit on my heels and snatch a chapter. It was true that I used the words I found, especially when I was with Frederick. It wasn't enough to read them. I had to try them out, and Mulla House wasn't the place for that, nor was home. But I see now that I did my mother an injustice in thinking that. I forgot how she'd loved the beautiful words of the songs my father sang. She would leave the back door open to the cold when he was in the yard, making some small contrivance for the house. I remember that. I must have been lying on the floor, playing. He made a shelf for her Bible, so that it could sit alone above all the other books. I remember that. My father always sang at such times, and even though I was only three years old when he died, I still recall words snatched here and there. Whole verses, sometimes. I think what makes me remember is the cold coming in and the music with it.

> When will you marry me, William
> And make me your wedded wife
> Or take you your keen bright sword
> And rid me of my life . . .

"You use too many words."

"What do you mean?"

Frederick shrugged. "I don't know. Forget it." His tone changed. "Forget it, my dear BB. I'm a blithering idiot." He smacked my arm, and I smacked him back. We jostled, and then we were rolling over and over in the sand.

He was learning to use only the right words, which were signals to others like him. Often what mattered was what he didn't say. Mr Dennis hadn't sent him away to school so much to learn things, it seemed to me, as to distinguish between them.

But for years, Frederick couldn't get enough of words. I never saw him read for pleasure, but he loved stories. He didn't want me to read aloud to him, although I was a good reader. Instead, he'd ask me to tell him the story of the book. He'd listen to the end and never let me stop until I had to pull myself away to dig the vegetable patch or help my mother with the mangle. We'd sit close, and sometimes, when we were deep in the story, we'd wrap our arms around each other's shoulders and huddle even closer, for delight.

"Why don't you read it for yourself?" I asked him once. You had to be private, inside a book, to get the best of it; I was sure of that. If Frederick gave *A Tale of Two Cities* half a chance, he wouldn't be able to stop. He'd be Sydney Carton, half-hero and half-villain, caught between the two sides of himself and never knowing which was going to win until that final ride to the scaffold . . .

"It's boring. I can't do the voices the way you can."

The voices were there in the book all the time, I thought. All you had to do was open the pages and they would talk to you. But Frederick wouldn't have it.

"It's not the same. Go on. You were up to where Sydney Carton finds out that Lucie is in great danger. In the wine shop. The Vengeance was speaking."

The Vengeance was French. I knew a French person wouldn't talk the way we did. Frederick knew some French but it sounded like nonsense, and I wasn't going to copy that. Instead, I made The Vengeance's voice like Ellen Tehidy's when she screamed at her children and made them cower. She was the worst woman I knew. Now the story was growing bright inside me, like a fire. "Oh, all right then," I said, as if I was doing Frederick a favour.

When Frederick was thirteen Mr Dennis sent him upcountry to board, at a school in Dorset. Truro wasn't far enough. Frederick and I stayed the same with each other when he came home for holidays, except one year when he brought a friend with him and they went about together. I kept seeing them every time I rounded a corner. I dodged away. I didn't want them to speak to me. The friend only stayed a week, but it changed the summer for me. I thought maybe that was the end. Even after I knew the friend was gone, I kept out of Frederick's way. After a couple of days of this, he came looking for me. I was up at my mother's vegetable patch, that I'd taken over since her illness. It wasn't big enough for potatoes, but I grew everything else beside. I still had my potato patch up at Mulla House. It was a summer evening, long and fine, and I was picking runner beans. Frederick's shadow fell over me.

"Why haven't I seen you?" he demanded, squatting down opposite me.

"Been busy. Some of us have holidays, some of us have a job of work to do."

"It's Saturday. You always have a half-day."

I shrugged. "I got to pick these beans."

"I can wait."

I sat back on my heels and brushed the soil off my hands. "Your friend gone home, then, has he?"

Frederick reached out, took a bean, nipped off the end and began to crunch it very slowly. I watched it disappear into his mouth, and that was the only time I came close to hating Frederick. I was boiling with anger and jealousy. I could have trampled down the row sooner than see him pick another bean.

Frederick knew it. No one was quicker than him. He was watching me intently and I caught my breath, wondering what he'd do. Below him, where the ground fell away in a slope to the sea, there were gulls tilting sharply through the sky. I thought: This is the end of it.

But Frederick's face changed. He was grave, eyes lowered as if he was in church. Slowly, he shuffled himself into a kneeling position and then bowed forward, and knocked his head against the ground. He came up, clasping his hands together in supplication.

"*I am not a Sahib. I am thy chela*," he said. He hadn't got Kim's voice right, but he'd remembered the words. I'd been reading *Kim* last Easter. I couldn't stop talking about it, and Frederick made me tell him the whole story, right through to the end. "Crease?" asked Frederick now, in his own voice. Very slowly, he began to tilt forward once more, until he lost his balance and fell into me.

"You bleddy addled, you," I said, heaving him off.

"Crease?"

"Crease, you dummock," and that was it. We were back to ourselves. Next holidays, Frederick came home alone.

If I used too many words, then I wanted to know which ones they were that were too many. Frederick couldn't tell me that. I came to disbelieve him, anyway. I thought that maybe you had to have too many, to have any chance of ever possessing what you needed, just as you sowed lettuce seed and then thinned out the seedlings.

It is the most soothing thing I've ever known, to stroke the collie bitch. She no more wants to go back to Venton Awen than she wants to fly to the moon, but I'll have to take her in case they come knocking on the door and see Mary Pascoe's empty bed, the scrubbed table with the little charred spot on it from last night's match, the earth that I've disturbed to dig Mary Pascoe's grave. I murmur, "Good girl. Good girl now," and I begin to slow my strokes, making them longer, lighter, preparing her for the end.

My mother had two books: the Bible and Charles Dickens's *A Christmas Carol*. They have her name written inside the front cover, in her fine handwriting. She was given the Bible as a Sunday School prize, and *A Christmas Carol* was a present from my father, on their wedding day. She wrote this on the flyleaf:

A Present from my Husband on the Occasion of our Marriage, 5th June 1897.

My father had no books, and never read any. He had only his wonderful memory for songs. He must have known hundreds, or, at least, my mother said that she never came to the end of his store. He had no family, only me and my mother. The magistrates in Bristol sent him to an Industrial School when he was seven years old, for begging on the streets. He never talked about it, my mother said; only told her once that he used to watch the ships going out of the docks, and think that one day he'd go with them. Maybe he did stow away, and ended up here, thinking he was in Australia already.

Each Christmas Eve my mother read aloud to me the story of the Cratchit family's goose, and the pudding coming in from the wash-house. I knew it so well that I would say the lines along with her, under my breath. I had my father's memory but I was a book-reader too.

My mother's Bible was in the bundle of her possessions that was left for me. It's in the deep windowsill at the back of the cottage now. I pick it up and take it out into the sunlight. She was given the Bible at Sunday School, when she was ten, as a prize for recitation. She did not need to open it in order to quote from it.

It's a long time since I opened it. There's a bookmark that has always been there, but right at the back, towards Revelation, there is another piece of thin card. The edge of it just shows above the edge of the pages. I take it out and turn it over. It's my school photograph, the only one ever taken.

I remember the day that the photographer came in, with his stand and the black cloth under which he vanished like a conjuror's rabbit. There had never been a school photograph before. Our teacher told the girls to wear clean pinafores and tie their hair with ribbons. If they had no ribbon, she would give them a length of white cotton tape. We boys must be clean and tidy, wear our Sunday clothes if we had them, and comb our hair down with water if it was unruly.

My mother polished my boots and scrubbed my face, neck and hands. We were to sit very still while the photograph was taken. If we moved, there would be a blur in the photograph instead of a face.

"It will look as if you were never in the class at all," said our teacher. "As if you were rubbed out with an India rubber." She bared her teeth, smiling.

I was determined not to be rubbed out. I hadn't been photographed since I was a baby. It was expensive to have a copy of the photograph, but my mother said we would order one. I had already taken the money into school in a brown envelope, and Miss Carlyon had put a tick against my name. I was proud of that tick, and glad that I wasn't Charlie Bozer or Susannah Caddy, with no tick and no photograph to come.

In the photograph, my lips are pressed tightly together. Like all the children, I'm sitting cross-legged, with my arms folded on my chest and my shoulders braced to take the weight of being photographed. I stare straight ahead, frowning with concentration. I don't remember anyone telling us to smile. It was a tense moment. We'd been drilled that when Miss Carlyon said, "Now, children!" we were to keep still as statues. We could move again when she said the word. *When I say the word, and not before.* She stood beside us, wearing her Sunday blouse, which we had never seen in school before. *"Now, children!"*

We froze. We didn't move or breathe or smile. There we are, rows of unsmiling children, looking straight ahead as instructed, the girls' hair plaited and be-ribboned, their pinafores as white as bleach and sunlight could make them. We boys are wearing our Sunday jackets and collars, if we possess them, and our hair is darkly plastered to our skulls.

When the photograph envelopes were given out we bore them home as if they were breakable as eggs. There was no larking about that day. Those who didn't have an envelope pretended not to care. I gave mine into my mother's hand, and stood beside her while she opened it. She looked at the photograph for a long moment, but said nothing, until I wondered if I had done something wrong. But I hadn't moved a muscle. There was no India rubber blur where my face ought to have been. It was clear as clear. I pointed to it, to show her.

"Look, that's me," I said.

"It's very like," said my mother. She was far away. I feared her in this mood, because I couldn't reach her, even if I was standing beside her. The photograph slipped into her lap, as if her hands were too tired to hold it.

The photograph was never framed. I thought my mother had lost it, when I thought of it at all, but soon I forgot that it had ever been taken. We had only one framed photograph, kept on a shelf of the kitchen dresser. It showed my mother, my father and me as a baby, with a waterfall thundering behind us and a rustic bridge to one side. For a long time I believed that I remembered the rush of that water, and the creaky sound of the bridge as the three of us walked across it, and then my mother explained that the photograph had been taken in a studio in Simonstown. My father looked proudly ahead. He was very handsome, I thought, and both my parents wore wonderful clothes. My baby self was swaddled in a shawl that fell like a second waterfall, halfway down my mother's dress.

But she had kept the school photograph all the time, and must have put it inside her Bible before she died. I know it wasn't there before, because the pages of that Bible were turned each Sunday. Its rhythms were as familiar to me as my own voice.

Behold, I show you a mystery; We shall not all sleep, but we shall all be changed. In a moment, in the twinkling of an eye, at the last trump; for the trumpet shall sound, and the dead shall be raised incorruptible, and we shall be changed.

The children in the photograph are not changed. I look at us, and all at once, for the first time, I realise why she never put it on display. I was not one of the boys in a Sunday jacket and collar. I was one of half a dozen who wore mended jerseys, and showed no collars below their scrubbed and shining faces. It must have cut her to the quick. Not because we were poor; we were most of us poor. We had been less poor once, when my father was alive, and we would do better again once I was older and able to work. Meanwhile my mother cleaned and mended, made broth with butcher's bones, worked all day in other people's houses and on spring and summer evenings dug and weeded in her vegetable plot at the top of the town until the light went. It was how we were and it said nothing about us, beyond that we had little. That photograph said too much. It said that this was how I was, a child who had no jacket or Sunday collar, and would never have one, as far as the photograph was concerned. It fixed what we believed was temporary, and made it the fact of our existence. But she hadn't destroyed it. I could not imagine my mother tearing up any photograph which contained my face.

We shall all be changed.

How those words used to run through me like fire. Whether or not I believed them didn't matter. They promised that the world was greater than I knew.

How many books had Mr Dennis in his library? Hundreds. Thousands, even. Frederick had textbooks, too. Kennedy's *Latin Primer*, Durell's *Elementary Problem Papers*, Panting's *English Grammar*, Laboulaye's *Contes Bleus* . . .

The Oxford Book of English Verse, edited by Sir Arthur Quiller-Couch. That was the most important of all. Later I found out that Sir Arthur Quiller-Couch was a Cornishman, born not forty miles away, up in Bodmin.

Frederick would toss the books to me when he was finished with them, as if they meant nothing. I could open *The Oxford Book of English Verse* at any page, and he would know nothing of what was on it. And yet he must have studied it. I was mystified, and then I would flatter myself with a touch of scorn for his laziness. It took me years to realise that Frederick was not lazy. I couldn't believe that he could fail to learn, if he wanted to, with everything he needed set in front of him. I never knew how to describe what it was that Frederick had. He made it seem as if the way he did things was the only possible way that they could be done. When I realised that he couldn't read a poem once over and know it, as I could, it made me think that there was something freakish in the gift. He laboured to learn the long lists of declensions that his school gave him. Mr Dennis read Frederick's school report and hired a tutor for the summer holidays.

I took *The Oxford Book of English Verse* from him one day when we were lying in a hollow above the cliffs. I read aloud the poem he was learning:

> Out of the night that covers me,
> Black as the Pit from pole to pole,
> I thank whatever gods may be
> For my unconquerable soul.
>
> In the fell clutch of circumstance
> I have not winced nor cried aloud.
> Under the bludgeoning of chance
> My head is bloody, but unbowed.

It was the kind of stuff that I liked then. I had just time to finish declaiming it before Frederick snatched the book from me.

"*You* haven't got to learn it."

"I know it already," I said.

"You infernal blowviator."

"It's true."

Frederick held the book against his chest, pages inward. He'd known for years that I could tell him any story through, if I'd read it once, but this was different. "All right then. Cough it up."

"Out of the night that covers me,
Black as the Pit from pole to pole,
I thank whatever gods may be
For my unconquerable soul.

In the fell clutch of circumstance . . ."

I went on to the end.

"Do that again," said Frederick, staring at me as if there was a trick he hadn't been quick enough to spot. He flipped the book open at another page and held it towards me. It was Lord Byron:

When we two parted
In silence and tears,
Half broken-hearted
To sever for years,
Pale grew thy cheek and cold,
Colder thy kiss;
Truly that hour foretold
Sorrow to this . . .

Twice more Frederick opened the book at a random page, and tested me. Twice more I recalled the words perfectly. Something changed then. I couldn't read his Greek but I could read Latin. I didn't understand it and I mispronounced it, but I could learn it as easy as breathing. Then I wished I'd never done it, because Frederick said that he would tell his father. For a moment my mind was flooded with impossibilities. Mr Dennis would clap me on the shoulder and say, "My boy, this is quite remarkable." He would send me to school with Frederick. I would leave Mulla House. I would become—

What would I become? Besides, Mr Dennis had no interest in poetry, or Greek or Latin. He hadn't read a single one of his own books. Frederick had to learn what a gentleman should learn. The things he learned had no importance in themselves. Mr Dennis would be embarrassed if I showed off my tricks to him, as if Frederick had brought in a performing monkey.

"Don't tell him," I said.

"You fatuous ape, why not?"

"You're the fatuous ape if you don't know," I said, using his words, feeling them go wrong in my mouth. I got up and left him. I didn't speak to him again for the rest of his holiday.

I have all those poems in my head. They swarm, crowding me like bees. I don't think that I even want them any more. I want the dead to be raised incorruptible, but I know that won't happen.

She's wide awake now, the collie bitch. She hasn't stirred but her eyes are on me. My hands keep on stroking her, as if they have a life of their own. She lies sideways, showing me her soft belly.

I might have gone through my whole life without knowing how good I'd be with a bayonet. Our bayonet instructor was a fat, overage sergeant who'd never been in France. He told us to go for the groin or the breastbone. But if you get a bayonet in a man's groin, he won't care what he does to get it out. He'll grab the blade and hold on even though his hands are cut to ribbons. And if you go for the breastbone, the blade will stick, or skid, and go nowhere. You need the knack, to see which way a man will go, and be there first.

Sergeant Flint's arse looked like a woman's. We called him Fanny Flinto. We heard that Fritz had bayonet blades that were saw-toothed, not like ours. I feinted, parried, struck. He had us charging uphill, bayonets fixed, yelling like lunatics.

I was good at it, that's all. But a live man doesn't work like a straw dummy. Your blade comes out of the dummy, clean as it went in. It's not just the blood and slime that comes out of a man, but the fact that he won't let go. Or his body won't. And in training there's Fanny Flinto screaming, "Stick un, stick the bugger! Get un in the guts!" but you don't think about what guts contain, because you don't know. You stick your bayonet in the right place inside a living man and it will come out with shit on it. It sticks to the blade, and you smell it when you clean your weapon.

I say that as if we were using our bayonets all the time, but we weren't. We didn't ever charge uphill, yelling, into a row of men like straw dummies. We used our bayonets at night, on patrol, because they were quiet. We used our knives, and Mr Tremough had his revolver.

That night with Frederick, in the dark of the shell-hole, it was a bayonet I was afraid of, more than a grenade

102

even. We'd failed. The raid was a disaster and those who could get away had gone. The rest were dead, or too injured to move, like Frederick. We were cornered if the Germans came and shone a light down. I had no idea where we were, although I could tell the direction of the line from the firing. We were in no-man's-land, and no-man's-land was as big as Africa once you were in it at night. There was water in the bottom of the shell-hole. Old rotten water, full of stinking things. There was a dugout in the side, where we were hidden. Wire ran from it up to the surface. They must have run a telephone wire out here, into no-man's-land, so they could crouch in the dugout, listening, and send back messages. On the earthen shelf, someone had left a tin mug. I hoped there might be water in the mug, but it was empty. It made my skin crawl, to think of that German coming back for his mug. This was his hole, and we were in it.

The lower part of Frederick's leg was bad. I lit a match from the box I carried in my tunic pocket, and cupped the flame to hide it. The calf of his boot was ripped open. Dirt had blown into the wound. There was shrapnel in it, and the flesh around was mushy. I saw a splinter big enough to grasp, but I didn't dare draw it out. The match singed my hand, and I dropped it in the water below us. I knew enough. I unfixed the blade of my bayonet, and gripped the leather of his boot in my right hand so I could cut it with my left. The blade was too clumsy. I had my knife, and I tried with that, but he groaned and shook all over until I had to stop. I lit another match, shielding it carefully with my hands, even though we were right into the back of the dugout. I couldn't get his boot off, because there was nothing above it I could safely get a hold of. There was a lot of bleeding, not pumping blood, just heavy, pulpy bleeding. I unwound the cotton tape from the top of my puttees, tied the pieces together and wrapped it around his thigh, tight enough to slow the blood. Frederick didn't seem to know what had happened to him. He'd been hit on the head too, which might have been the reason. I felt his forehead and there was a bloody ridge. He wasn't unconscious though. I could just about see his eyes, and his pupils shrank from the light of the match. I was afraid that any moment he would start to feel his leg and make a noise so that they'd be bound to hear us. I wound off more of my puttees and made a gag ready.

The Germans must have been in this shell-hole all the time, listening to us, while we thought that they knew nothing of the raid. Once the shelling stopped, that would be the time for them to retake their dugout. I had my rifle. I fixed my bayonet again. But it was more than likely they'd lob grenades down before retaking it. That's what I'd have done. Our one chance was that they wouldn't know we were here. They'd think they were retaking an empty shell-hole, and that could wait, now that the raid was over. Besides, they wouldn't want to blow up a listening post that had already proved so useful.

The collie whines. She's had enough of this. I lift my hand off her, and she gets up, shakes herself all over as if she's been in the water, and whines again. She wants to go home.

"All right, my girl," I say, stooping over her, but she doesn't like me as much as she did. Sometimes I think a dog can see right through you, into the thoughts you hide even from yourself.

CHAPTER
EIGHT

As regards dress and arrangements generally, no part of the training should be perfunctory, that is to say, nothing should be left to the imagination.

This time there is a smell of food in the hall of Albert House. Felicia comes to the door with the child in her arms. The two of them look at me out of eyes that are shaped the same, then Felicia smiles as if she's glad to see me.

"This is Jeannie," she says, and the baby turns her head into her mother's shoulder. Her hair is as fine as thistledown, and pale. There was never hair like that in the Dennis family. It must come from Harry Fearne.

"It's all right, Jeannie. Daniel's our friend," says Felicia, but Jeannie won't look up. "She's tired. I was just going to put her to bed."

I watch Felicia move about the kitchen with the child on her hip.

"She still has her bottle at night," she says, and heats milk in a little pan before pouring it into a newfangled-looking feeding bottle. I watch everything she does. Her hands move surely. Of course they do, she must have done this hundreds of times. Felicia being a mother is new to me, but not to her.

"I won't be long," she says, and goes off with the child and the bottle. I look around the kitchen. The range is lit, and a pot is simmering on one of the plates. A dense, savoury smell rises with the steam. My mouth floods with saliva. It seems a long time before Felicia comes back.

"She's hard to settle. I sit and sit, and as soon as I move, she rears up."

I know nothing about little children. I thought they lay down and slept when it was time for bed.

"Will you have some chicken soup?" asks Felicia.

"Did you make it?"

"I'm learning. I ask Dolly what to do, and I write down what she says. She brought up a boiling fowl this morning, and cut it into joints. I did the rest."

"It smells good."

"I hope so." Felicia picks up a pot-holder, opens the lid and steps back as a gout of steam blows at her. She approaches the pot again, cautiously. "I don't know what it's supposed to look like," she says.

"Let me see."

"All right," she says doubtfully, and passes the pot-holder to me. I look into the pot, where four quarters of chicken swim in yellow globules of fat. There are carrots and onions, and a bunch of thyme and bay, tied together.

"What my mother used to do was take off the fat from the surface with a piece of bread," I remember.

"Could you do that, Dan?"

"Cut me off the heel of the loaf."

I take a large fork, lower the bread and skim the surface of the soup with it. Sure enough, the yellow globules of fat are sucked into the dough. I lift the bread before it can dissolve, and lay the soggy slice on a plate.

"What did you used to do with the bread?"

"Eat it."

The soup is too liquid, but the chicken is already cooked through. "The stock needs to be boiled down," I tell her, "but you don't want to cook the chicken to rags." I lift the chicken pieces one by one, with the fork, and put them on a board. "How does the range work, Felicia? Is there a plate that's hotter than the others?"

"I'm not sure."

Families like the Dennises live in their own houses like children, not knowing how things work. And now that all the people who used to run the house for them have gone, Felicia is next door to helpless. I pass my hand over the iron plates and judge that the front left one is the hottest. I move the pot across. Sure enough, after a few minutes bubbles start to swarm beneath the surface. My mother put barley into soup, to thicken it, but Felicia doesn't know if there is any.

"It'll taste as good without," I say.

Felicia cuts more slices of bread, and when the soup has boiled thick enough, I drop the chicken pieces back into it to heat through.

"There's so much of it," says Felicia, as I fill our plates and put them on the kitchen table. She's right; there seems to be almost as much soup left in the pot as there was before.

"You can eat it tomorrow," I say.

"Will it keep?"

"Soup keeps for ever, as long as you boil it up every day." That was what my mother used to do. Every day, she would feed our soup pot with carrots and onion, sliced potato, some barley, maybe a piece of fat bacon if she had it. This soup could have done with the bacon: it tastes bland. "Did you salt it, Felicia?"

A faint colour comes up into her face. She rises, fetches the salt, and passes it to me. Some spills on the table and so I reach out, take a pinch and throw it over my left shoulder. Felicia tucks in her lips, the way she used to when she was trying not to laugh.

"That's sent him off with his tail between his legs," I say.

"Who?"

"Old Nick, of course."

Felicia doesn't add salt. She'd sooner swallow tasteless soup than admit that it needed seasoning. Here we are, eating together at the same table again. I watch the movements of her hands and the dip of her head as she brings the spoon to her mouth.

"Do you still grow flowers?" I ask her.

"I clear leaves and cut things back when they grow over the paths. Josh comes up once a week to mow, in season."

He came every day, before. I wonder how he lives without his wages? He wasn't called up because of his foot. They grew grapes in the glasshouse before the war, and melons. It was nothing like the scale of Mulla House, but the Dennis house was always full of their own flowers. Now everything is pared, as if a knife has gone round and round an apple without knowing where to stop, so that it isn't only the peel that has been taken away, but the whole fruit. I wonder if they're short of money; or rather, if Felicia is, now that Mr Dennis and his wife and coming child have left her to make their own separate household. But he will have done well out of the war. A man like him, an engineer who employed more than three hundred men before the war — he trained up women to replace them, and the work went on. Mr Dennis would have had to throw money over his shoulder, like salt, if he didn't want to get rich in the war years. Perhaps he forgets Felicia, because his attention is elsewhere. And then I think: all this house, for one girl and a baby. The remarkable thing is that any of them should think it's right for her to be here alone.

The narrow spaces of the cellars are directly underneath me now. I'll go down there, because I promised Felicia, but if she doesn't mention the furnace then nor will I. I'd rather be up here. Her hands move delicately, lifting her spoon, bringing it to her mouth.

When I finish, Felicia ladles more into my plate, with another piece of chicken. The white and brown flesh has melted from the bone, and long fibres of it drift in the liquid. Felicia has finished eating. The noises of my jaw and teeth and tongue are loud, but I'm still so hungry that I have to hold back from leaning over my bowl and supping like a dog.

Felicia's left hand cups the stem of her glass, her right plucks at the crumb of her bread, which she hasn't tasted. She sits so still that you'd think her calm, but I know her better than that. I remember her on her knees beside the little patch the gardener gave her. She would make spells with sticks and stones and shells, incanting to herself. Frederick used to say that she was a witch.

Felicia didn't know enough to realise that the gardener had given her a poor patch of soil, where marigolds and nasturtiums would flourish, but little else. She had her fork and trowel and she was so absorbed in digging that she didn't hear us creep up behind her. Frederick shouted "Boo!" and she jumped, but then she flushed with pleasure, because we had sought her out.

We ran away from her too often. I don't know why, now.

Felicia clears the table, while I go to the lavatory. I know that word because of the Dennises. My mother would say "out the back". My father had another word for it, which I do remember. I think it was a Bristol word from his childhood. He would say, "I'm off to the jollyhouse." That word I thought was apt for the Dennises' lavatories and their glorious bathrooms, one on each of the upper floors. This big downstairs lavatory has green tiles with dolphins leaping on the narrow border. There are black and white chequered tiles on the floor, and a high cistern with a long brass chain. The door fittings are brass too, with a soft, deep sheen on them. The hook on the back of the door still has a bag of lavender hanging from it. I crush it, but the smell is old and dusty. I used to love the rattle of the chain and the roar of the water refilling the tank, and then I would wash my hands in a deep basin of hot water, soaping them all over. Today, the water in the hot tap is cold and runs thinly. These taps used to spout like whales. I ought to ask Felicia where the tools are kept.

"Do you know what a Ouija board is?" Felicia asks. She has poured me another glass of wine, the same elderberry that we drank last time.

"I've heard of them."

"I hate the thought of it."

"It does no harm. It's a lot of nonsense."

"Of course it does harm," says Felicia. She is silent for a long while, then she takes a sip of her wine, which so far she's barely touched. "But I know why they do it."

I wait.

"It's because they haven't a grave to go to. Because there wasn't a body to wash and bury. All they have is a telegram, like we had about Frederick. And then a letter. We had a letter from a Major Puttington-Bott — can that have been his real name?"

"I should think it was."

"Father liked the letter, but when I read it again, I thought it might have been written about anybody. I don't believe he even knew who Frederick was. That's why when I got your letter—"

I have nothing to say to that. "What made you think of Ouija boards?"

112

"My old French teacher asked if I'd like to go to a session with her. Her nephew was killed. She goes every week, but he hasn't come through yet."

"My God."

"I know." Felicia looks suddenly weary. She gives a little shiver, and rubs her arms.

"I ought to see to that furnace. It's what I came for."

"It's getting late. It doesn't matter, I'm not cold. The range is lit in here now, and I've got a fire laid in the morning room." The morning room. Of course. I'd forgotten that was what they called it. They had so many words for things, the Dennis family, but I suppose that, in their lives, such words were necessary and had been devised for a purpose. That is, they described what was real to the Dennises.

"Is she better?" Felicia is asking, and I stare at her for a blank second. "Mary Pascoe. Is her chest better?"

"Yes," I say, before I've thought about where the sentence might take me, "at least, she's not as bad as she was."

"Is she out of bed? Can she go outside?"

"Not yet."

"I ought to visit her, Dan. She needs a woman to see to her."

"I can see to her as much as she wants."

"But there are things—"

I push back my chair. Something must show on my face, for Felicia says quickly, "I'm sure you look after her very well."

She thinks I'm annoyed with her. What if I'd told her the truth at the outset? I almost wish that I had. Felicia might have believed me. I think she would understand how an old woman might die like a bird at the bottom of a hedge, and that it was right for Mary Pascoe to be buried in her own land, instead of under a stone among strangers. It wasn't a terrible thing, compared to how men lie rotting. But it's too late now. Felicia will want to believe me, but I'll see her wondering how it can have been, and why I didn't tell her the truth from the beginning.

I could ask Felicia to come with me now. We could stand together by Mary Pascoe's grave. But what if she was afraid? What if she stumbled away from me with her arms outstretched in panic, and her skirts catching on the bushes? I don't want Felicia to be frightened.

"Do you still play the piano?" I ask her, but she shakes her head.

"Not for a long time."

She learned the piano, and French. She had singing lessons. It was what girls like Felicia did. She wanted a telescope. She read Frederick's Euclid, although he snatched it away from her and told her to stop pretending she understood it.

"You could go to night school, Daniel," she says now, following some swerve of her own thoughts. "With all you've read, and the way you talk—"

"There's nothing I want to learn," I say.

"Oh!" she exclaims, as if I've hurt myself. "There must be something."

114

"Only how to live quiet, and make the hens lay better," I say.

"You're not very ambitious."

"Trouble with me, Felicia, I've fulfilled my ambition, and now I don't like the look of it."

"What was your ambition?"

"To stay alive." I say it meaning to hurt her, meaning to hurt her doubly, maybe. I've stayed alive, and Frederick and Harry Fearne will stay dead. I'm eating at their table, as she must long for them to do, but I don't care a fig for it.

"So you'll stay at Mary Pascoe's for the rest of your life, if she'll have you," says Felicia sharply. She gets up and clashes our soup bowls together as she takes them to the sink. She runs cold water into a pan and hoists it on to the range to heat.

"And you won't ever go to Cambridge," I say to her back.

We are enemies. I look at her and see the warm quick shape of Frederick moving inside her like a ghost.

"We could come to an agreement," she says, turning. "You go, and I'll go too. I went to night school, you know. I didn't tell you that. I was the only girl there."

"You said you didn't want to leave here—"

"I know. I say all kinds of things. But he's not here, is he? I could pull the house down brick by brick and I wouldn't find him."

"Could you do so, Felicia?" I say, looking at her tender, narrow hands.

"I could cause it to be done," she says grandly, in the way she would talk with her head in the air sometimes

115

after we'd teased her too long. *Oh my blessed Felicia,* said Frederick once, and he caught hold of her, squeezed her tight, lifted her off the floor. I saw his face, surprised with love, and hers, radiant; and surprised too, because she didn't know what she'd done to please him.

I want to say it to her now but I don't dare. I was jealous of her then. I wanted Frederick to look at me like that, not at Felicia. "I'll come tomorrow," I say instead. "Have you any tools, or did they take them?"

"There's a rack full in the cellar. I don't know what you need. I think there are some special ones for the furnace. Nothing's been moved. I could come down with you and hand them to you as you needed them. But I must be able to hear Jeannie. If she cried and I didn't hear her—"

"You can't go down there. Those tunnels must be filthy." I remember the way the furnace squatted in the middle of the cellars, with tunnels leading from it, like veins. I would have to crawl down them to clear the hot-air passages to the vents. If they've been neglected—

"There might be fumes; or bad air, anyway," says Felicia. "You shouldn't go down there alone."

"How long since the furnace has been lit?"

"Not since January. It wasn't working well, even then. The hot air came out of the vents in the hall, but not in any of the bedrooms. We've made do with the range and fires."

"Then the main upstairs flue must be blocked. That could be why the furnace keeps going out."

We look at each other. We have a plan. I'm to come tomorrow, and then maybe another day there'll be another thing to mend. I have the freedom of the house now. I can go into all the rooms. I used to meet Frederick in the garden, and come into the house only when Mr and Mrs Dennis were absent. The house had an engine humming inside it, which was their life. I barely saw it, after the second Mrs Dennis came to the house. I crept into their library, secretly, with Frederick as my lookout. When it grew dark Frederick and Felicia sat together in her schoolroom, while the gaslight hissed. He said to her: *My blessed Felicia*. He never saw Jeannie.

I think Felicia has forgiven me for saying that she won't ever go to Cambridge. At any rate, she comes and sits at the table with me again, resting her chin on her hands.

"You should go away," she says. "Do you remember my grandmother, Dan?"

She wasn't really Felicia's grandmother, but her great-grandmother. She was more than eighty years old, shrivelled and silent. I never remember her speaking, but I saw her eat. They gave her bread-and-milk which she mambled round and round with her gums, because her teeth were gone. She came from another time, before the Dennises were rich and built Albert House. One day she died and was put into a little coffin, like a child's coffin, and buried. The mist was down and I peeped at the mourners over the graveyard wall. Felicia, draped in black, stared back at me.

"She left Frederick ten thousand pounds," says Felicia, "and now it's come to me."

"How did she get that?"

"I don't know. My great-grandfather was in India. I want you to have half of it, Daniel."

The breath is sucked out of me.

"It's what Frederick would have wanted. You could study. You could do as you liked. You could go where you liked. You've no one to keep you here." She looks up at me and I wonder if she knows how harsh it sounds, as if she's nothing to me, or doesn't want to be. As if there's no relation between us. But Frederick—

I am back underground.

Frederick breathes heavily, snoring almost. I have him propped against me. Of course they will retake the shell-hole. Some of us must have blundered back to safety, those that aren't dead or trapped like Frederick with legs that won't move them. I saw Charlie Hassell crawling the wrong way, with blood in his eyes. Going side to side like a cut worm. I did nothing to help Charlie, didn't even wipe away the blood so he could see. This morning he'd made tea in a billycan, thick and black and sweet, and I'd dipped my mug into it.

"Frederick," I say in his ear, "don't go to sleep. We can't stay here."

They'll lob grenades down, there'll be no risk to them. That's what I'd do. The shell-hole's deep, but not deep enough to hide us. The dead, rotten smell of water. The smell of Frederick's blood. A wet wall of earth at our backs, squeezing out drops of slime.

Felicia waits.

"Your grandmother never spoke to me," I say. "She didn't know I was there."

"She was the same with all of us," says Felicia quickly.

"She must have talked to you sometimes."

"She told me to sit up straight. I can hear her now. *Sit up straight, miss.* I used to wonder if she knew my name."

I remember the old woman's rusty black dresses, and yet she'd had ten thousand pounds misered away. If she had taken out her banknotes then and given me a hundred pounds, I would have pelted home. I'd have burst into the house, barely able to speak. That night we'd have had lamb chops, my mother's favourite. We'd have piled our fire with coal. My mother would have rested at home instead of going out to clean. A hundred pounds might have kept her alive. And now Felicia says I can have five thousand.

"I don't want it, Felicia," I say. Black anger breaks bubbles in me, like road-menders' tar. I don't know what I'll say if I stay here another minute. I scrape my chair back and stand up. She stands too, and clasps her hands tight in front of her.

"I've offended you," she says.

I can't answer her. I want to pull down the house, brick by brick, as she said. I'm not angry with Felicia. The clear oval of her face is turned to me, her eyes black with trouble. I remember how wild she was, like a poppy or a marigold, some tough, constant little flower that grew by itself on the edge of things. I remember how she would run in spurts along the garden paths, with her dusty handfuls of treasure — stones and shells I think, she would never show them — and then she would lag by the gooseberry bushes, singing to herself hoarsely, a song without words. She was always at the corner of my eye then; I rarely looked at her straight, because my vision was taken up by Frederick.

CHAPTER
NINE

To gain a decisive success the enemy must be driven out of his defences and his armies crushed in the open.

I knew he would be at the foot of my bed tonight, and here he is. His head is bowed. His back is turned to me, and he's deep in thought, away by himself in that place where you can never reach even those you know best. That's how I realised what a soul was, when I was young. I'd sung about it in hymns, along with everyone else. I had a soul, I knew that, just as I knew I had a stomach. But it meant nothing until one day I saw my mother sitting in her chair by the unlit fire, her eyes open as if she was looking at the wall opposite. But she wasn't. If I'd made a sound she would have turned and become my mother again. I didn't make a sound. She was away, and I couldn't come to her. I saw something then: loneliness, like a frost that burns your hand when you touch it. I knew she was away, and I couldn't come near without breaking whatever it was that held her. When I first read "*My soul, there is a country/Far beyond the stars . . .*" I knew what it meant. It was about how lonely we all were, trying to come close but something always stopping us, that something inside us that was as far away as the stars. From that time on, when I looked up at the night sky I couldn't feel that the stars were companions. I saw a forest of lights, going away into nowhere.

"Frederick," I say, but he doesn't turn. The frost holds him. Tonight I'm less afraid of him than I've ever been, but farther from him too. He stands and dreams, lost in himself, and my voice doesn't touch him.

We are together in the shell-hole. He's propped against the back of the dugout. I've had to push and shove to get him safe, and I'm afraid I've hurt him, but this is the best place he can be. He doesn't cry out, but his breath whistles through his teeth. Even though there's no water in the dugout, it oozes damp, and stinks of raw earth and gas. I am wet and cold with sweat. The noise of shelling is not so loud now. It smells of blood down here too, like a butcher's shop. It takes a while before I understand where the smell is coming from. A rat scampers, close by, then goes still before I know where it is. It will have smelled the blood. I kick out, in case it's by my foot. Nothing happens.

I prop my rifle beside me, then think again, take it and lay it across my knees to examine the firing mechanism. Frederick's equipment was blown away into the mud. I've got his revolver.

If they haven't come by dark we have a chance. If Frederick rests he'll be strong enough to move. I can get him out of the shell-hole. Once we're out, the flashes from the guns will show me where the line is. Men have come back long after everyone's given them up. Spike Rowe did. He crawled from shell-hole to shell-hole. He fell asleep in one, he said, didn't know how long he slept, maybe a day and a night and day, then he came on. The worst danger he was in was when our sentries shot at him before he started singing out in English. His eyes were white all round and his body black with earth that had blown into him from the shell-blast that ripped his tunic and trousers off. All he had on him was rags. Every grain of his skin was full of dirt.

"Where's that fucking Sunlight Soap to," said Dickie Fadge, as he knelt beside Spike and unwrapped, very gently, the last rags of his puttees. Spike didn't flinch. He looked down at himself as if he didn't know what was there.

"Cleanest fighter in the world, that's the British Tommy, did you know that, Spikey," said Jack Peach, and he held his can of cold tea to Spike's mouth. It gaped open and the tea ran down his chin.

My head pounds and I begin to believe that I'm wounded too, even though I know I'm not. They'll come back. They will retake the shell-hole. There's nothing to stop them. Maybe they already know we're down here and they are muttering, out of hearing, deciding what's best. Chuck in a couple of grenades first, to flush us out. They're safe in their trenches, which are like palaces compared to ours. Twelve foot deep at least. Their sandbags are darker than ours. They dig good drainage channels under their duckboards so they're not slopping in muddy water. I've never been in a German trench but Blanco says they're like blooming Buckingham Palace. For a moment I let myself think of

123

us coming back like Spike. Cold tea on our chins. The blessed slop of mud at the bottom of the trench.

"Frederick," I whisper, and shake his shoulder gently. Nothing happens. His head lolls. For a moment I think he's dead and my animal self leaps up in relief: Now I won't have to crawl. I can run. Now I can get away.

But a bit of breath smoors out of him, on to my hand. I light another match, cup it, look around in case a rat is watching us. They won't attack a man that they know is living.

Five thousand pounds, Felicia says. If I want, she will give me five thousand pounds. I wanted to laugh in her face. Felicia said: *I've offended you.* The old woman in her rusty black had that money all the time, but she never spoke a word to me. The fees for the grammar school over in Simonstown were six pounds a year. I don't know what the fees were for the schools that Frederick attended. That doesn't matter. I never wanted what he had. I never begrudged him any of it.

We caught a pony in the fields above Senara and rode it on the high road, turn by turn, all the way out to Bass Head, getting a hold of its mane and sticking on to its hot, burry sides with our knees. Frederick had chocolate and I had three Woodbines. The sky was high blue but there were mares' tails streaking in from the west. We tied the pony to a post and took the footpath down to the old mine. Frederick said you could hear men's feet tramping there, morning and evening, but we heard nothing. We cast ourselves down at the cliff edge and smoked the last Woodbine. Frederick stared out to sea, his eyes narrowed against the glare. I looked westward where sometimes the Scillies show themselves, looking like damsons on the water, but there was more cloud coming in, twenty miles off. By evening, there'd be rain.

Frederick looked as if he was smiling, but I knew it was a trick of his face, the way the bones were set in it. He was dark-skinned. At school they called him a Red Indian, and he rose to it, showing them how to track through the school woods and how to make fire from a handful of damp wood. Maybe he had Spanish blood in him somewhere, from the Armada vessels that were wrecked against the coast. Felicia had the same black hair, but her skin was pale.

"Tell me one of your poems," he said, but I didn't want to. It was enough to be there with Frederick. He passed me the Woodbine and I dragged deep on it until I was dizzy. It would be a long way back. We'd be lucky if the farmer hadn't missed his pony. He'd thrash us if he caught us. We might get home before the rain fell, but there'd be no moon or starlight, with all the cloud cover. We'd have to follow the whiteness of the high road rather than take the field paths.

"Let's sleep out here on the cliffs," said Frederick.

"It's going to rain."

"We can make a shelter."

I never begrudged Frederick anything. I didn't want what he had, and so I could think about it all quite easily: Albert House, his school, the darkroom he and Felicia had for their photography, the smell of food in the hall. But the grammar school was different. It was close at hand, and boys I knew went there. It opened the year that I was eleven, in January. I had been at work for seven months then. Already it seemed a long time since I was a scholar, but although the work at Mulla House was hard, it never crowded my mind, and I had the long walk there and back, morning and evening. I went through *Sketches By Boz*, which I'd read from Mr Dennis's library. Boys like me streamed to work along crowded pavements, going from Camden Town or Somers Town to Chancery. I had a London in my head then made up of carts and wagons coming to Covent Garden, which I thought must be pretty much like Simonstown market, only bigger. Boys darted through thick fog, drunks jostled with policemen, yards were packed with ostlers, hackney coachmen, and boys my age, who worked like me, but in hats that were too big for them, and dirty white trousers. I had many of the scenes off by heart. All the poems I had learned were in my mind too, as whole as eggs. I chanted them aloud to the tramp of my boots, as I walked to Mulla House:

The Assyrian came down like the wolf on the
    fold,
And his cohorts were gleaming in purple and
    gold;
And the sheen of their spears was like stars on
    the sea,
When the blue wave rolls nightly on deep
    Galilee.

I looked behind me as I chanted. I was up on the top of the hill, and could see the crease in the land where the town lay, with the winter sea beyond it, bluer by far I thought than any Galilee. There was the lighthouse, floating in the bowl of the bay, and the hump of land northward. I was the Assyrian.

Like the leaves of the forest when Summer is
   green,
That host with their banners at sunset were seen:
Like the leaves of the forest when Autumn hath
   blown,
That host on the morrow lay withered and
   strown.

There were no forests where I lived. Instead of leaves, I saw the host flying like the scuds of foam that were blown off the tops of waves in a storm. Next day it was calm again and you'd barely believe how wild the sea had risen. I thought it would be like that after a battle.

For the Angel of Death spread his wings on the
   blast,
And breathed in the face of the foe as he passed;
And the eyes of the sleepers waxed deadly and
   chill,
And their hearts but once heaved, and for ever
   grew still!

The Angel of Death must be like a buzzard looping the sky above the valley, searching for food. But I knew that the rabbits a buzzard took didn't heave once and then grow still. They screamed, and a mess of fur and claws was left after the bird had sated itself.

I knew more than a hundred poems by heart, not to speak of the hymns I'd taken in like breathing. I went up and down my tables like a ladder. I made the names of the Kings and Queens of England blaze across my mind like banners: *Edward Edward Edward Richard Henry Henry Henry Edward Edward Richard Henry Henry Edward Mary Elizabeth James* . . .

One morning early, I reached the turn of the lane that led up to Mulla House, but did not stop. Instead, I kept going along the road that led to Simonstown. It was a long walk but I reached the grammar school by the time the boys were arriving. I hung about by the gate and watched them go in. They didn't notice me. It seemed to me that there were hundreds of them streaming in from all directions, and I thought of the Sermon on the Mount and how it must have been a morning like this, with the February sun sharp and making everything new. Even in our town there'd been talk about the new grammar school and of boys who were going there. But you had to have two pounds a term for the fees, they said. You would have to have money for the uniform.

I could have gone. There were scholarships which paid the fees, if you were clever enough, and I was always the cleverest in the class. I could have made up the months of school I'd missed since I left for Mulla House, and taken the scholarship examination. But they didn't pay wages at the grammar school.

Andrew Sennen was getting a scholarship. He hadn't read any of the books I had read. He never knew all the answers in class as I did.

I stayed near the gates until they'd all gone in. The first bell rang and then a second for warning. They barged and jostled through the gate, and I was pushed aside. A minute later they had all vanished, and the street was empty. Whatever was beginning in there had swallowed them up. I listened, but all I could hear through the open window was a murmur like a beehive, mysterious as the noise bees make when they go to their work. I thought that when next September came, Andrew Sennen would be one of them. I took hold of the iron railings with both hands, and clung to them.

It was the only time I ever failed to go to work, and lied about the reason. I walked back the way I'd come but instead of turning up the lane to Mulla House, I went and lay down in a hollow of the furze where the sun was trapped, and shouted all the bad words I knew up into the empty sky, and then cried, and then fell asleep. The next day I said to Mr Roscorla that my mother had been taken ill again and needed me to stay with her. I thought she'd never know, but I hadn't reckoned that the day's pay would be docked from my wages. When my mother asked me about it, I turned sullen and said I'd wanted a day's holiday for once. She looked at my face and didn't question me further, but became busy about something.

The day of the fight was soon after that, and it showed me something that had swarmed beneath the surface for years, like the bubbles in Felicia's soup. My mother was a Camborne girl, not from the town. My father was an upcountry man, from Bristol, and dead. When the net of family was cast, I was by-catch. I went about with Frederick, not the knot of boys I'd gone to school with, even though I was poorer than any of them. I had a book in my pocket, and when I forgot myself I used too many words, for the pleasure of tasting them in my mouth. But the other boys would have left it at that. There was an easiness in the town that would have made room for me if I'd let it. It was my fight, and I brought it about.

Andrew Sennen got his scholarship, and he was going to the grammar school the next September. He was a big fair boy, humorous, with a slow smile that changed his heavy face. He liked himself and others liked him. His father kept the ironmonger's and there was money there. We were never friends but he was his same easy self with me as he was with everyone.

I picked the fight with him. I was a wasp, buzzing around his head. The poison in me was bursting and burning, and I saw his look change. He knew he was stronger than me but he didn't know how strong the poison was. I saw him going in through that gate along with all the other boys of the grammar school. He would be one of them. I wasn't stupid, and I knew that even if he wasn't as clever as me, he would soon go to places where I couldn't follow him. He would be part of that hive-noise of learning. Andrew Sennen had got it so easy. He didn't even want it. He'd have sat the scholarship only because he was told to and because they had the shop and didn't need his wages.

We shoved and pummelled ourselves to the back of the Parade Hall, with more and more boys crowding up to us, and girls too, the noise of them all sawing in my ears.

I would have killed him. I felt the wickedness in me leaping and making me as strong as twenty men, like in the Bible. I got him on the ground and battered him, not the way we fought in the playground but real. I locked myself on to him and banged his head on the ground so that he jerked all over like a dog in a fit. I was on top and he was down but I wouldn't stop. He flapped his left hand. The noise changed. My name was being screamed and Andrew's too but in a different way, frightened now. Suddenly the air above me darkened like a cloud of gulls coming down on a fish-head and hands came down on me, pulling me off him. It was Mark Relubbus and two other bigger boys who had hold of me and there was Andrew on the ground, holding his face, twisting with his knees up, jerking side to side while his sister pushed forward and knelt by him with her pinafore in the dirt. I hung forward sobbing for breath.

"You bleddy addled, you!" screeched the sister.

They got me for it three days later. I saw them coming as I went down Redeemer Street. Five Sennen cousins, all of them bigger than me. I ran and swerved but they got me out into the open like dogs flushing a fox. There was the chapel ahead. I was fast but they might trap me there by the rocks, coming at me all ways. Better to race for it over the beach. They were bigger than me but that made them heavier too and I would go faster on the sand. But the wind was against me, pushing in from the southwest, and now my lightness was dangerous because they had more weight to push against it than I did. I ran on with fire spreading through my lungs and my legs pumping slow like legs in a dream. They were behind me, spreading out like a net. I was making for Bullen's Head and the cliff path and they knew it. I'd be quick and light on the rocks and if I got into the furze I could cotch down and they would never find me. But they had thought better than me. They were running me down to the margin of flat wet sand where the sea was. There they could close on me. I glanced back and three were still behind me but two had peeled off and gone higher up the beach. I saw them running to my left, gaining, ready to come down on me. I began to twist and jink, as if I could slip myself through them, but my boot caught. The heel churned in the sand and brought me down, and then they were on me.

I thought they would kill me. I rolled myself into a ball, closing my arms around my head, screwing my eyes shut so I could see nothing. They kicked me, their boots in my back and ribs and arse. But they could not open me up without getting hold of me as I squirmed in the sand. I went far inside myself where there was not even a sound, although at the same time I could hear the noises I was making and the grunts and curses of the Sennen boys. There was a last kick that drove my face into the sand and I felt myself jerking all over like Andrew Sennen, but I held tight so that the ball of me only shuddered a little way along the sand.

"Let's throw un into the sea," said one.

I thought they would do it. Maybe they would have if I'd been sprawled on the ground, and they could have picked me up by my arms and legs and swung me out into the waves. But curled up as I was like a sowpig, they couldn't get at me, or else they didn't want to. I lay still. Maybe I frightened them for I heard muttering and then they were on their way, voices growing louder again with distance, telling themselves what they'd done.

I lay for a long while, until a spill of water pushed against my face. I coughed as the salt caught the back of my throat. The tide was coming in. I could keep on lying if I wanted, and it would cover me. I rolled over, away from the water, to get my mouth clear of it. I had to uncurl myself if I was going to crawl away, but the clench of my body was too strong for me. I rolled again, a little way up the beach. I tried to be like an adder I'd seen once on the coast path, whipping itself from side to side to get into the furze. The shuddering in me grew stronger. Maybe I was cold or maybe it was the force of the blows. I shook so hard I bit my lips and tasted blood. After a long while the shaking stopped and I knew I had to get away from here before I was too cold to move. The wind scoured every drop of warmth from my blood, and the sea was coming in fast. I didn't think about my mother. I thought about my father, although all I remembered of him were the memories that my mother told me. If he saw me now in the far distance, like a heap of rubbish that the tide had spat out, he wouldn't know it was me.

I don't know when it is that Frederick leaves me. I would swear I never took my eyes off him, but one moment he is there at the bed-end, and then he is not. He has never stayed with me for so long before.

Frederick is the only person, besides myself, who knows that Mary Pascoe is lying at the top of the field, under a deepening fuzz of green. He knows everything I've done. I wonder, if I went up there now, if he'd come with me. He'd look into the green earth, at the grave he'd never had for himself. He wouldn't begrudge her that quiet space. Frederick would look consideringly, measuring up the bright oblong of new grass. Under it, her bones lie as they should. Her arms are crossed over her breast, and her eyes are closed. I laid her out straight and sure. It's not an easy thing to bury a grown woman, even one who's light and shrivelled with age and sickness. I had to climb down into the grave with her, to be sure she was laid as she should be, and I folded the canvas over her so that no soil would touch her bare face.

I did what I could. You are the only person who understands that. There was nothing. Nothing to be done. I turned and you were gone. You were a rain of earth, a fine rain and wet with your blood, your body, every bit of you gone into it. You threw me back. I thought it was you and not the shell-blast. Your arms shoving me into safety. I cried out *Frederick!* but my mouth was stuffed with earth.

If we were at Bass Head now, and you said, "Let's sleep out on the cliffs," of course I'd say yes. We could build a shelter easy enough. We could lie hearing the sea breathe beneath us, and the gulls that cry out in the middle of the night. I wouldn't be so bloody soft as to unhitch that pony and plod all the way back home.

CHAPTER
TEN

The essence of the following games is that they should he conducted with the utmost amount of energy and the rigid observance of all the details connected with them. Executed in this way, they inculcate discipline and develop quickness of brain and movement, whereas, if carelessly carried out, they may do more harm than good.

"Felicia?"

The front door is ajar, wedged with an iron doorstop. I push it open. After the sheer spring light, the hall is dark.

"Felicia?" I call more loudly. The flags are wet. Someone's been washing the floor. Dolly Quick, of course: I'd forgotten her. That's why the door is open. I move away. I have no wish to meet Dolly Quick. Behind me, footsteps crunch on the gravel. It's Felicia. She's wearing an old blue jersey of Frederick's, and her skirt is kilted up. Her boots are covered with earth.

"We're in the garden," she says. "I'm digging over the moon beds." I follow her to the crescent flowerbeds that used to be filled with lilies, phlox and sweet williams. Felicia has been turning over the soil with a spade, clumsily, leaving the clods full of weeds. She has spread out a blanket for Jeannie on the grass, but the child squats in the dirt, poring over something in the cup of her hand.

"Jeannie, leave that!"

"What has she got?"

"She's playing with a worm. She'll eat it." Felicia crouches down, eases open the child's fist, takes the worm and flings it away. Jeannie's face goes purple, her mouth squares, and she roars like a bull. "Leave her," says Felicia, "she'll get over it. She wants to eat everything, that's her trouble." The child turns into Felicia's skirts and butts her head furiously against her mother's legs. "She's trying to bite me, but she won't be able because this skirt's too thick."

"I wouldn't bet on it."

"Do you think roses here? Or lilies, maybe?"

"You've got to get the weeds right out first. You need a fork, not that spade."

"I'll fetch one."

The storm's over. Jeannie follows her mother to the shed, hiccuping but calm. The sun catches on Felicia's hair, which is never pure black when she's out in the light. There are sparks of red in it, and even blue. How can there be blue in a girl's hair? Her baggy clothes hide her body, but she moves inside them the same as ever.

The fork isn't as clean as it should be.

"You should tell Josh to oil your tools. He's not doing his job. There's rust on the tines." I wipe them carefully on a tuft of grass, wishing for an oily rag. Felicia watches, and all of a sudden I'm thrown back ten years. I'm the gardener's boy, a crouching shape you barely see as you walk around the lawns with your friends.

"Have you ever been to London, Felicia?" I ask her, and the gardener's boy slips out of sight.

"I was going to," she says quickly. "On Frederick's next leave, I was going to meet him—"

Why the hell did I start talking about London? Because I wanted to make it clear that I wasn't the old Daniel, who'd never done anything or been anywhere. I rub at the rust, to give her time to settle her face, then plant the prongs deep in the bed, rock down on the fork and ease it through the soil, taking care not to break the taproots of dock and dandelions. There's couch grass and creeping buttercup. Jeannie and Felicia stand there watching me, hand in hand, their hair and skirts blowing in the spring wind.

"You can pull out the weeds as I dig them loose," I tell Felicia. "You have to keep going over the bed until the soil's clean, or else the weeds come back."

Felicia makes a heap, and Jeannie pulls it about. As I dig I think of little Felicia scratting in the earth, planting her nasturtiums and love-in-a-mist. "So what's it to be then, lilies or roses? You could have both."

"I don't know." She sits back on her heels and smiles at me. The wind has blown her hair loose from the knot at the nape of her neck, and there's a streak of earth across her cheek where she's pushed back the tendrils. "I thought I'd ask you. No, Jeannie, not in your mouth."

I glance up at the sky. "It's about the sunniest bit of your garden. Good for roses. If you planted 'Ophelia',

say, you'd get the scent through the back windows."
"Ophelia" would be the right rose for these beds. The
scent would drift all over the garden, there's not
another as strong and sweet. And it's like Felicia,
somehow.

"What colour is it?"

It is like Felicia's skin, now that the sun and wind
have blown some colour into it.

"White, with a bit of pink in it, not much. Not sugar
pink, more brownish. Maybe even a bit of green on the
curl of the petals."

Felicia makes a face. "Sounds wishy-washy to me."

I bend to my digging. Maybe she says that because
she knows what I'm thinking: that the rose is like her.
She doesn't want the comparison. She's pushing me
away. My hands sting from gripping tight to the fork
handle and I can't look at her. I'm back at Mulla House
with the ladies faffing endlessly to Mr Roscorla about
what should be planted and where, when none of them
knew any more about roses than how to spend a whole
morning massacring them into vases. My thoughts
must have shown on my face that day, for Mr Roscorla
spoke harshly to me after: *Don't you ever forget who's
paying your wages.*

"I've made you cross, Daniel."

"I'm not cross."

"You are. I'm sorry. I'll get Mrs Quick to make us
some tea."

"Don't trouble her, she's scrubbing the floors."

"Daniel!"

I lean on the handle of the fork. Jeannie is clambering in her mother's lap, reaching up to stroke her face. Felicia leans down towards her. Their foreheads touch, and knock. The baby crows with laughter, expectant.

"Again!"

"She always does that," says Felicia.

"I didn't think she'd be able to talk."

"She says a lot, but I don't always understand it."

"*Again!*"

But this time Jeannie throws herself forward much too hard. Her head cracks against Felicia's, and she screams.

"Oh God," says Felicia, taking hold of the flailing child. "It's always like this. Every game she plays, it ends in tears. It's all right, Jeannie, don't make that noise. She goes on as if she's half killed. She's so — she's so *intransigent*. And so are you, Daniel."

"What's that when it's at home?"

"Don't pretend you don't know."

"All right. You tell me what roses to plant, Felicia, and I'll plant them."

Felicia folds her arms around Jeannie. The sobs die down with the drumming of Jeannie's little boots against her mother's thighs. Felicia wipes her hair off her forehead wearily.

"It's all in your head, Daniel, not mine."

"What do you mean?"

"You get so angry."

"I'm not angry."

140

"You are. Just as you were about the five thousand pounds."

"Felicia, I'm—" But I'm not sure what to say. *"I'm your friend, how can I be angry with you? If you think this is anger, then you don't know much."* I can't say that. "I'm not against you, Felicia."

"I know you're not. But you think that people are against *you*."

"Maybe they are. Maybe it's a habit I can't break, from having thousands of 'em shooting at me."

"I'm not shooting at you."

I nearly laugh, looking at her fine, clumsy hands.

"I'm not shooting at you, Daniel."

I shrug. "I know that."

"You don't act as if you do." She reaches out, hoisting Jeannie sideways on to her hip, and takes the fork from me. I let it go. I don't want us tussling. "I don't want you to do this any more," she says. "Besides, Jeannie needs her tea."

The weeds are already growing limp. The bed isn't half finished, and the day is spoiled. Felicia is stubborn, I know that. They would put her into a frilled white pinafore and she would glower. She would run away as far as the edge of the lawn, and I would peep through the leaves, out of my hiding place, and see her. They would call her, and she'd pretend not to hear, but she'd have to go at last, laggingly, looking behind her. She wanted to be with me and Frederick, in the shrubbery. We were little then, too young to go raking over the downs and cliff tops, and we were building a secret wigwam in the bushes.

141

Felicia knew that as soon as she was corralled into the drawing room with the visitors, Frederick would run away to join me where I waited, hidden under the gunnera. The Dennises didn't know I was there, nine times out of ten. I remember the sound of rain falling on the gunnera leaves above me. Those leaves were as good as an umbrella. I waited for a long time, it seemed, and then there was a rush through the branches of the laurels and camellia, and Frederick was there, triumphant. "I've shaken them off!"

Felicia never gave us away, although she must have been tempted.

I knew how to climb the wall and glide through the garden like a Red Indian. No one saw me. If Frederick couldn't come out, I would creep inside the wigwam, and where the sky showed through I would thatch it with twigs and moss. The wigwam lasted a summer, maybe less.

I want to go back to the moment when she smiled and said, *I thought I'd ask you*. But she's busying herself with the child, setting her down on the ground again, folding the blanket. I see Dolly Quick before Felicia does. Neither of us heard her coming, and I don't know how long she has been there, five yards from us. She has her coat on, and her felt hat is stabbed into her hair with a jet pin.

"There's squab pie for your supper, on the slab," she says, addressing Felicia, slipping me a glance. "I'll finish upstairs on Monday."

"Oh, thank you," says Felicia, too effusively, as if there's something to cover up. But there's nothing. Only Dan Branwell, digging up a flowerbed, as he's done all his working life. Dolly Quick most likely thinks Felicia's found some work for me, at the expense of Josh, for old times' sake.

"Daniel thinks we should plant roses in this bed," says Felicia.

"I wouldn't know about that. And I'll make a start on washing the loose covers."

Her eyes are on me, then on Felicia, then on me again, as rapid as blinking. She has those dark, curranty eyes you can't look into.

"That'll be lovely," says Felicia, flexing her own thin fingers, as if she, too, is ready to plunge into the suds. She's too eager, Felicia, trying to be what people want of her. It never works. Dolly sniffs, and snaps the clasp of her bag. And there's Jeannie, staggering towards her with a pile of weeds in her arms. She drops them at Dolly's feet. The lined face softens. She bends down, picks up the child and presses her close. I see how red and raw her hands are. Dolly Quick touches Jeannie's soft cheek with her knuckle, then strokes her hair. "And did you do all that, then, my lovely?"

"She wanted to eat a worm. I expect you heard her screaming," says Felicia.

"Did she? No, my bird, you don't want to go eating a worm. You'll get a bellyache." Still stroking the child's hair, but in a different tone, she says to me, "You're back with us, then, Dan."

"As you see."

She nods towards Felicia. "She'll have told you they've all gone away upcountry, but we keep an eye here, me and Quicky."

She always called her husband Quicky. You would hear her asking down the street as the men came up from the lodge: "You got Quicky with you?" Everyone took it from her and he was Quicky all over town. He was a little, lugubrious man, unless he'd had a drink, which was seldom since Dolly was strong chapel. I'm thinking of all this when I see the smile that Dolly Quick gives to Felicia, and the one from Felicia that answers it. Dolly Quick has no daughter, only the two great lumps of her sons. Jabez and Jethro Quick, both prone to fits and exempted by the Tribunal. I remember their mother knuckling their heads even when they were great boys, twice the size of her. I also remember that Andrew Sennen is Quicky's sister's son.

"I ent seen Mary Pascoe in a long time. Used to get my eggs from her."

"She's been ill," says Felicia. "Daniel's been looking after the hens and vegetable garden."

"I dessay." Slowly, she disengages Jeannie's hands, kisses her, and sets her down. "Dolly's got to go now, my chiel." Gratifyingly, Jeannie starts to cry. "You going to come along down mine for a while then?"

"It's a trouble for you," says Felicia quickly.

"It's no trouble. She can watch the boats come in. I'll see you later."

"If the Lord spares us," I murmur, and catch an ungodly glint from Dolly Quick. Off she goes, to work her black seam of gossip. We listen to her and Jeannie,

144

their voices mingling and growing fainter. Felicia rolls down the sleeves of her jersey, and settles the ribbed cuffs on her wrists. Her hands, which looked so fine and pale by lamplight, are chapped. Her wrists are narrow, and the bones prominent. I wonder if the jersey still smells of Frederick. He used to wear it when we rowed in the harbour.

"She's always wanting to go to Dolly's," says Felicia. Her face is clouded. "We seem to have so many quarrels."

"What, you and Jeannie?"

"Yes."

"Does she know enough words to quarrel?"

"She screams, she throws herself on the ground, I have to hold my hands down sometimes so as not to slap her. Sometimes I wonder what she *will* say to me, once she can talk properly."

"She'll have grown out of wanting to eat worms, at any rate."

"She'll have thought of worse things. No, it's only that sometimes I'm not sure she even likes me."

"You're her mother. Of course she does."

"Dolly was there when she was born, did I tell you that?" Felicia sighs. "Never mind. Let's go in and have tea."

I wipe the tines of the fork clean, and take the weeds to the heap. "You've mud on your face, Felicia," I say, coming back to her.

"Oh! Where?"

I touch my left cheek. "Just here." She dabs at the wrong cheek, mirroring me. "No, here."

I reach out to show her, without quite touching her. Quickly, she scrubs at her skin until a red mark comes.

"It's all gone."

I smelled her skin as I came close. It's not like roses at all and I don't want it to be.

"She'll have left a cake too," says Felicia, as if she needs to tempt me.

I suppose we'll eat in the kitchen again, but Felicia loads up a heavy tray with tea things and cinnamon cake.

"There'll be a fire in the morning room," she says.

The fire is laid, but not lit. A fine spatter of rain hits the window as Felicia kneels to put a match to the coils of paper. They catch, and lick the kindling. We watch, without speaking, as the fire grows. There's the noise of the rain and the puckering of flames, and then Felicia pours tea into the cups. The Dennises have the smallest, thinnest cups I've ever seen. You can drink them off in two gulps. It's like a doll's tea party, until Felicia cuts thick slices of cake with the black-handled knife that I remember the knife-grinder sharpening, with all the rest. It's good cake.

"Have another piece," she says, lifting it towards me on the knife blade. She refills the teapot from the hot-water jug, and pours me another cup. She seems to be pouring and handing every five minutes. I lift my cup, take a drink, and it's empty.

"I know," she says, catching my eye. "We could have had the big kitchen cups, but I thought—" And then she blushes, as I've never seen her blush before. Suddenly I understand why. She's not wanted to bring

146

in the kitchen cups, in case it seems she thinks they are good enough for Dan Branwell. She's used her fine china. She'd have given Frederick his tea in a kitchen cup, I'm sure of it.

I watch her thin, clumsy fingers and my heart slides in my chest with longing, but I still don't know what I want. This room ought to be comfortable. It smells of damp, but the fire warms it, and the brass fender gives back the dance of the flames. There's a clutter of children's toys on the hearth: bricks, rag books, and a knitted cat. A rag doll.

"Is that Pip Lily?" I ask.

"Fancy you remembering. She's a bit the worse for wear, but Jeannie likes her."

Most of the paintings that used to be on the walls are gone, but there is one left that I remember: Frederick and Felicia, hand in hand, golden-curled as I'm sure they never were. Mr Dennis must not have wanted to take the portrait with him. Felicia has followed my glance.

"Isn't it hideous?" she says quickly.

"How old were you?"

"Mother had it done, not long before she died. We sat for it in this room: look, you can see where he's painted a corner of the fireplace. But he wasn't a very good painter. Father always thought it was sickly."

"He painted what he thought your parents wanted."

I look at the four faded oblongs on the wallpaper. "What's happened to your photographs?"

"They're not here any more."

They must be with her father and the new Mrs Dennis. It's raining heavily now.

"Dolly won't bring her home in this," says Felicia. "I'll go down for her after our dinner. And then there'll be another screaming match. She won't want to come home. Dolly makes such a fuss of her. Jeannie has a little bed made up down there, and her own cup and bowl."

The heat of the fire is making me drowsy. I think of the long walk back, battered by wind, with sheets of rain swaying in across the sea. Sometimes it feels as if the sky is down on you like a lid, and you can't get away.

"I'll put the pie in the oven," says Felicia, and leaves me alone in the room. I gape into the fire, and eat more cake, and picture Felicia moving around the kitchen. The minutes lengthen. This is the afterlife. This is what we dreamed of, in France. Fire, and four walls, dry feet, a belly warm with food. Children's toys on the floor. We talked about such things as if they were gone from the earth. You couldn't believe in them. I still can't, even though I'm here. I say Frederick's name, but the room doesn't answer. The grinning yellow-haired boy in the painting doesn't know who I'm talking about. I hold out my fingers and squint at the firelight through them. I'm in Mrs Dennis's own room. I used to scuttle by under her window, head down so she wouldn't see me. But there's no victory in it. I'm tired, that's all.

Felicia's been in the kitchen a long time. Maybe she's seeing to the pie. I don't know, though. Something in her absence makes me uneasy, as if I've no right to be in the house unless she's with me. The Dennises are gone, I tell myself. There's no tall black roaring man behind the study door.

I wait a while longer, then go to the door, open it, listen. There is only the house, creaking and settling as the wind rises. I pad across the hall, through the green baize door and into the kitchen. There's no one here. The kettle is drawn to one side of the plate, and singing very quietly to itself. There on the slab is the pie.

My boots clop on the flagstones as I go back through the hall. I remember the old days, when I would flit about the house in my stockinged feet so that no one would hear me. I bend down, unlace my boots and put them aside. The stairwell rises into shadows. Felicia must be upstairs. She wouldn't have gone down to fetch Jeannie without telling me. I could go back into the morning room and wait for her. No. I want to find her.

These stairs. My feet know every tread. I go up lightly, feeling the give and creak of each stair beneath my weight. On the first landing, the staircase divides, curving left and right. Right is to Frederick's room. My feet are already moving towards it when I remember that Mrs Dennis turned Frederick out of his bedroom. She didn't think he'd need it again. She put him in the Blue Room.

I know where that is. It's the little room two doors down from Frederick. My mother told me it was where the baby was going to be, the one that died along with Frederick's and Felicia's mother. She'd made it into a nursery, but then everything was taken out again, the walls were stripped and afterwards there was blue paper put on. Visitors slept there sometimes.

The clock in the hall strikes the quarter, and I stand stock-still. When the house closes over the sound again, I move forward. Felicia's room was right at the end of the corridor. I suppose she must be there. On my left a door stands wide, into an empty room. Part of the carpet is cut away, as if it used to be fitted around a piece of furniture, and there is newspaper over the bare boards. The curtains have gone. They used to call this room the night nursery. All those names they had.

Felicia's room has a white china doorknob with forget-me-knots painted on it. The door is closed. If I knock, she won't know who it is. She might be afraid. I turn, and go to the door of the Blue Room. I put my hand on the doorknob, gather it into my palm, and very slowly, very cautiously, I begin to turn it. It goes easily, without a click. I push, just a little, until a line of light appears between door and frame. I push farther. At the same moment there's a noise from inside the room. A stifled, animal sound. My hair crisps. I want to turn and run but I look down at my hand and see that it is pushing the door wider. I open the door.

Felicia is lying on her stomach, across the bed. The room is full of stuff: piles of books, photographs, Frederick's school trunk with his initials on it in red, a heap of clothes in the middle of a sheet on the floor, as if someone was sorting them. Cricket pads lie on the windowsill. Chairs, desk and wardrobe are stacked

150

against the wall. There is hardly room to move around the bed.

Felicia's face comes out of the pillow, swollen with weeping. Red patches have come up on her skin. She pushes back her hair, looking bewildered, as if she doesn't know where she is.

"Felicia, it's only me."

She rolls over, clutching the pillow to herself.

"Why did you come up here?" she asks angrily, as if I'm a stranger.

"I didn't mean to frighten you."

"You didn't frighten me." She sits up, swings her legs over the side of the bed, and punches the pillow back into place. "I didn't expect anyone to come up here, that's all."

This is a junkyard, not a bedroom. I can't believe that Frederick ever slept here. They pitched his stuff in anyhow, and left it.

If the Dennises were poor, this would never happen. A room wasted, not taken care of, possessions strewn anywhere. There's no feeling in it. There are his schoolbooks on the floor under the window, textbooks and exercise books thrown down in a heap. I pick up an exercise book. It smells of damp, and the pages are stuck together. There's another smell too, that makes my skin prickle. It's not coming from the exercise book. I take a deep breath, to steady myself, and peel the pages apart. *The whole of Gaul is divided into three parts . . .* On it goes down the page, in Frederick's awful handwriting. For once, there are no drawings in the margins. I stoop, and replace the exercise book on the slipshod pile.

"What were you doing in here, Felicia?"

"I keep thinking I ought to sort it out."

"It's best left, I should think."

"I can't. These are Frederick's things."

Frederick's things, thrown down as if they are nothing. A pullover with empty sleeves. A cricket bat no one will handle again. They pitched the lot in here, and shut the door on it. But Felicia opened the door. She couldn't keep away.

"Look," she says, pointing, "there are his things that they sent home."

I see it then. The squat bundle of his kit, by the end of the bed. That's what the smell was. Everything that's been near that mud smells of death.

"Haven't you opened it?"

She shakes her head. "I can't."

"They're not the clothes he was wearing when he was killed," I say, and at once I realise I've said too much. But she doesn't seem to notice.

"They sent Harry's kit back too," she says, "but that was all right. I went through it to see if there was anything I could keep for Jeannie. I thought there might be a postcard, or a souvenir he'd picked up. But there wasn't."

I watch Felicia's hands, turning over and over. Her chapped knuckles, her thin wrists coming out of her too-short sleeves. There's that smell again, that you never know before the first time you go up the line. Raw mud, old gas, cordite, shit, rotting flesh. I don't

152

suppose these windows are ever opened. It's airless and the room is too small. I glance behind me. The door is still open.

"You shouldn't come in here," I say to her. She doesn't answer, just looks at me with unreadable eyes. I reach out and take her wrist. "Let's go downstairs."

She takes a deep, noisy breath and a smile quavers over her face. Gently, she withdraws her hand. "I wish he'd stayed in his old bedroom," she says. "But you wouldn't recognise it now. It's got wallpaper with lambs and daffodils all over it."

It's cold in here. Even the books are cold. Felicia ought to come away. The cold is getting into me. I step back from the books, stumble over the edge of the trunk, and catch my balance by grabbing the bedpost. The iron is icy.

"Felicia," I mutter. My lips are thick and clumsy now. "Let's get out of here."

I step back through the open door, and into the corridor. I am trembling and although I am freezing cold, sweat is starting out all over my body.

"Felicia."

I've got to get her out, but I can barely speak. I hear the bedsprings and then her footsteps on the drugget. I sink to my knees and cover my head with my arms and rock myself to stop the trembling. I think that I cry out.

I daren't look up. I rock and rock, easing myself, with my eyes screwed tight shut so I see nothing. There's a bad taste in my mouth. I hear footsteps going away and then coming back. Something cold and wet touches me. I open my eyes a chink and see an old enamel mug full of water.

"Drink this," says Felicia.

My hands shake so much as I bring the lip of the mug to my mouth that lumps of water jolt over my clothes. Some goes into my mouth. I look only at the mug. There's a chip in the enamel.

"Can you stand up?"

I shake my head. She's kneeling in front of me. I look a little way beyond the mug. I see her wrists, and the dark blue wool. We stay like that for a long time, while my heart steadies.

"Don't go in that room," I say.

"Hush. It's all right, Daniel. It's only a room."

"Don't go in there again."

I am able to look up at her now. The red patches on her temples are fading. She can be ugly and she's ugly now, pale and draggled, the bones of her skull showing through her skin.

"I'm sorry."

"Can you get up now?" she asks me.

Can you get up now? Can you move your arms? Your legs?

The stretcher party came for me, but not for Frederick. There was no sign of him anywhere. Only blown, sticky mud over everything. A shudder takes hold of me again, as if I'm a child being shaken by a grown man. "Felicia," I say, very quietly so no one will hear, "is there anything behind me?"

"Only the door."

"Is there anything on my hands?"

"What do you mean?"

"Touch my hand. There, like that. Now wipe your hand across. Is there anything? Can you see anything?" I can still smell it. Raw earth, raw iron, meat, explosive. It rains around me but it is invisible. Felicia's hand is clean. "That's good," I tell her. "Look again."

"There's nothing there."

"Felicia. Hold me."

I'm shaking now. If she holds me now, I'll be still. She takes hold of my shoulders, patting me clumsily.

"Hold me."

She doesn't know how. "You're trembling," she says.

I don't answer. I'm trying to keep my teeth from chattering. I'm ashamed. I was never this bad, not in France. It washes over me like the hundredth wave and I cling to the rock. When I come to, our eyes are inches apart. She is still crying, but silently now. A tear slides down to her mouth, and she licks it away.

"I didn't mean to frighten you," I say.

"I know."

"I would never hurt you, Felicia."

"I know."

"I want to get the furnace going for you, so that you and Jeannie are warm."

"Not now. You must come downstairs with me, by the fire, and get warm. We'll eat the pie, and then I have to go and fetch Jeannie."

"All right. Don't cry any more, Felicia."

"I can't cry when Jeannie's here. It frightens her. And then I think that if Frederick could see me, he'd think I'd forgotten him — and then *I* get frightened. I might forget his face. I can't see Harry's any more. I told you that, didn't I?"

"Yes."

"Well then." She takes my hand, just for a second. Her clasp is warm and quick, and then gone. "That's why I come here."

We go down through the empty house. I can't help thinking of that woman, the French teacher, going into someone's stuffy front room, week after week. I've never seen a Ouija board, and I don't want to.

Here's the chair on the landing, where Felicia used to sit, fidgeting, while my mother knelt to fasten her little black boots that buttoned at the sides. Downstairs there was the smell of cooking, the clip of hooves in the yard, the clang of pans from the kitchen. Sunlight lay on the flagstones where the front door was wide open. We heard the drone of Mr Dennis's voice behind his study door. That was before the day he came out, and beat Frederick.

Most of what I remember at Albert House comes from before that day. Maybe I make those times better than they were, by going over and over them in my mind. But I don't think so. A memory like mine is more a curse than a blessing. It cuts into the past, as sharp as a knife, and serves it up glistening. The chair creaks as Felicia fidgets. Frederick hides his new catapult behind his back, so my mother won't see it. He slides a glance at me. We'll be free in a minute, cantering on the gravel before we plunge across the lawn and into the wilderness of camellias and tree ferns and gunnera. My mother is always afraid that one of us will take out the other's eye. How my fingers itch to test the tension of the catapult's elastic.

CHAPTER
ELEVEN

Men removed masks at times when they thought that
the gas had disappeared. As a result of this continued
removal and adjustment of the mask, the men must
have breathed a certain amount of gas.

Gravy spills out of the squab pie as Felicia cuts it in
half. She gives me the larger piece. I hold my knife and
fork as she does, but I can't copy the slowness with
which she eats.

"It's a long time since I tasted proper squab pie," I
tell her. "They put pigeon in it upcountry, did you
know that? I had it once in London. I couldn't eat it.
London pigeons, they're like vermin. You wouldn't
want to put the flesh in your mouth."

The thick, fat taste of the mutton is cut with apple.
They'll be from the old tree on the back wall. Pig's
Nose. That's good keeping fruit.

"You may as well finish it, Dan."

"You and the little one will want it tomorrow."

But she heaps pie on to my plate. When I've finished,
she rises and goes to the larder, comes back with an
earthenware jug covered with a muslin cloth.

"I asked Dolly to fetch me a jug of beer. I don't
know what she must have thought."

I know exactly what she must have thought. There
she is, my blessed Felicia, with her thin wrists and an

expression that gets wiped off the faces of most kids before they're ten years old. She's innocent, that's what she is. Never mind the death of Harry Fearne, the birth of Jeannie. Frederick's death.

I push my chair back and take a deep drink of the beer. This is how it must be, if you're married. Felicia moving around the table, clearing plates, wiping the wood. But if we were married, she'd have made the pie herself. She's playing at something she doesn't know how to do. Same with the baby. Maybe that's why Jeannie cries to go down to Dolly Quick's, because there's a sureness in the old woman that Felicia lacks.

She carries the plates out into the scullery, for Dolly Quick to wash tomorrow I dare say. She leaves the door of the scullery open. It must be damp in there, because a smell creeps out. At first it only touches my nostrils, like a coil of smoke, but then it thickens. I cough, and put my hand up to my mouth. It's all around me now, thick as fog. Gas gets into the earth and stays there. Nothing could flourish in that soil, except rats. There's chloride of lime, or creosol, and the ooze from the latrines. We stink worst of all when we unwrap our puttees. No wonder the rats are close enough to lick our hair-grease. They eye us up like chums. You'll do, they say. You're worth coming back for.

Did you know that a rat gets finicky if he's overfed? He'll eat the eyes and liver out of a dead man and leave the rest. He'll pop out of the hole he's made in a dead man's cheek. As dainty as a cat and about the size of one, but he comes through that hole like water.

She's still in the scullery. I can hear the plates. Drink your beer, Daniel. Drink your beer, old son, and have a coffin-nail.

"Do you mind if I smoke, Felicia?"

"Of course not. I like it."

She likes it because it reminds her of Frederick. I taught Frederick to smoke. He was green as grass the first time. Pallid and sweating before he chucked up his breakfast over the sand. But he kept on going, and soon he wanted a Woodbine as much as I did. You get used to things, that's the curse of it.

I draw in the smoke from my cigarette, and look at Felicia. She smiles. That's her innocence.

"I'll finish this, and then I'll take a look at that furnace. Unless you want to fetch Jeannie first?"

She glances at her wristwatch. "It's still raining," she says. "Maybe it's better if she stays. Dolly will like to have her . . ." She hesitates, rocked this way and that by different thoughts. I wish she would go and get the child, and yet I want her to myself. "It's too late, really," she says. "She'll have told Jeannie she's staying the night. I'll come down to the cellar with you."

The way you get to the furnace is through the cellar. Felicia takes candles, tapers and a lantern, and goes ahead. Albert House has fine dry cellars. Mr Dennis, being an engineer as well as a gentleman, gave a lot of thought to the construction of his house. The architect's drawings used to be displayed in a case in his study, with his own handwritten remarks on them.

160

There are eight steps down, then a turn, and four more steps.

"Wait until I light the lamp," Felicia calls to me. Seconds later a gas lamp on the wall hisses into light, and I see the good order in which everything's kept. The coal cellar and the coke cellar sit side by side, and a wood store beyond. Tools are ranged on shelves and hooks.

"My father's wine cellar is through there," says Felicia. "I don't think we ever went into it, did we?"

I did, with Frederick. He wouldn't allow us to taste the wine: we had to take a whole bottle, he said, otherwise they would find out. We drank it on the clifftops, but I didn't like it, and Frederick only pretended to. We poured the rest of the bottle away, dark red until it sank into the earth.

"They took the wine with them. All of it. Even the claret that was laid down for Frederick's twenty-first birthday." Her face and voice are expressionless.

"But they left you the coal."

She smiles faintly. "The house is mine, did you know that?"

"Yours? You mean, because you're living in it?"

"No. It's really mine. It was my mother's money that paid for building it, and it was always in her name. You didn't know that, did you? No one did. Everyone thought my father was the one who made us rich, out in Australia. Well, he did make money, but she *had* money. The house came to me and Frederick. It was held in trust, until he was twenty-one."

"He wasn't twenty-one when he died."

"My mother thought of that. In case of Frederick's death before he came of age or had an heir, the house came to me. She tied up everything, so that it couldn't be unpicked."

"Your mother thought your father would marry again, mostly likely."

"She must have known he would. He tried to have her will overturned, you know, after Frederick's death. He went to lawyers in Truro, and when they said the will had to stand, he went up to London to the Inns of Court. He came back in a black temper, because they told him there was no doing anything about it, and he'd spent all that money on lawyer's fees. *She* went up to London with him, and when they came back I knew we couldn't live together any more. She'd changed, as soon as she knew they were going to have a baby. They blamed me for the will. They wanted me to sign some documents, giving them a lifetime interest in the house — the right to live here — but I wouldn't. It was my house, from my mother."

She had resisted them. I've got it all wrong. I thought Felicia was left here alone and grieving, clinging by her finger-ends to her childhood home. Abandoned. But it was Felicia who told them all to go. She had the power.

"You know how my father was always talking about *duty*," says Felicia. "He had a duty to me as well, but he didn't care about that. All he thought about was himself — and her and the baby they were going to have, I suppose."

"People are like that, most of 'em."

162

"When I die, everything will go to Jeannie. I've made my will." She stands there, mostly in shadow, with the light from the lamp coming sideways over her shoulder. She's been to a lawyer and made her will. I've seen blokes scribbling down things on bits of paper, saying who was to have what. I never bothered.

Felicia points, and the shadow of her arm leaps on the whitewashed wall to my right. "You remember where the passage is, Dan, behind this door. I'll come with you if you like."

"You stay here. I'll have a dekko at the furnace, and see what tools I need."

"You'll need the lantern. There's no gas in the furnace room. Some light comes through from the ventilation shaft in daytime, but it's getting too dark now."

They have whitewashed the brick passage-walls that I remember so dirty. I have to duck down, but then I'm tall for round here. They put all the short-arses into bantam regiments, like hens.

The passage opens into the furnace room, and there it is, a big, cold thing squatting like a toad, waiting to be fed. There are dials and gauges. It looks as complicated as a ship's engine. Mr Dennis was like that: he didn't want things easy, he wanted them perfect. I can't help thinking of the river of money this house has swallowed.

It's the kind of furnace that ought never to be let go out. You can regulate the flow of hot air to the ducts, or even switch off the flow entirely, so that the furnace only heats water in summer. The furnace room is cold, but it still smells baked and cokey, and the air catches at the back of my throat and makes me cough. The lantern throws a fair light. It'll be a long job to work out what's wrong, and what's needed to fix it. I'll come again first thing tomorrow. Dolly Quick can think what she likes.

CHAPTER
TWELVE

Men's faces and hands should be darkened. Khaki woollen caps or Balaclava helmets have been found a suitable head-dress. Woollen gloves to be worn while crawling forward and thrown away on reaching the enemy's parapet have been found useful.

Men should be armed according to the tasks they are to perform. Bayonet men should carry rifles and bayonets and fifty rounds of ammunition. Revolvers, knobkerries and daggers have been used. Men to carry revolvers must be carefully trained in their use.

Electric torches tied to the rifle with black insulating tape have been found useful for men detailed to clear dugouts. The insulating tape conceals the bright metal parts of the torch and prevents short circuiting.

The raiding party should be provided with the most powerful wire cutters available. Men for wire cutting should be provided with leather hedging gloves.

It seemed from what we learned at Boxall that we'd be fighting most of the time. We marched and drilled, stabbed and shot, until you'd have thought we'd be killing Germans night and day. It wasn't until we got to France that we knew the war was the biggest job of work there'd ever been. You had to wait and see where they were going to slot you in. And then you waited some more. Ned Causley worked in a paint factory up in Plymouth and he was a union man. He said that if they ran a factory like they were running this war, there wouldn't be a can of paint out of it this side of Christmas.

First there was getting there. Weeks it seemed to take, not days. The cloud was down when we marched out of camp. It clung to us, greasy and dripping, all the way to the station where we were to entrain. The thud of our boots was hollow in the fog.

Our train went slow at first, jolting and stopping for long halts at Saltash and then Plymouth. When we crept over the bridge I knew that we were leaving Cornwall, which I'd never done before. We were coming into new, broad, fat country, and the train ran faster. From Exeter it was a troop train, that would take us straight through with only a change of engine. There was a long wait between London and Dover. No one knew why, but rumours went up and down the train that we were being held for the passing of hospital trains. We were in a siding for two hours, but the trains that chuntered past us looked like passenger trains to me. It didn't matter. We'd been given two days' rations, besides what we'd bought from the camp canteen. We were packed in and still jolly. There'd been girls to see us off, and the town band had played outside the camp as we marched. There were crowds at Exeter station, milling about. Lots of women in black, and men with black armbands. You noticed it more outside Cornwall, because there were more people.

There was a long wait at Dover, before our train slid into the shed next to an empty hospital train, marked on the sides with red crosses. They said a hospital ship was being unloaded. We couldn't see anything, but the thought of it quietened us. They marched us away and then we were fallen out to kip down on our packs on the pier. Our escort was still out in the middle of the Channel, so the sergeant said. We were all weary, or what we thought was weary then. The sea was a dark, dirty grey, slopping about like water that clothes have been washed in. There was a destroyer lying close in harbour, which had come in with the hospital ship. Late in the afternoon the sun shone and made the sea gleam like a pewter mug. But it was nothing like the sea at home. We could hear the dockers shouting, and men giving orders. The hospital ship was white with a green band around it. It was such a huge ship that you wouldn't think there could be so many wounded to be brought home at one time.

I saw cattle put into a boat for the Scillies once, at Newlyn. I'd never thought of live cattle being transported by water. They were swung out one by one, in a sort of sling, lowing loudly. They were big, fat Friesians, not like our wild little Zennor cattle. You could see the shit fall from them as they were swung.

I wondered if the war had forgotten about us, although I knew it couldn't have done. A man in overalls shinned about in the girders above our heads, tapping nuts and tightening them. He didn't care a bit about the drop beneath him. It seemed queer that all this ordinary business was going on. The man whistling, and the tap of metal. Then there was an order: we were to march to another quay, where the troopship lay.

I'd never imagined a vessel as tall as that one. It looked as if it could carry a city of men. Some were already up there, moving about like ants. Khaki ants. But my feet were still on solid earth. I wondered how I should ever come back. It seemed like a dream, that the ship was going to take all of us away with it, to another country, and that maybe we'd come back in that white ship with its green band, or maybe we wouldn't come back. I wondered if the others thought of it, but no one said a word except about when we'd next have a brew, and what the tarts were going to be like in France. The crossing was roughish and we had to wear life-jackets in case of mines, or maybe submarines. Some of the boys were sick. We sat on deck and smoked, and saw England sidle away backwards, as if it was trying to escape. Rain was spattering out of the clouds, but not much. Being on that boat was something and nothing. We were in the army, but the army doesn't fight on water. We weren't in England and we weren't in France. I didn't mind how long the crossing lasted.

When we landed, we were in France. After all the talking and training, there it was, an ordinary town with gulls flying up against the houses and people going about their business, not stopping to look at us because they were so used to the sight of us I suppose. It smelled different from England and the houses were higher and narrower, crowding together. The sky was white and it showed up the peeling paint and the posters that were coming off the walls. The notices were all in French, which surprised me, though it shouldn't have done. Some of the lads began to sing "Inky pinky parlay voo" in a defiant kind of way, as if they were daring the French to know that we'd only just got here. We marched through the town to the railway station, and I wanted to buy some cakes a girl had in a little tray around her neck. She ran alongside us chattering all the time in French, about the prices I should think, but no one knew how to work it out and I didn't want to give her English money in case she cheated me. I can see her now. A clean, dusty-blue apron, and seven or nine little cakes, round and glistening fat, on a nice sheet of paper. It was an odd number of cakes, I do remember that. I wanted one so much that my mouth watered, but I never got it.

They put us in cattle trucks. Some of the lads made mooing noises and shouted, "Get on up there, Daisy!" but it stood to reason, really, that there couldn't be enough railway carriages in France for all the men that were coming through. Our train ran along briskly for twenty minutes, showing us country that looked much like what we'd seen on the other side, as we came through Kent. The fields were bigger, though, and they laid their hedges differently. We stopped again, in the middle of nowhere. I thought: This is France. I'm in another country — but I couldn't feel it. I only had the same knot in my stomach I'd had for days, and on top of that a peaceful feeling, because I couldn't do anything about anything any more.

I peered through the chink. A woman was scrubbing her doorstep, far enough away that she could ignore the

169

shouts and whistles. She looked up, shaded her eyes, and waved her scrubbing brush as if she was shooing away flies. I licked my finger to pick up the last crumbs of chocolate from a bar of Five Boys. I was always hungry then. I suppose I was still growing.

We'd all heard about the Bullring, and that the instructors were fucking bastards who would drill a man until he fell down unconscious, so there was a groan when we learned we were going to Étaples. As it turned out, we didn't stay there long. The camp was jammed. The latrines overflowed on to the concrete floors because of an outbreak of dysentery. They were trying to clear the camp, not put more men into it. We drew our weapons there, and then we were put on to yet another train, that jerked and stopped and jolted us to the front: or at least we thought, in our ignorance, that it was taking us up the line with our brand-new rifles. The thing I remember most about that train is that someone had got hold of a bag of oranges, and we made false teeth out of the peel. Then we were in another base camp well behind the line for more courses on gas and assault training, and training for night work.

We paid attention when it sounded like something that could get you killed if you didn't. Most of it was the usual: drill and bull, hours of it, but no one fell down or died of sunstroke as we'd been told. It wasn't a bad life.

As soon as I'd been at the camp a day, I knew I should have had a trade. The carpenters and joiners were put into workshops to make box loopholes, knife rests, floor gratings and all the rest of it. They made signboards, too. The camp was like a town, with all the streets marked. Everybody except us seemed to know what they were meant to be doing. You had to look sharp.

If you got into a brigade workshop, you were a made man. Blacksmiths and farriers had more work than they had at home, what with all the pack animals. Then there was laying telephone wires, driving the brass to and fro behind the lines, cooking the rations. Skilled men had their hands full, and weren't likely to find themselves in the fire-trench. But there wasn't any call for a gardener. You'd be marched through a village which had been knocked to bits by shelling, and all there'd be left of a hundred gardens was a bit of green straggling out of a gash in a wall. The fields hadn't any hedges, most of the time. At first, when the word "wood" was mentioned, I expected to see trees, but I soon learned that it meant a place where a wood had been, and that there might be a few stumps left, or not.

I'd heard a lot of stuff about the fields we were fighting for, before ever I saw them. For me, fields were small and sharply green, with stone hedges around them and cattle plotting how to scramble a way out of them. Once you got up near the line, there wasn't much you could recognise as a field, any more than the woods were woods. It was all a jumble. It took a while to make sense of it. There'd be patches where everything was going on as normal. We'd be marching and the French would be ploughing. Other parts, there was only the war.

Everybody else seemed to know where they were going and what they were doing, and so we kept our mouths shut. Half of what was being said, I couldn't even understand at first. I thought it was French, but it was mostly what the regular soldiers learned out in India. You soon picked it up. I was always quick with words.

There wasn't any gardening, but there was plenty of digging. We were always at it. Trenches, pits, dugouts, latrines, graves. We were more like navvies than soldiers, with our picks and shovels, sandbags and rabbit netting. The first time we went up the line it was wiring parties every night, because they were expecting another German offensive. We never stopped having to repair the wire, or lay down new wire, or get things off the wire that oughtn't to have been on it, or cut the wire where a patrol was going out. The worst bit was fixing the corkscrews in silence while the wire leapt about in the dark, sweating, heaving, knowing that if you could see what you were doing, then so could the Germans. They were waiting. They only had to get lucky once, while we had to be lucky all the time.

I could have been sent to Army School. Sergeant Mills was right about that, back in Boxall. It would have been a trade, but it had drawbacks. Fritz might be trying to kill blacksmiths, chefs and mechanics and farriers and all the rest of us — but not always very hard, and only in a general way, just as we weren't always trying very hard to kill them. However, they were always trying very hard and in a very particular way to kill any sniper they could. Just as we were. I was

172

in the Riflemen section of my platoon and took my turn at sniping, but that wasn't the same as creeping out into no-man's-land and hiding in a fake tree trunk in full sight of the guns.

Fritz might bob up, careless, as any of us might, even though it was drilled into us to keep our heads down. He might be caught short, hurrying to the latrine, or he might be thinking about a letter he'd just had, telling him his best girl was off with someone else. That was your chance. They'd do the same for us, we knew that. Sometimes, for no reason, we'd hold back. Other times, we wouldn't. I was the best. Everyone knew it. I'd get the nudge: *One for Danny over there.* The company didn't want me in a sniper detachment any more than I did. I was more use where I was.

It was Frederick's coming that mucked it up. The months I'd spent head down, part of it. We moved and ate and drilled, nursed up our jokes, sweated and ached and itched and shat, all the same. We were all different and we were all the same. I'd never been part of anything before, not like that. If you had a new pair of socks sent to you, and your mate's socks had holes, that was it. He had the socks. You didn't think about it. We were paired up to look after each other's feet. Looking after your own feet wasn't sufficient incentive. You'd think selfishness would be the stronger force, but it turns out that isn't so. Tell a man to unwrap his puttees, take off his boots, dry each toe individually, examine his feet for sores and rub them all over with whale oil, and tell him that if he doesn't he'll get trench foot which will cause his feet to go black and stink and maybe even

173

have to be cut off — well, you'd think he'd do it. But he doesn't. He's cold and wet and dead beat and all he wants is to get some kip. Tell him he's responsible for the feet of the man next to him, and he does it.

It was strange for me, since I'd always been separate all my life, off by myself. Here, I could forget about that. I had to, and it felt easy. I'd hear myself roaring out songs some nights in the estaminet when we were on rest, while a weaselly little boy ran about with glasses and we all despised him together. We'd drink their rat's-piss vin blanc because the beer was such that even we couldn't drink it, until we could fool ourselves we were drunk enough, and stagger back arm in arm. We hated the French a hundred times worse than the Germans, because they spent their lives dunning us while we were supposedly fighting for them. If they had as much as a bad egg, they'd haggle you into paying twice what a good egg was worth. The French bints were dirty, or that was what Sergeant Morris told us. We had talks about diseases but usually the lecturer couldn't make himself heard over the shouting and whistling.

Frederick was posted to A Company, to command our platoon, after Mr Tremough was killed. Frederick turned me back into what I used to be, even though he didn't know he was doing it. He'd been in the Third Battalion since he got his commission, until his company was smashed up at Fellancourt Wood. They were trying to retake a salient near the Soutines Ridge, which the Germans had taken from us three months previously. Frederick explained the plan of attack to me later. Our heavy artillery was to have knocked out the German heavy artillery position with gas shells, and then they were to shell the two machine-gun emplacements that had been identified. Our light artillery would pin their men in their trenches. The Third would then advance behind a creeping barrage. It was a good plan of attack, he thought, or would have been if they hadn't thrown in a smokescreen as well. Frederick's platoon must have got ahead of itself. Timing was everything. For a few seconds they might have thought they were being hit by short-falling shells, then they must have known that they were ahead of the timetable and up in the barrage. Frederick was knocked out by shell-blast.

"The smoke was clearing," he told me later. "I didn't know where I was and something was on top of me, pinning me down. It seemed to take hours to work out what it was. I was on my back and the thing across my face was a hand. Not my hand. Do you know, I had a queer idea that it was yours. And the body that belonged to the hand was crushing me. I was squinting through someone else's fingers. I had some sort of idea that he was pushing me down into the earth. Burying me. I'd forgotten about the war. I started fighting with him, trying to get him off me. I pushed and shoved in a most awful panic but he wouldn't budge, and I couldn't get an arm free to pick his fingers off my face. I twisted my head round and that got his hand off me, and then I could see that he couldn't stir because there was another man lying across his legs.

175

"There were six of them. All from my platoon, but I didn't know that then. All I wanted was to get them off me. You've no idea how heavy they were. I would have done anything to get them off me.

"There was such a mess everywhere. Everything was jumbled up, you couldn't recognise it. I did know Hicks, because his face wasn't touched. He was covered in earth up to the waist and he had his arms flung up beside his head as if he was sleeping, but he was dead too. You remember Pip Lily — how Felicia used to throw her across the room? She'd land anyhow, wouldn't she? — legs folded up behind her so it didn't look as if she had any. They looked like Pip Lily, all of them. Doubled over, heads down. Helmets still on. Like some awful game. I picked up a rifle — mine had gone. The firing was only sporadic by then. When I crawled out there was mess all over the place and a few men stumbling back to our line. The barrage had stopped. I knew something had gone most awfully wrong."

Seventeen men from Frederick's platoon were killed, and six more seriously wounded. It wasn't only his platoon but most of B Company. In all, more than a third of the battalion was killed, and another two hundred men out of action. It shouldn't have happened, Frederick said. He kept repeating that it was a good plan of attack, even though the outcome was a disaster. Losses like that were exactly the kind of thing the new tactics were designed to prevent. There were pockmarks on his forehead, where bits of shrapnel had been blown in, and the muscle under his right cheekbone jumped when he spoke.

Frederick was posted to the Second, given how many men they'd need to bring the Third back up to strength and the time it would take. The sniper had got Mr Tremough, so we needed another officer. We'd heard about Soutines and thanked Christ we'd been out of it. Frederick seemed to bring some of that disaster with him. Nobody talked about it but everyone thought of it.

He'd always been Frederick. Now he was Mr Dennis, in command of our platoon. He was watching me. I was watching him. I felt as if the skin had been taken off me. I was back on my own, the way I'd always been, fighting my own corner, walking the high road, saying my poems aloud. But there were men around me day and night and their feet were my feet.

I kept my head down. I didn't catch Frederick's eye if I could avoid it. I thought he would appreciate the reasons. Ours was a good platoon, one of the best, not sloppy. I said Frederick and I were from the same town, because it was clear that we knew each other. Everyone understood that with him an officer and me a private, being from the same town didn't mean much. As soon as he opened his mouth you could tell he wasn't my kind. His kind and mine lived parallel, not together. Why that wasn't true of me and Frederick, nobody knew, or needed to.

I didn't know what to do. I was hypnotised by the sight of that muscle jumping under his cheekbone. He was drinking, I knew that, but nothing out of the way. All the officers drank whisky. I looked at him and saw how different from the rest of us he looked. His skin.

His uniform. The way his hair was cut, and the way he stood. I saw all those things as if I'd never seen them before. As if someone was pointing them out in a lecture.

I didn't know how to be all the things I was meant to be, to Frederick, to the others, to the war. It brought me back to myself, and I didn't want that. I talked like the others, wrote my letter on my knee like the others and gave it to him to be censored, drank my tea thick with sugar to hide the taint of petrol or worse, and swilled out the latrine bucket which was full of our shared piss and shit. It was the others I needed, not Frederick. Or so I believed. I wanted him away from me, where I could write him letters. He'd still be Frederick and I'd be Daniel, the way we used to be, with no divisions between us.

He didn't get on with Captain Morton-Smith. They grated on each other and that grated on all of us. Mr Tremough, before the sniper got him, was a man with the same kind of easiness Andrew Sennen had, and so all the men liked him. Even the captain couldn't manage to quarrel with him. Also, Mr Tremough would play Twenty-one with him. Captain Morton-Smith never niggled us, and had the sense never to say a wrong word to Sergeant Morris. He prided himself on the way he got on with the men. But he niggled his junior officers. It's bad when officers don't get along.

The first time Frederick and I talked properly was when we were billeted at Estancourt, for five days' rest. I was in the Cat Fur with the others, and we'd settled in to make a night of it. The place was packed out, fugged with smoke and frying fat. I'd had my egg and chips and then gone out for a piss. For some reason I wandered off round the corner and there was a door in the wall. Nothing new there: there'd been the same wooden door in that wall two days ago, when we marched past, but it had been shut and locked. Tonight it was ajar, and I couldn't help being curious to look inside.

It was a garden. Not much of one, but still a garden. There were gravel paths, espaliered pear trees, a big quince. There were no leaves in that season, of course, but I knew them all by their shapes. The garden wasn't well kept; in fact it was knocked about a bit, but it had things growing in it, and it smelled of earth from the beds that had been dug over, by the wall. Not mud: earth.

There was a crunching on the gravel, and I saw that down by the end of the garden there was a man walking, and then that the man was Frederick. He saw me too. I saluted, and he came over and said, "Don't be such a fatuous ape. There's no one else here."

I didn't dispute that, although I could have said that it was as well to keep to habit in case you forgot yourself later on. It was still and quiet, as if the garden was its own little world. I didn't want to disturb it.

"All right," I said.

"So we're still friends," said Frederick, like a child, with laughter bubbling in his voice. He sounded so like the old Frederick that my heart leapt up, and I said, "Of course we are."

"Dear old boy," said Frederick. I had never heard him say anything like that, not since he once said, "My blessed Felicia." I wasn't used to soft words, not from him nor anyone. They melted me so that I could have fallen down there on the gravel path. I was glad it was dark, to hide my face. Then he said, clearing his throat, "Felicia's married, did you know that?"

"Yes. My mother told me in a letter." I didn't tell him that he'd written to me himself, about the marriage. I supposed he'd forgotten. Shell-blast could knock memory out of a man, I knew that.

"I don't know what kind of man he is. But I suppose Felicia knows what she's doing."

"I suppose she does."

There was a long pause, then: "Tell me one of your poems, why don't you?" he asked suddenly.

I could have resisted him, but I didn't. I nodded, although I'm not sure that he saw it in the dark. I felt softened and sleepy and wide awake, all at the same time. There was only a sliver of moon. I waited, to see which poem would rise in my mind. All my poems lay deep down. That was the way they kept themselves whole. And then these lines did rise, I don't know why. Because it was night, maybe, and we were both of us soldiers in France:

"The sea is calm tonight,
The tide is full, the moon lies fair
Upon the straits; on the French coast the light
Gleams and is gone . . ."

180

I stopped, and cleared my throat. It would take too long to say the whole poem. Frederick would get bored.

"Go on," he said.

"It's too long. I'll give you the last lines."

The dark was soft all around me, touching my eyes and lips, getting into my throat.

> "Ah, love, let us be true
> To one another! for the world, which seems
> To lie before us like a land of dreams,
> So various, so beautiful, so new,
> Hath really neither joy, nor love, nor light,
> Nor certitude, nor peace, nor help for pain;
> And we are here as on a darkling plain
> Swept with confused alarms of struggle and flight,
> Where ignorant armies clash by night."

Frederick listened intently. "*Ignorant armies* . . ." he said. "That's very good, isn't it?"

He spoke as if he really wanted to know.

"I think it's very good," I said. But it was another line that echoed over and over in me.

"Who wrote it?"

"Matthew Arnold. It's on your father's shelves."

"If you haven't chucked it over a cliff."

We both laughed.

"It beats me how you can spout reams of it, just like that."

"It's just a knack."

"The guns cut across the lines rather, don't they?" I hadn't noticed. His clipped voice was carrying us further and further from the poem. "I can't say that Estancourt is much like the land of dreams," he went on. "Although this isn't a bad billet, is it? Are you comfortable?"

"Yes," I said.

We had clean straw mattresses in the loft of a barn, clean water, a village that was more or less undamaged to walk about in, the Cat Fur for the evenings. We could watch women working in the fields, as if there wasn't a war at all. It made me realise that up the line it was a new kind of country, man-made. No one had ever seen it before, and no woman had ever been there. You could get fresh eggs and milk every day in Estancourt, if you didn't mind being cheated. Better than all of that, we had three more clear days' rest.

"You seem to get on all right," he said, his voice strange. "I can't believe how well you've got yourself dug in."

"What do you mean?"

"I suppose I wasn't expecting you to have changed."

"We've all changed."

"I suppose so."

There was silence. I felt that he was disappointed in me, and I was angry with him for being disappointed, even though I knew why it was. Why hadn't he wanted to talk about the poem?

"I hated poetry at school," said Frederick, and now I heard the appeal in his voice. "I'm all right as long as I've got you to explain it for me."

My throat had tightened up again. I cleared it, and said, "*Ah, love, let us be true / To one another . . .*" There's nothing difficult about that, is there?"

"I suppose he wrote it for the woman he was in love with."

All the night noises came clearer than ever. There were shouts from the Cat Fur, and an engine revved somewhere farther off. The wind rattled the twigs lightly. No heavy firing, just the odd burst. Enough to make you glad you weren't there, and a bit anxious too, as if you ought to have been. As if where the firing came from was the only place that was real. But that was all rubbish. Frederick was so close that I heard the little catch of his breath before he spoke.

"There's a bit of a push coming," he said. "We're having another shot at that ridge."

"Soutines Ridge?" I couldn't believe it was happening again.

"We can't let them hold a position like that," said Frederick, as flat as a pancake. He shouldn't have been telling me any of it. It was for officers to know and men to be told in due course, preferably only hours beforehand so they didn't have time to get the wind up. I'd heard rumours, but hearing it from Frederick's mouth was a different thing.

"If at first you don't succeed," said Frederick, "try, try and try again."

I said nothing. Fritz could hold on to Soutines Ridge for the rest of eternity as far as I was concerned, if the alternative was the same happening to us as had happened to the Third. In our present position we

183

couldn't advance, but we were lucky. It was a quiet sector. We kept our heads down. It might seem strange, looking back, that all we wanted was for nothing to happen, because that would have meant that the war would go on for ever. We'd be rotating in and out of the line until kingdom come. But we knew that the fewer big ideas the brass got, the better it was for us.

"D'you fancy a trench raid?" asked Frederick abruptly.

"What?" I was still thinking about Soutines.

"I need volunteers."

"You can't retake Soutines Ridge with a raiding party," I said stupidly.

"No, you blithering idiot, this has nothing to do with Soutines. It's not very likely they'd be asking a second lieutenant to recruit for that, is it? Soutines is a pleasure for the future, like Christmas. This is a minor company enterprise, a little piece of night work just for us. One officer, Sergeant Morris, a couple of corporals and forty-eight men picked from all four platoons. Volunteers," he added, after a pause.

He kept his voice light, with its bantering edge, but I knew him better than that. He'd been cut up at Soutines, even though he only had those shrapnel fragments in his forehead to show for it. They'd healed, but they gave him a queer look. There was something in him now that all the men felt. No one put a name to it. He'd lost his luck, you could say, if you wanted to, but that wasn't it. You might call it the war, but it was more than that. It was what happened when nothing mattered, or everything mattered in the same dull, ugly,

184

pointless way, day after day after day. It was how I'd felt for a long time, after the fight with Andrew Sennen. But I didn't feel it that night in Estancourt, not as Frederick did. I suppose it was knowing that when I went back into the Cat Fur they'd all budge up on the bench for me and there we'd be, packed in, swallowed up in noise and heat and fug. No one in our platoon said anything to me about Frederick, but they didn't warm to him.

Still I said nothing. I knew enough never to volunteer, but at the same time, as sure as if I'd been shown a picture postcard with my face on it, I knew I'd be there.

"There'll be two days' training," said Frederick. "It's a tricky piece of work."

"Just to get a prisoner?"

"It's a bit more ambitious than that."

Two more days behind the line, in a cushy billet. Most trench raids, you were picked a few hours before, when you were already up the line. I wondered what was so special about this one. Two days' training. That must mean that we were more than usually likely to get our heads blown off. And then I thought: Why not? My death was waiting for me somewhere. Maybe not yet, maybe not here. I was careful, or as careful as I could be, but that made no difference. I didn't want to stir death up, by trying to outwit it. That was the kind of logic I used to convince myself. But deeper than that, I knew that if Frederick was going on a night raid, then I was going too. The thought of the raiding party made my guts crawl, but I was used to that.

"You never know, we could get a Blighty one before Soutines," I said.

"Bugger Soutines," he said. "Are you on then, BB?"

"Looks like it."

"Wot Larks," he said.

I was startled. But then I remembered one morning when we walked over the downs together, with shadows bulking at us out of the mist, and I told him about Pip and Magwitch, and he liked it so much I went on to tell him everything I could remember, about Joe and Pip in the chimney corner, and each of them biting a shape out of his bread and butter and holding it up to show the other, and Joe sending his message to Pip after Pip thought he was already more than half a gentleman: *Wot Larks*.

Those days had vanished like smoke. But Frederick was real, even in the ghostly gloom of the garden. He was always more real than anyone. There he was, scrabbling at gravel in the dark with a stick, drawing lines and rubbing them away as if they were sums that wouldn't come out right. *Nor certitude, nor peace, nor help for pain . . .*

I touched his arm, to bring him back from whatever dark place he'd gone. "All right, boy?" I said.

"All right? Christ!" He shook off my hand. "I've had enough of this. I need a drink."

A man drank if he had the money for it. It was natural, given where we were. I thought of the red wine we'd taken from Mr Dennis's cellar, spilled on the ground because we didn't like the taste.

"You go down that whisky bottle fast enough," I said.

186

"What the fuck do you mean?" He barged against me. I wasn't expecting it and I went sprawling. The gravel would have been all right, but I struck the back of my head on an edging stone and bit my tongue so hard that a rush of salty blood filled my mouth. It tasted like iron filings. I rolled over, spat it out, retched, spat again. Frederick was down on the ground with me, trying to pull me up, asking me if I was all right and if I could see straight. It was too dark to see at all. His breath was in my face, hot and quick. His hands came around my face and held it.

"Can you hear me?"

I grunted.

"Christ," he said, "when I heard your head crack on the stone like that, I thought I'd killed you." His hand slid around the back of my head, exploring it. "You're bleeding."

"It's nothing," I mumbled thickly, through the blood in my mouth. It hurt, but somehow I wanted to laugh. It was ridiculous, the two of us. Me and Frederick, fighting in the middle of a war. And as well as wanting to laugh, I wanted his hands to stay there, holding me. I didn't want him ever to move.

"You old blowviator," said Frederick in relief, "I believe your head's made of iron."

"Put a round into me, all you get's a hole in the bullet."

We were laughing. He was hauling me up. We staggered together and I could smell the drink on him as well as on me. I felt drunker than I'd been all night. I don't know what happened then except our faces must have got close. I tasted my own blood and then his mouth, his spit and the taste I seemed to know already because I knew the smell of him so well. Him, himself, as if we'd come out of the same womb. How good he tasted. We were no use on our own, either of us. If I was ever going to be myself, I needed him.

We pulled apart and I tried to look at him, but he was all shadows.

"You old fucking blowviator," he said. His hands dropped to my shoulders, and he shook me, lightly, as if to say: Here you are. I could hear him breathing. I wondered if my blood had got smeared on him somehow. We were already blood brothers, from long ago. We belonged to each other, I knew that now for sure.

"I'll look after you," I said, God knows why. He'd be leading the raiding party, not me.

There was a roaring from beyond the garden. It took me a moment to realise that it was my name they were calling.

"*Danny! Daaaannnnneeee!*"

It was time to get back to the others. They wouldn't leave off calling until they found me, for fear I'd dropped down drunk somewhere and would end up put on a charge.

"*Danny! Daaaannnnny. You there, boy? DAAAANNNEEEE!*"

I didn't have to say to Frederick: You wait here, I don't want us to be seen coming out of here together. He drifted into the shadow under the wall, and I saw a spurt of flame as he lit a cigarette. I thought of it in his mouth as I went to the wooden door, passed through it, and made my way into the world outside.

CHAPTER
THIRTEEN

It is seldom advisable to persevere in a minor enterprise
if the enemy are found ready and prepared.

Yesterday seems a long way away. Today there's a
beautiful morning, with the sea so bright you can't look
at it straight. I eat my porridge and drink a mug of
milk. I was late back last night and I felt ashamed when
I heard the goat bleating her distress across the field,
tethered as she was.

I lay the morning's eggs carefully with yesterday's,
ready to take to Enoch. One of the hens is bloody
from a pecking, and I take her out of the run. Once
the other hens start on her, they won't leave off. I
keep a small, separate run for any hen that shows
signs of sickness, and I put her into it. At once she
begins to run up and down, squawking, as if I've
done her harm. After milking, I take up the goat's
post and tether her in a new spot. I decide to take
some eggs to Felicia, choose four fine ones and lay
them in straw in a brown paper bag. Let's see if I
can get them to Albert House without as much as a
crack. Maybe, if that henpecked fowl can't settle with
the flock again, I'll wring her neck. Felicia can have
her for the pot.

I know Felicia can go into the shops and order
anything she has a mind to. She doesn't need eggs from

me. I suppose I like to do it. You get tired of looking out for yourself.

I go the long way round, to avoid the town as much as I can. It's the brightest, purest, sunniest morning imaginable. It reminds me of when I used to slam the house door shut behind me and run up the street on my way up to Mulla House, my boots striking on the cobbles. My mother had iron tips nailed to them, sole and heel, to make them last. I dashed them down, and they rang on the stones. I was earlier than the schoolchildren but not as early as the fishermen, who were gone already on the tide. I used to feel a flash of pride when a man nodded to me, "All right, my boy?" knowing that I was off to work. All I had to carry was myself, since we were given dinner in the back kitchen. Maybe a cart would go past me and I'd get a ride.

Felicia comes to the door. She looks preoccupied, not welcoming as I'd hoped and half expected. She has Jeannie by the hand, dressed in a little velvet coat and hat. Jeannie looks up at me with her finger in her mouth.

"Oh, Daniel." Felicia shades her eyes against the light. "I was just on my way to church."

"Church?"

"It's Sunday, Dan." She expands, as women do when they want to put you off, with their tender way of explaining how the world works. "Surely you know it's Sunday."

And sure enough, the bells are banging away, down on the quay. I hadn't noticed until she spoke.

"Do you always go to church?"

She looks down. "Not as often as I should. I take Jeannie sometimes."

"*Should?* What do you mean? Why should you do anything you don't want?"

Jeannie sees a baby sowpig crawling over the threshold. She lets go of Felicia's hand and crouches down to watch it. She puts her finger out and I'm afraid she'll crush the little creature, but she doesn't.

"I do want to," says Felicia. "It's good for Jeannie. She likes watching everybody, and it gives me time to think. It makes me — I feel nearer to Frederick."

"Nearer to *Frederick?* Because you run when the bells ring?"

"I don't run, I walk. I'm not a little girl now."

The bells rise to a clamour, and then they stop. Felicia doesn't move.

"One thing I do know," I say, jerking my thumb churchwards, "is that Frederick's not down there."

She tugs on her gloves. "Do you think I don't know that?"

"I came to mend the furnace, but I suppose you won't agree to it, given it's Sunday."

"Oh! I'd forgotten. I'm sorry, Dan. I ought to have remembered."

"Yes, you ought," I say. "You can't go forgetting things you've agreed with other people, not if you want to keep your friends."

"Are you my friend, Dan?" she asks, soft and wheedling, and smiling a little too, as if she thinks it's funny to be the Felicia who can speak to me like this.

"That's not up for discussion."

She laughs outright, a crow I haven't heard out of her for ten years maybe, and then she strips off her gloves. Jeannie looks up at the sound of her mother laughing, and abandons the sowpig. "You'd better come inside," says Felicia. "Jeannie, come here. Let me take off your coat and hat, and you can play with your horse."

"Seeing as you've just damned your immortal soul, maybe you don't need the furnace lit after all." And then I remember the eggs, and lift them out of my coat pocket tenderly, and give the bag to her. "New laid this morning," I say. She puts her fingers into the straw and strokes the shells.

"They feel warm," she says. "Do you think they'd hatch, if I put them by the range?"

"They're for you to eat."

"I've got enough to eat."

"You don't look as if you had."

"I'd like to keep chicks."

"They're work, Felicia."

"I know that. But it would be nice to have them running about. Jeannie would like it. We haven't even got a dog. I haven't got a dog," she corrects herself.

"You could get one."

"Of course I couldn't. I don't know where I'm going to be. You know I'm going to sell this house."

This chills me so much I'm silent. Felicia's life alarms me. She camps in the house as if she's been billeted there, not as if it's her home. She might forget to eat. She's thin and pale enough as it is. When she piles her hair up on her head like that, and puts a hat on top, she looks as if the weight of it will break her neck.

"I saw girls with bobbed hair in London," I say. "Running for omnibuses."

Felicia makes herself busy with Jeannie, and doesn't reply. I follow them into the house. Felicia takes off the little velvet coat and hat, and hangs them up carefully. I watch the bend and sway of her, and the line of her body as she stretches up to the peg. It's hard to believe this child ever came out of Felicia's body. I turn my thought away quickly. Under the coat, Jeannie is wearing a red woollen dress with smocking. Felicia takes a pinafore off another peg, and buttons the child into it.

"Now you can play," she says.

"You should have a peg low down for her, so she can reach it. She'd soon learn to hang up her own things. I'll put in a peg for you if you like," I say.

Jeannie's horse is a battered plush horse's head on a pole, with a mane of real horsehair. I remember Felicia riding it. Jeannie is too young for that, but she sits on the floor with the horse's head in her lap, and croons to it.

"She loves that horse," says Felicia. "She takes it into bed with her."

"Can you leave her to play here, while we go down to the cellars?"

Felicia laughs. "Of course I can't. You don't know much about children, do you, Dan? I'm with her every hour of the day, unless Dolly has her. But I went down early to fetch her home, because I didn't want Dolly taking her to chapel. Jeannie'd be frightened if I went down to the cellar and left her. I can carry her. It'll be an adventure for her."

"I'll carry her, if you like."

"You can try."

I can see Felicia doesn't expect the child to come to me. I pick her up, and she's stiff in my arms at first, resisting, her face turned away. I'm afraid she'll cry, so I gentle her as if she's a pony we've stolen out of a field.

"You'll come down with me, won't you, Jeannie? Your mother's going to hold the light and we're going to follow after her. You'll be able to see her all the while."

After a minute, I feel her body yield and curl into my shoulder. Felicia's looking at me, her face softened.

She leads me back to the cellar steps. I duck down, shielding Jeannie's head against the low doorway. This time Felicia has brought two lanterns, in spite of the brightness of the day.

"I'll show you where the tools for the furnace are kept."

There are shovels, and curious long pokers with the end at right angles to the stem, brushes, wrenches, pliers, a selection of flue brushes. I hand Jeannie to her mother and go back and forth with the tools until everything I might need is laid out on the stone floor in front of the furnace. There's a tool which levers open the furnace door. Inside, there's the dry smell of combustion. I empty everything: Josh has laid the furnace with paper, wood and coal, then coke in a pyramid above it. The paper has caught, but the wood is singed, no more. I riddle out under the grate, and remove the clinker. There's not much there. I take the flue brushes, the longest first, and angle it up the chimney. I jab it as far as I can from side to side, but there's no rush of soot, as there was in the cottage. Some dirt falls, again not much. I go back down the passage, to see if Felicia's waiting with Jeannie, but the cellars are empty. She must have taken the child back upstairs.

We used to be able to crawl into the passages that led to the hot-air ducts. We could only do it when the furnace was cold, in summer. They were wide enough for a child. And maybe wider than that. I remember us scampering down them like rats, not having to squeeze ourselves.

It's cold down here. I hunker in front of the furnace again, and contemplate it. There must be a blockage deeper in the system, which is making the furnace shut down before it's properly alight. I lift the lantern high. Over in the corner of the furnace room, there's a gap at the side of the inward air shaft, where the chicken wire that should cover it is broken. The gap is big enough for a rat, or a bird. If a creature came in and flew about, it might become trapped; but where? It would need to be within some sensitive part of the mechanism.

The furnace sits like a spider in the heart of its web. We used to play games in the tunnels. I remember sitting tight for what seemed like hours, barely breathing, listening for footfalls or the shuffle of Frederick on his hands and knees. The biggest tunnel is

196

opposite the furnace. I don't know what its purpose is. Unlike the other ducts, its brickwork has no metal lining. Maybe it was built for a purpose that was later abandoned.

The tunnel draws me to it. I know I won't solve the problem of the furnace by scrambling about in the bowels of the house, but I want to. Felicia is upstairs, far away. This house is too solidly built for me to hear any sound from above ground.

We used to put a wooden box beneath the opening of the tunnel, so that we could climb up and then inside. I remember that now. Even for a grown man, the height is awkward. I put my hands on the brickwork, heave and haul myself upwards. It's much more effort than I remember, and I'm too big. My body fills up the space and my head bangs against the roof of the tunnel. I scrabble for a handhold, wriggle, kick myself inside. Now I'm lying full length, and it's easier. There's not enough room to get up on all fours, but I can push myself along, using my elbows. It's not dark in here, not truly dark. I feel safe. The tunnel doesn't narrow, but it comes to an angle where my body remembers turning once, easily, eeling with a child's elasticity around the corner. I can't do that now. I turn on to my side, tuck my head down and lead with my right shoulder, pushing myself forward with the tips of my boots. I'm moving. I'm going round.

Halfway, my boots lose their grip. I am wedged. I'm not going to make the turn. I can't go forward, and as I flail my feet for a grip, I know I can't go back either.

197

There is nothing to push against. I'm in the wrong position.

Slow. Slow. Think about it. Don't let yourself panic, boy. You do that, you're stuck for sure. Inch by inch, grating the side of my head against brick, I turn my head. The head is the biggest part, you've got to get that through.

O dream of joy is this indeed O dream of joy is
this indeed O dream of joy O dream of joy O
dream

Don't let yourself think beyond the line, Dan boy. Don't go beyond the line. There's nothing behind you. Breathe steady now. Go steady. Go on.

I come round that corner like a fish, as if something's pulling me. Now it's dark for sure. The tunnel's widened out somehow. I don't remember it being like this. I feel behind me. There's chicken wire over the brickwork. Or is it brickwork? It feels too cold and damp for that. There's a smell of rotting sandbags. Damp has got into this house for sure. Maybe old Dennis built it over a stream without knowing it.

This dugout is like the Savoy.
You've never been in the Savoy in your life, you
old blowviator.

"Frederick?"
I shuffle until my back is against the wall. He slumps beside me, head down to his chest. The effort of getting

into the dugout has exhausted him. I've done most of the work, pushing and shoving, holding him so he doesn't fall into the mud and water at the bottom of the shell-hole. I'm afraid for his leg but more afraid to leave us exposed.

I put out my hand and feel the rough brickwork of the tunnel underneath Albert House. I'm in a muddle. Tiredness does that to you. You think you're doing one thing when you're really doing another. You even think that you're awake when you're asleep. Men have been shot for that. You can march asleep on your feet.

I'm in the dugout in the side of the shell-hole. I'm under Albert House. Those two things are true, and I go in and out of them. The thing that doesn't change is that Frederick is here. I shift position, and he also shifts. He's sleeping, after all the effort of getting here. The weight of him is a real thing, slumped against me. I put my right arm around his shoulders, to support him. He is dense, heavy, cold. This is how I know he isn't a ghost. You can put your hand through a ghost, and not feel it. He won't feel it either. But even though he's so deeply asleep, Frederick knows I'm here. He sighs, and turns his head in towards me.

Why didn't I think of looking for him here? Of course a man would come home to his own house.

"Frederick," I say again, not expecting an answer, just wanting to say his name aloud. He isn't ready to speak yet. He only wants to sit here, leaning against me, drifting deep. I hitch myself more comfortably, and get a firmer hold of him so that he won't slip away. Maybe I'm imagining it, but he seems a little warmer now.

199

"You're all right here with me, boy," I tell him. "We'll cuddy down, shall we?"

I can feel him smile against my arm. I know why he's smiling. It's because I'm talking like me, not like him. Not like any of those books in the Dennis library either. I hold him as close as I can and rock him, hardly moving him because I don't want to hurt his leg. I rock him in the same way that blood rocks inside the body without showing on the surface, on and on. All the while I'm opening inside myself, the way I never have before. I don't know even what there is inside me. Darkness, maybe, more and more of it, velvety and not raw the way it is when you stare into the night, full of the dread of morning. I rock Frederick even more gently. We're neither of us moving now.

I don't think we're in the cellars of Albert House. The sides of the shell-hole are wet. There's a hell of a noise outside, like a thousand furnaces exploding. I feel it coming through the earth. Perhaps it's time for the evening hate. As long as they don't come to retake their listening post before dark, we have a chance. The whole day has passed and they haven't come. When it's dark, we can crawl. I can carry him on my back. I'm strong enough for that. I'll get him out somehow.

"How's the old leg now, Frederick?"

He doesn't answer. Saving his energy, I know. He understands about the dark coming down again, and that the night is our chance. We can't stay here. He does smell of blood. It'll be drying now, crusting over. Down in the water at the bottom of the shell-hole there's the plop of a rat. It might be a frog. At night you hear them croaking. There are hundreds of them in the shell-holes. Creatures come from all over. They're perfectly at home, even though this place is like nowhere the world has ever seen. Frogs and crows, rats and beetles, the fattest bluebottles you ever saw in your life. Cockroaches. As for magpies, the churned-up clods are thick with them. It beats me where they all come from. When you put out your hand in the morning there are slugs all over the sandbags.

Blanco had a slug trail across his face, right to the corner of his mouth, and the slug was in his hair. You should have heard him yell when I told him. His hands flailed up in his hair. I'd have said a rat was worse. But mostly rats won't bite a living body. They'll walk over you but they know the dead from the living.

Frederick does smell of blood. Better leave it until we can get him to a dressing station. A light wound you can dress. Anything more serious, leave it be unless you know what you're doing.

"Not long to wait now," I say. "It's getting dark. We'll soon have you out of here."

I think I've been asleep. Time jumps forward, then it joins up again. My mouth feels swollen. I want water. There's water in the bottom of the shell-hole, shining. If I go down I'll never be able to climb back. I'm sure there are rats in the water. They swim with just their whiskers showing, and their eyes. The dugout is high up in the slope of the shell-hole, not far from the top. The Germans have even cut steps up to the lip of the crater, so as to get up and down easily. This shell-hole does them credit. They were listening to us all the while. Telephoning to their artillery the time of our attack. A very thorough approach, as Mr Tremough used to say.

Frederick's leg has stopped bleeding. That's good. If that was the evening hate, it's over. Time to go.

I've thrown away my rifle into the water at the bottom of the shell-hole where it will be no good to anyone. It was like throwing away part of myself. The knobkerry went a long time ago, I don't even remember. I never had faith in it, any more than Sergeant Morris had. I've still got my knife, and Frederick's revolver. You can be shot for throwing away your weapons. I can't carry anything but Frederick.

We're over the lip of the shell-hole, crawling through mud. Not too deep, thank God, not the kind that pulls you down. I'm crawling with Frederick on my back, my spine on fire from the weight of him. I keep having to stop and spit out the stuff that gets in my mouth. I can see the flash of guns and the trails of Very lights going up. I'm afraid of going round in a circle so I keep having to stop and check. German lines behind me. Ours ahead. I think I'm right.

We go on and on. I think we crawl for hours, half a yard, half a yard, half a yard. Frederick groans but he never lets out a cry. I feel as if I'm drowning. As if we're sinking down to the bottom of the world together. We wallow through the darkness, bumping into things. I don't know what the things are. I don't want to know. Posts and wire is all I care about. There are dead men all over, out here in the darkness. This is where they live. You can bury them, but they rise up again with

202

every bout of shelling. That's someone else groaning, not Frederick. I hear the patter of a voice, reciting to itself:

> "Four times fifty living men
> (And I heard nor sigh nor groan)
> With heavy thump, a lifeless lump,
> They dropped down one by one.
>
> "The souls did from their bodies fly, —
> They fled to bliss or woe!
> And every soul, it passed me by
> Like the whizz of my cross-bow!"

It's been dark for a long while now. The voice has gone away. Sometimes there's a chatter of fire. Windy. None of it's close enough to make that furze-fire noise in the air above us. Maybe it'll be dawn soon. Stand-to. The morning hate, then the livelong day, and then the evening hate. All in order, like church services.

I have to rest, just for a moment. I lay my face down sideways, to keep my mouth out of the mud. Frederick crushes me down, but I can't move him off me. We lie still for a long time. I must have fallen asleep, because the next thing I know, Frederick has rolled away. I dab around frantically, and there he is, lying on his back not two feet away, with rain on his face. I can feel wetness all over his skin, cold. But under it he's warm, I know he is. The warmth has gone deep inside him, where he needs it. I whisper, "Frederick," but he doesn't answer. I shuffle over, dig myself in under him and try to roll him back on top of me so I can crawl on. He rolls clumsily, too far, and topples over on the other side. I can't get a proper grip on him, he's so stiff and heavy.

I'm crying with the frustration of it. He doesn't hear me. He's not helping me now, the way he was at first. I know he won't be able to keep himself on my back. All kinds of stuff surges in my head. The noise of the rain on the gunnera leaves above me. Our wigwam right and tight so we can peer out of it at the rain while we are dry. *We could live here for ever,* Frederick said. We looked at each other. The joy of it went up like a Very light.

"Frederick!" I say, covering his ear with my mouth. He doesn't stir. He's unconscious, that's what it is, and no wonder. Better for him that way. I'll have to go backwards, dragging him. I'll get a hold under his arms, and shuffle along close to the ground so we won't be too visible. It looks as if the dark's thinning out, over to the east where the Germans are. Dawn's the worst time. Everyone's jumpy, firing off at anything that moves.

I feel Frederick's face again. I thought it was wet with rain but it's too sticky. It must be mud. His mouth is open. I feel round it for his breath against my hand, but my hand is so cold and numb that I can't feel anything.

"You'll be all right, boy," I tell him.

I hadn't reckoned on the wire. I know we cut ours. We went sideways down the line afterwards, like you do in the sea when the current's dragging you to the diagonal. This wire hasn't been cut and it's thick as hell. There are gooseberries in it too.

I let Frederick down on to the earth. I know that I can't drag him all the way back up to where we cut the wire. I'm done in, shaking, my skin pushing out sweat that freezes me. I turn my head aside to throw up on the earth, away from Frederick, choking out mud and vomit.

I suck in some deep breaths and then take my cheek off the earth, and wipe myself. I reach for Frederick and feel him all over to be sure he's safe. I try to settle him close to the ground like I was settling him in a bed. I make sure his face is turned up out of the mud, and his mouth and nose are clear. He'll be all right here. No one can see him. The wire hides him from our front line, and there's no reason for Fritz to know he's here.

"You'll be all right now, boy," I whisper to him. I tell him I'm going to crawl as fast as I can around the worst of the entanglement. There'll be a way cut through it somewhere, for patrols. Once I'm through, it isn't twenty yards to the fire-trench. I'll be close enough to call out for help before they shoot me. Can't call too soon in case a sniper finds me. Can't call too late in case our sentry thinks I'm a dawn raiding party. Frederick's head is on one side, facing towards me. I put my mouth back where his ear's got to be.

"Can you hear me?" I say, the same as he said to me in the garden. "You'll be all right, boy. I'll be back with the body-snatchers before you know it." He doesn't reply, but I'm sure he's heard me. When a man's unconscious, he'll say afterwards that he remembers every word you said.

I move quickly without him, like a rat darting from hole to hole. I've got to get help. I must go as fast as I can, away from him. I keep my head down and close to the wire, and pray for a gap. I don't think I'm anywhere near where we cut it, but I come to a place where it's been shelled and I shove myself through it, under it, my arms around my head to shield it. The wire lashes and catches me but I tear myself away. I wriggle from post to post on my belly, the wire scourging me, my whole skin prickling for fear of bullets. And then I'm through, crawling on, downhill now and so quick and light I can barely believe myself, as if a hand is behind me, shoving me. I cry out:

"Don't shoot! For Christ's sake don't shoot! I been out here all night!"

I'm scuttering over the open ground on our side of the wire and nobody's firing at me, and then I'm falling over the parapet, and still no one's firing at me, and I'm alive as I bump down against the sandbags and crash into the water at the bottom of the fire-trench.

There isn't time to wait for the body-snatchers. It's still dark but it won't be for long. Maybe there are dawny streaks here and there. There's no chance they'll find Frederick without me. Two men say they'll go with me. I gulp rum as the order to hold fire goes down the trench. They know the way. We scuttle back, canted low to the ground, ducking this way and that through the wire. It's getting lighter by the second and the lumps of darkness are turning into dips and shell-holes.

I see Frederick, twenty yards ahead. He hasn't moved. If you didn't know he was there you'd never find him. You'd think he was part of the earth.

"There!" I whisper, pointing. "There he is."

"Where?" They turn to me, their faces grey and grainy now. I see how much the darkness has weakened.

"There!"

I remember that. I don't see or hear the shell-burst. One minute I see Frederick. The next I am punched into the earth.

We survived, the three of us, because there was a slight ridge in the ground between us and Frederick. So I couldn't have seen him, even though I was right about where he was. It was the blast that threw me back.

If I'd dragged him even a bit farther, a few yards, twenty yards, Frederick would have lived too. He'd have been over that little ridge. I can't remember why it was that I left him just there, exactly in that place. Why did I do it? I crawled away from him so fast, like a rat flicking from hole to hole. I was fetching help for him.

For a long time after the shell-burst I didn't hear anything. I felt the rain of earth, not cold but warm, sticky to touch, going on and on. It pattered down all over me.

They got me into a dugout and I had tea with rum in it. I didn't know why my clothes were rags on me. I was black all over, too, without knowing it. I could see the eyes of the man opposite, moving in his black face. I thought: He's corked his face. I sat there until I started to shake so much I had to curl up like a sowpig. They laid me on a blanket. I've never felt silence like it, as thick as night, coming down over me. I tried to say that I wasn't wounded, but I couldn't hear my own voice. A sergeant I didn't know bent over me and his mouth opened and shut as if he was drowning. I said your name but I couldn't hear it. The sergeant's face was close and then it was distant, and I put out my hand to stop him going, full of terror that he hadn't heard me. I cried out your name again and again but it was like crying out in a dream where there is no sound. I could not wake myself, and the sergeant was already moving away, as if he knew everything that he needed to know.

CHAPTER
FOURTEEN

The value of concealment cannot be overestimated.

The thing that stopped the furnace from lighting is simple, as it turns out. The cold tap that feeds the water tank has been turned off. Although the furnace is a warm-air-duct system, it also heats the water and there is a safety valve. It shuts down the system if the tank is empty, so that it can never boil dry.

It was too complicated for Josh. The kind of system that a man with too much time and money on his hands would come up with, and leave behind for people who don't understand it. I come on the cold-water tap by chance, and think it strange that it would be turned off, when the system was built to feed every hot-water pipe in the house.

I shuffle myself out of that tunnel easily enough. I was making it out narrower than it really was, in my mind. Panicking. Of course Frederick was never there, but when I come out I feel different.

I open the cold tap as far as it will go, and then set about lighting the furnace. I don't know the proper way of it, but everyone knows how to light a fire. I open the bottom vent wide, to give it a good updraught, and lay the fire in order. The flame catches, such a thin blue thing that you wouldn't think it'd come to anything, but of course it does. It licks all around the kindling, tasting it, then goes up with a roar you'd never hear from an open fire. I squat beside it, feeding it until its insides are red. When it's safe to do so I close the vent and fill the furnace full of coke, enough to keep it going all night. How Felicia is going to feed and empty it, I don't know. She'll have to get Josh in more regularly, or else I'll do it for her. At any rate, she'll have her warm house, for herself and the little one.

The smell in the furnace room changes. It's warm and cokey now, with smoke in it. This is how it always used to smell, so that we'd creep in here for comfort on a cold day. The ventilation system is good. I check everything, as far as I am able. He was a proper engineer, Mr Dennis, one of those inventors who made the mines and the machinery that was in them. They made dynamite and pumps, steam engines and safety fuses. They made their fortunes too, out of their cleverness, or at any rate they made fortunes for the men who had the money to invest in their inventions. Maybe if the war had gone on another ten years, all our trenches would have turned into tunnels, deep underground, like the mining tunnels. There was plenty of work for engineers out in France. We could have lived there like rats, had our children like rats, watched them learn.

The furnace will want riddling, stoking and filling night and morning. I make a note to come down and mend that chicken wire too, in case a bird flies in and does mischief. I have no idea what time of day or night it will be when I go up to Felicia, like a miner coming out of the earth.

*　*　*

Felicia is studying in the kitchen, elbows on the table, hands cupping her face.

"Jeannie's having her nap," she says as I come in. "You've been down there a long time."

"I've got that furnace fixed," I say, and she actually jumps up, scattering her papers, and claps her hands together.

"You haven't!" she says.

"I have. Come here."

There's no heating vent in the kitchen: it wasn't necessary, with the heat coming from the slab. I take her out to the hall and hold my hand over the vent in the polished floor, in the corner. Sure enough, the air is starting to come up warm. Felicia kneels beside me, and spreads out her fingers to catch the heat.

"That's wonderful, Daniel," she says. "I thought you'd never get it going."

"Give it half an hour for the tank to heat through and you'll have hot water too, as much as you like."

I have never felt so proud of anything, as if I'd invented the furnace, the ventilation system, the ducts and all of it. I look up and notice that the sun is flooding through the coloured glass in the fanlight over the front door. It's a beautiful day. These spring days can be as good as summer, when the wind drops. I can't help smiling at the thought that the furnace is working again, just when Felicia won't be needing it. I look down at my hands and see that they are filthy. Most probably my face is, too.

"You'll need hot water to wash," says Felicia, and we go back into the kitchen. She swings the kettle off the range, unhooks it and hands it to me with a pot-holder.

In the jollyhouse I pour cold water into hot. I look at my face in the mirror, almost believing that I'll find it blackened, but there's only a bit of dirt from the furnace. They have fine soap that smells of lavender. I work up a lather, then swill my face and arms and dry myself carefully on the roller towel. As an afterthought I wet my fingers again and comb my hair into place with them, before going back to Felicia.

"Were you doing your mathematics?" I ask her.

"I don't get on well, without a teacher. I need to go back to night school."

I think of the rows of night scholars at their desks, learning after the day's work. They wanted to get on. They knew they could make something of themselves. I never joined them. Maybe I scorned to do so, out of some boy's idea that if the world wouldn't give me what I wanted, then I was damned if I'd snatch the crumbs from its table.

"Why should you go to night school?" I ask her. "It's not as if you needed the qualifications."

"I want to learn. There's too much in my head, going round and round. Mathematics is so cool and clear. Everything else goes away, when I'm thinking about it."

There's a shout from upstairs. Jeannie. "I'd better get her up," says Felicia. "She can play in the garden. It's such a beautiful day."

"Why don't we take her down to Gwidden?" I say boldly. "Let her run about on the sand."

212

It's the first time I've walked through the town in broad daylight, instead of skulking against its walls like a thief at night, or taking the long way round. I walk with Felicia at my side, carrying her basket. Jeannie's on her other side, held tight by the hand. I don't look to right or left. I keep my face set ahead, for people to stare at if they want to. We go down the hill, through the mazy little streets, and down the long road where the cloth factory stands. Everywhere there are children, and women popping in and out to watch them. There's not a face that I don't know, but I feel safe walking with Felicia. She walks lightly, greeting people here and there.

We go down the slipway and on to the sand. There are boys on the rocks as always, throwing themselves in and out of the water in spite of the season, but they're a good way off. The tide's on its way out, so the sand is packed and clean. Felicia takes off Jeannie's shoes and stockings, for her to run about, and then she takes from the basket a child's wooden spade, and a tin pail. They are scraped and battered. Jeannie runs to the water's edge and stands there stock-still, watching the boys. Her pinafore blows about, and her hair too. For the first time I see something of little Felicia in her.

It's one of those days that could be the heart of summer. There's heat in the afternoon sun, and the sea dazzles as if it's been cut for diamonds. Felicia sets down a square of mackintosh, and I spread out my coat over it, for us to sit side by side, looking out at the water. A lugger comes round from the harbour, then passes beyond the rocks. Inside the little bay, the sea is flat, with small waves turning over at its edge like shells.

"I could never go away from here," says Felicia.

"Not even to Cambridge?"

"It's a pipe dream, Dan. I study five hours a week if I'm lucky. I seem a bit clever, but that's all it is." She looks sideways at me, and smiles. "They'd laugh at me in Cambridge." She's wearing a jersey that looks like one of Frederick's cricket jerseys. Her wrists are narrow inside its turned-back cuffs. She stretches her arms up above her head, then down. I see the line of her body show against the thick creamy wool, and then hide itself again. I have to turn aside and dig my fist into the sand. I am hot with confusion.

"Isn't this a beautiful day?" she cries. Felicia was always like this. If we came down to the sea, she would sit as close to the water as she could and watch it for hours, while Frederick and I messed around fishing with bits of limpet on thread. Jeannie is edging forward into the shallows. She steals a glance behind, at us. "She won't go far," says Felicia, and we watch Jeannie bend down and start to fling handfuls of sand and water at the horizon. My heartbeat settles.

"She'll be soaked through," Felicia murmurs.

I get up, go to Jeannie and pick her up, swooping her on to my shoulders. She's too surprised to protest. Her father would have done this, so would Frederick. I settle her, and run her up and down the water's edge, giving her a horseback ride as I've seen fathers do. She laughs, and clutches at my hair. I like the sound of her laughing. It sounds reluctant somehow, as if laughter has been shaken out of her against her will. We gallop up and down the beach until I'm out of breath. Jeannie bumps forward, clutching my neck. Her breath is on my skin and she's still laughing. I swing her round, wriggling. Suddenly, as quick as an eel, she flips herself and digs her teeth into the cushion of flesh at the base of my thumb.

"You young limb," I say to her, "I'll spifflicate you." She laughs harder, and ducks her head down to bite me again, but I don't let her. I think she'll be crying soon, if this goes on, so I put her down on the sand and walk her back to Felicia.

"What was Harry Fearne like?" I ask, as I sit down by her again. "Why did you marry him?"

She takes Jeannie into her lap and holds her there, bending over her. "He was very nice," she says at last. "He came and said he wanted to marry me, and I was a bit surprised because it was so quick, but he wanted it so much. My father didn't like it, but he couldn't say anything. Harry had embarkation leave, and we got married."

She stops and turns aside, just as I did earlier. A slow colour comes up in her cheek. "He was nice, Daniel. You'd have liked him. You know how it was then, everything had to happen so quickly." The colour deepens. I think, for the first time: She isn't a girl. She's been married. Of course I knew it, but now I feel it and I blush, like Felicia, in a dark, painful tide like the blood coming back into a dead limb. It seems as if I'm seeing her body inside her clothes.

"And now there's all the time in the world," says Felicia. "Jeannie, don't put that in your mouth."

I watch her as she busies herself with the child. She wants to change the subject and so do I.

"I used to fish off those rocks," I say, remembering later times, serious times, not limpet on a thread but hooks and bait and the long struggle for fish to take home and make my mother smile.

"I know. You and Frederick." She draws a ship in the sand, for Jeannie. "I used to be so envious. I wanted to fish more than anything."

"You did, surely." I remember her figure in the distance, heading for the rocks with her net and pail.

"Not properly. You had fishing lines. You caught real fish."

"Me more than Frederick. It was play, for him."

"You let me bait up your line once, do you remember? Frederick said I'd flinch, but I didn't. When you brought the line up there were three mackerel hanging off it, and you jerked it — like that — to bring them over sharp on to the rocks."

"Gwidden Rocks is a good place for mackerel."

"You can make a fishing line for Jeannie when she's older," says Felicia, getting up. "She's hungry. We'd better go back."

"I'll have to get back too. Got a goat to milk."

"Oh — of course," says Felicia, sounding startled, as if she's forgotten about my life.

As we walk up the long road I see a familiar figure. Dolly Quick. She'll be coming or going from some Sabbath service. I'm carrying Jeannie, and I see Dolly's sharp eyes go from me to Felicia, to the child, and back to me again. Her face doesn't soften. Jeannie is tired and grumpy, and instead of smiling, she turns her head into my neck and hides her face. Dolly Quick pinches in her mouth.

"Thank you so much for having Jeannie last night," says Felicia, over-effusive again and awkward. "She had a lovely time, didn't you, Jeannie?"

Jeannie says nothing.

"Cat got her tongue," says Dolly grimly, staring at me.

"Daniel has mended the furnace. It's roaring away beautifully. There'll be plenty of hot water for the washing tomorrow."

"I dessay."

Jeannie keeps her face buried in my neck. I can feel her breath snorting against my skin.

"She's tired," says Felicia. "She's been running about on the beach."

Dolly ignores this. Instead, looking straight at me, she says, "They were saying after chapel, the doctor ought to go up to Mary Pascoe's, or else send a nurse. It ent right, her up there alone, without a woman to do for her."

"I do everything for her."

"I dessay you do, Dan Branwell," she says, with a wealth of meaning in her voice. "You living in that cottage, tending her chickens, digging her vegetable plot."

"Daniel doesn't live in the cottage," breaks in Felicia. "He lives in the outbuilding, don't you, Dan?"

"That's right."

"What does she do if she wants something in the night, then?" demands Dolly. "Say what you like, she needs a woman there, even if it's only calling in. Or else be brought to hospital."

"I can go and see her," says Felicia, with her quick sensitiveness that knows I don't want anybody else there.

"And take that child where there's catching illness? Mary Pascoe's chest been bad all winter, you say. It could be she's in a consumption. Taking the child, there's no sense in it." She jerks her head at me and speaks with open hostility, careless of what Felicia thinks. She must know that Felicia needs her too much to fall out with her. "*He* should find lodgings in town, and let Mary Pascoe have proper care up hers."

I say nothing. I hold on to Jeannie, maybe too hard because Jeannie doesn't like it. She wriggles and pulls away. Dolly Quick puts out her arms and Jeannie slides into them.

"There you are, my girl. Why, you're all wet. You feel her hem, Mrs Fearne, it's sopping."

"I'll change her when we get home."

"You got to go careful, this time of year. They can get a chill. I always kept mine in wool until May was out."

She is coddling Jeannie as she speaks, turning her away from me. "I can take her to mine if you want. It's closer. I've got a change there and she can have a warm by the fire."

"No," says Felicia. "It's very kind of you, but we'll take her home now."

218

That's it, I think. That's torn it. I keep my face impassive. I don't reach out to take Jeannie, I let her go to her mother. But as I walk away beside them, I don't need to turn round to know how Dolly Quick is staring after us, nor to guess at the expression she wears.

"It's getting late," I say, when we reach the house.

"You should get rid of that goat."

"She's not mine to sell."

"You should ask Mary. She might need the money from the sale."

"I can't go bothering her with things like that."

"I *will* come up and see her," says Felicia, with sudden decision. "If she needs it, I'll pay for a nurse. No, don't argue, Dan. Dolly's right, even though she means it wrong. If anything should happen to Mary, think what people would say."

CHAPTER
FIFTEEN

Every artifice should be used to mislead the enemy.

You wouldn't think there could be such a run of mornings, each one finer than the last. The sea is flat, with a few boats working their way across the fishing grounds. I deal with the goat and hens, then walk up to the edge of the plot I've cultivated. Today, I'll break the next patch, working my way slowly outward through land that's been let go to bracken and brambles. No-man's-land. Why shouldn't I claim it back? I work with my back to the rising sun, and it's almost hot. There's a sharp smell from the crushed bracken and black soil. Every so often I take out stones that lie in the earth like potatoes, and fling them away. I want this land clean.

Felicia intends to give Josh the job of looking after the furnace. He'll be glad of the work, and besides, I couldn't be there night and morning. It's impractical. I have enough to do here. I could get more hens, as the egg money builds up. I could grow enough to feed myself, and more to sell besides. I could live here.

It seems as if I've been half asleep all these months.

She and Jeannie will be up by now. I wonder if they're eating my eggs. The thought of it makes me hungry, and I leave my work, put one of this morning's eggs into the little saucepan and balance it on the grid over the fire. When it's coddled enough, I swill away the water and dance the egg as I peel it, so as not to burn my fingers. There's no bread. I mash cold potato into the egg, and salt it. I eat fast, and wish I had more. The sun's come round to the doorway now, so I make a mug of strong black tea and prop myself against the frame to drink it. All the sea eastward is shining now, too bright to look at. I close my eyes and sup the tea, which is why I don't see the doctor's hat moving along the furze, not until he hails me:

"Daniel!"

I know that voice. It gives orders. It shifts lives.

"Daniel!"

You can be shot for sleeping on duty. I can't feel my rifle. You can be shot for throwing away your weapons. But it's Dr Sanders, lifting his stick in greeting as he comes off the path and stands before me. He has his black bag in his other hand. I reach behind me, get hold of the door handle, and pull it to as I step out towards him. There he is, in his tweed suit, and looking older. The same creased, shrewd face as ever. Sweat trickles inside my armpits and my heart is banging. I stand sideways so that he has to face into the sun and squint.

"This is a bad business, Daniel," he says, as familiar as if we're in my mother's kitchen and I'm going for a gardener's boy. As if the war never happened. But I fold my arms and lower my head to look at him, bullish. I want to tell him how lucky he is that I didn't have my weapon. Coming on a man like that, when he's half asleep. You've only yourself to blame if you get shot.

"Which business would that be?" I ask him.

"Mary Pascoe lying ill all winter, and no one sending for me," he says bluntly. "I only heard of it yesterday. A bad business. I should have thought you knew me well enough to knock at my door."

I have to marvel at the way Dr Sanders doesn't know things that have simmered through the town for weeks. The Dennises were the same. They hear no more about what goes on than a child does.

"She's been cared for well enough," I tell him.

"I dare say she has, as far as you are able," he says, looking as if he doesn't think that's very far. "She ought to have had a nurse. Never mind. What's done is done. No use standing here talking. I'll go in and see her." He steps forward, as if to skirt around me to the door of the cottage. I shouldn't have stepped sideways to dazzle his eyes. I move back, lightly enough, and block him.

"You won't find her here." My heart is still beating so fast I'm afraid he'll hear it, and yet I'm glad, somehow, that the reckoning has come. It sweeps away everything into a kind of wildness. I have the better of him. He's never been there, where dawn comes between one breath and the next, and we have the advantage of the light. We see the German lines plain against the ribbon of raw light at the horizon. Or at least the sentries do, with their periscopes. We're too close to risk it otherwise. I look to the right and left of me. Glimmer of faces all turned the same way, every muscle in them stretched tight, flat, the way you never see a face at home. The clinks and shifts of equipment. The sudden reek of chloride of lime, old gas, rottenness, all pouring into your nose at once as if you've never smelled anything in your life before.

I will outface Dr Sanders. I straighten up, look him dead in the eye, and say, "The morning was so fine, she asked me to walk her up to the high road, and she's gone by cart to Morven."

"Morven!" The doctor looks confounded, as well he may.

"She has a sister at Morven. She'll stay a month there, maybe more, with her sister looking after her."

"I was told she couldn't get out of bed."

"She was in bed most of the winter. But once the spring came, she took a turn for the better."

I look at him steadily, daring him not to believe me. My heart has quietened itself now. In my mind I can see the high road, and the cart, and Mary Pascoe clambering aboard. I even see the red flash of her flannel petticoat. Why shouldn't it have happened?

"Walked to the high road, you say?"

"Well, I say walk. She was leaning on me. I half carried her, if I'm honest. But she was set on going."

Call me a liar, I dare him silently. Call me a liar, and I'll knock you down. All my fear has burned off like mist.

"Are you living in the cottage, Daniel?" asks the doctor abruptly, catching me off guard. There is smoke coming from the chimney, and he must have seen it.

"Until she comes back. Otherwise I'm staying there," and I jerk my head towards the corrugated-iron shack.

There's a silence. He looks about him with his quick doctor's eye, noting the freshly dug earth, the chickens in their run, the goat nuzzling at the stone hedge. From here I can see the rise of the field, where Mary Pascoe lies under her green coat. I almost think that the doctor will hear my thoughts, and see what I see. He considers me.

"What's the name of this sister in Morven?"

"Pascoe. Ellen Pascoe."

He makes a slight movement of the head, and shifts the bag in his hand. Suddenly he says, "Daniel?" in quite a different voice, softer but as if he's a bit afraid of me too. As if I might have some illness that he doesn't want to diagnose. I don't answer. "Daniel, I ought to have come to see you before now. Your mother—"

I cannot hear it. I turn aside, chopping the air with my hand. He falters, but only for a moment, then he shakes out a white handkerchief, takes off his glasses and wipes them slowly and carefully. He wants time. He wants to think what to do next.

"I'm sorry you had your walk for nothing," I say, and I mean it too. Dr Sanders got me out of school a year early and found me work as a gardener's boy. I have a lot to be grateful for, as my mother often said. But in my head I hear Frederick laugh and say, "It'll do the old walrus good to walk. Get his fat down."

"You should come into the town more," says the doctor. "It's not good to be alone out here."

"I've had enough of all that. I'm better here." The morning sun searches out every crack and crevice in his face. He's getting old. And soft too. He'd rather believe me, because it's easier.

224

"You'll be wanting work," he says. "I can put in a word for you."

It's boiling up in me now: the hate. The morning hate and the evening hate. "I've got all the work I need."

He nods slowly. "You know Georgie Sennen lost his right leg."

"I heard," I say, although I haven't.

"He has wonderful spirit."

"I dessay."

That's what they like: *wonderful spirit*. Men with no legs selling matches outside theatres. Men with their hands shaking so that the tea towels they sell door to door dance in their hands. And grateful with it. I should have said I didn't know where the sister lived. Morven's too small. It's easy enough to find out who lives there, and who doesn't. I can always say I was mistaken.

She told me she wanted to lie here, and not in the graveyard under a stone. I did what she asked. She was light to carry, but since then I've been heavy. It lies inside me like the stone that might have lain on Mary Pascoe. I stare at the doctor and think the same as I thought when Felicia came here: What if I told him? What if I took him up the field to where Mary Pascoe lies, and told him how it happened? But I know I won't. I could tell him how there isn't anything between life and death, not when you come to it. You wake dead beat, wipe yourself as best you can with a mug of water. Billy Ransom crouches at the back of the dugout, coaxing up a clear flame from splinters of wood, to boil up the dixie. You all want your tea. It's been raining, and it looks as if it's going to rain again later, but for now the sky holds clear. You think of sugar, and a fag. It's been a quiet night. Billy says, "Bugger this, I need more wood," and wriggles out of the dugout. He doesn't put on his tin hat. Off he goes, crouching, because this is a shallow trench. Head down, just as it ought to be. He disappears round the angle of the trench. You scratch your armpit, and once you start you can't stop because it itches like fire. You want to tear your own skin off. A few minutes later, back comes Billy, grinning, with a bundle of sticks scrounged from God knows where. For some reason no one will ever know, when he's a couple of yards away he lifts his head. Maybe he's smelling the rain. At that exact moment a rattle of machine-gun fire crosses the spot where Billy Ransom's forehead rises above the rim of the earth. Earth and stuff out of Billy flies around like a blizzard. He folds up backwards without a sound. There he is: dead, his face, thank Christ, turned the other way. In an instant, in the blinking of an eye, he's not Billy Ransom any more. His little fire is still going. And what I feel isn't shock or anger or even pity for him: it's annoyance. It sounds a simple enough thing: a wet grey morning and Billy Ransom here one minute and gone the next, but I can't get past it, and no one who wasn't out there can get anywhere near it. What were the odds? Ten to one, a hundred to one, a thousand to one? It made no odds.

Here I am, upright in the sunshine, and they're gone. I've walked past them. I've watched the rain dropping on their faces as if they were split pigs hung up outside

226

the butcher's. I've seen them put in their graves and then blown out again. They dung the fields.

There was an old man called Michael Finnegan
He grew whiskers on his chinegan
The wind came out and blew them inigan
Poor old Michael Finnegan begin agin

Why shouldn't I be punished? Billy Ransom did nothing but go for a bundle of sticks. I watched as the stuff flew out of him and then I turned away. I touched my own head after. His fire still burned and I drank the tea. If I tell the doctor now, I will be punished. They'll take me to Bodmin gaol. They could hang me there.

"Do you sleep well, Daniel?" he asks me quietly. The question catches me, but I don't show it.

"Well enough," I say, "and now if you'll excuse me, doctor, I've work to do."

I watch him down the path, his hat bobbing where the furze hides his figure. As I'm about to turn away, his hat stops moving. His voice hails me again: "Daniel!" I don't answer. Even when he's as still as still, the hat stands out. A perfect target.

CHAPTER
SIXTEEN

Labourers working in the fields between the armies have been detected giving information.

I haven't had time to take up my spade again before I see Felicia coming, with Jeannie in her arms. I go forward to lift the child's weight from her, but Felicia holds on. She won't meet my eye, and at once I know that she's met the doctor on the way, and that he's told her my lie about Mary Pascoe.

"You shouldn't lug Jeannie all this way."

"She's not heavy. Daniel—"

"No, Felicia."

"What do you mean, 'no'? How can I not? Dr Sanders tells me Mary Pascoe's gone to Morven, to her sister's, when you told me she was lying in bed too ill to move or see me. What are you saying, Daniel? What are you doing?"

Jeannie squalls, and clings to her mother's neck like a monkey.

"You're frightening her," I say. "Come inside and I'll get her a drink of water."

"So I can come inside now, can I? She's not too ill to see me?"

"She's not here."

"I know she's not here. Dr Sanders told me that. I'm just wondering what other lies you've told me."

"I haven't told you lies. Not meant as lies, Felicia." I am up too close to her, and a spark of fear lights in her eyes. She steps backwards, clutching Jeannie. I let my hands drop to my sides and step backwards too, away from her.

"I'll show you," I say.

We turn, and walk up to the top of the field. First you can't see it, and then you can. The brighter green oblong in the after-winter dullness of last year's grass. I go ahead and they walk in my footsteps. The long grass brushes wet on to my boots, from the night's dew. I halt by the grave. I think Felicia will understand at once, but she doesn't.

"Here," I say, pointing down. "She's here."

All the colour goes out of her face. She is so white that I'm afraid she'll fall, or drop the child. She sways back, but recovers herself. I daren't touch her.

"Who put her here?" she says at last.

"I did. She asked me to, when she was dying. She said she didn't want to lie in the graveyard, under a stone. She wanted to be here."

There is a long silence, or you could call it silence although it's full of noises. I hear the gulls as they wheel out over the sea. The close drowsy burring of a bee. Farther off, a buzzard's cat-like cry. All the while the stirring of wind and water.

"Did she tell you that?" asks Felicia.

"Yes."

I don't know that she'll believe me. I think she won't.

"How did it happen?"

"She'd been failing. It was her chest, like I said. She knew she was dying. She didn't want the doctor. I asked her and she shook her head. She said she wanted to lie here. She asked me to stay with her."

"And then did she die?"

"Not straight away."

"Were you with her?"

"Yes." I think of Mary Pascoe's skull, so visible, with its frail wisps of hair flattened by the sweat of dying. Her nose poked out like a bird's beak. Her tongue was thick in her mouth and I dipped a cloth in water and held it to her lips. I'd seen plenty of men die, but never an old woman dying in her bed, day by day. It was quite different. It looked like hard work that she was engaged in, and had to finish.

"I think she had pneumonia," I say. "She was dark all around here," and I touch my own lips.

"And you buried her." Felicia can't help herself: she gives a shudder and it runs all through her, head to foot, at the thought of what that burial means. She is seeing me lift Mary Pascoe, and carry her, and dig out a grave deep enough for her, then lay her into it. I can see how terrible it might appear to a girl like Felicia.

"I covered her," I say, "I wrapped her in a sheet of canvas so that the earth wouldn't touch her."

Felicia is silent, looking down at the green, dinted ground. Jeannie, too, looks down as if she understands what is being said. She puts out her hand, and points, then throws her head back and crows with laughter.

"Did you say a prayer for her?"

"No. I said goodbye to her, and then I covered her face."

"Don't you think she should have had the choice?" asks Felicia angrily.

"I did what she asked."

Jeannie wriggles in her mother's arms. She's had enough of us talking. "Set her down," I say to Felicia. "Let her run about a bit."

Felicia puts Jeannie on the ground, but she doesn't run about. She stands there, holding fast to her mother's legs, looking at me warily out of eyes that are the shape of Frederick's, though not the colour.

"Dr Sanders didn't believe you," says Felicia.

"I didn't tell him what had happened."

"I mean, he didn't believe that she had gone to Morven."

"Did he say so?"

"No, but I could tell. Daniel, is it a crime?"

"What do you mean?"

"To keep her from being buried in the churchyard."

I almost smile. *My blessed Felicia*. It has not even occurred to her that I might be suspected of a worse crime than that.

"She ought to have had a doctor," I say. "Her death ought to have been certified. You know all that."

Felicia nods, then looks down at Jeannie, who's whining now and dragging off her mother's hand. "Stand up straight, Jeannie," she says sharply, and to me, "I ought not to have brought her."

"I'll get her a cup of milk. Does she like goat's milk?"

It seems not. Jeannie screws up her face when she tastes the milk, and tries to dash the cup down. "That's not the way," I say to her. "This is good milk, Jeannie. Look at the goat over there that's given it to you. She wants you to drink it, not waste it." Jeannie does look. She is sharp for her age, I can see that. She sees the goat's roving yellow eyes and maybe she thinks that the goat will be angry with her and bite her. She sups the milk noisily until it's all gone, leaving her with a milk moustache that Felicia wipes away.

"I don't understand how you could do it, Daniel," she says to me over the child's head.

"You mean burying her? It wasn't hard. It's heavy work but it's not hard. I've done it a few times."

"In France, you mean?"

"Yes. Think how she liked to be alone. They lie cheek by jowl in the graveyard."

The wind stirs again, ruffling Jeannie's pinafore where she sits on the grass, tugging at stalks. Felicia kneels down and kisses the nape of the baby's neck, so that her own face is hidden. She says, "Did you bury Frederick?"

I can't think what to say. I try to remember what I wrote in the letter I sent to the Dennises. What story I told. "No," I tell her, "I didn't bury him. There was a burial party that day."

"And did they have a proper graveyard?"

"It was like this. Part of a field. They put up wooden crosses with the men's numbers on them."

I want her to see green and quiet. A grave with the air washing over it, like this one.

"One day, I'll go and see it," says Felicia.

I say nothing. There's no need. Time enough for whatever discoveries she may make in the years to come. I don't believe she'll go anywhere, not to Cambridge, not to France. Jeannie will grow up here, as we did.

"I think that you were right to do what Mary wanted," says Felicia, frowning.

"Wrong or right, it's done now."

"Look, Jeannie, a rabbit!"

I want to shy a stone at it, but not in front of them. Rabbits'd strip the world bare if they were let. It sits up, quivering. Jeannie throws out her fist with a shout, and the rabbit disappears.

"You used to catch rabbits, you and Frederick."

Yes, and we'd pull the skin over their heads, like pulling off a jersey, while they were still warm. It was a knack. I'd take the rabbit home and my mother would joint it for the pot.

"Daniel, I think you need to go away from here."

I was wrong: she understands everything.

"Where would I go?"

"To London?"

"What would I do in London?"

"You'd be safe there."

"I'm safe enough here. Nothing's going to hurt me."

"Dr Sanders will go up to Morven, or he'll send someone."

"I know that. I'll say I was mistaken. It must have been some other place where her sister lived."

"They won't believe you. Even if they do, it won't be for long. Look at the colour of the grass over the grave. It's different from the rest. They'll come up here and they'll see it." She looks around her at the wide sweep of the land: so bare, it seems. But we both know that it isn't. "People might be watching—"

"I know that."

"Frederick would have wanted you to take the money. You could stay as long as you wanted in London. You'd have enough to rent a place. You could even go abroad."

"To France, do you think? I'll stay here, Felicia. Let's not talk about it."

"All right. You tell me what else we're going to talk about."

"Don't be angry."

"I'm not angry with you. I'm angry because of what you've done to yourself. No one will believe you now. Look at me, Daniel. I'm a widow. I'm not twenty and I'm a widow, and Jeannie's got no father. It's like something out of a book, isn't it? But with a book, you can read it and close it up and go back to your own life. I can't remember Harry's face. I have to try to get it back by looking at Jeannie."

I've been allowing myself to believe that Felicia only married him because of the war. I've never once considered that she might have loved him. He wanted her: I understood that. But the thought that Felicia might have wanted him is hard to bear. I have to think of her differently, and in a way that troubles me.

"He hoped we'd have a baby."

234

I can't answer. There's Jeannie, curled in the grass like a hare in its form, cuddling her mother's boots.

"He wanted that because he knew it might be all he'd get. And then he never even saw her. Frederick was gone too and you were away. There was no one for me to show her to. They'll take you away, Daniel." She bends down, picks up the child and rocks her on her hip, to and fro, to and fro, comforting Jeannie, comforting herself. She looks so age-old and desolate that I don't know what to do. In spite of the rocking, Jeannie wails and wails.

They sit at my table, Felicia with Jeannie on her lap, and I give them mashed potatoes with a poached egg each on the top, and chopped-up dandelion leaves. Felicia asks me what the greenstuff is, and I tell her that dandelions clean the blood. Jeannie eats everything, but Felicia only swallows a couple of mouthfuls. She's tired, she says. She sits sunk in on herself, attending to Jeannie automatically. I make her tea, and put in the last of my sugar to give her strength for the walk back. I'll buy more tea and sugar before they come again. I'll buy biscuits for Jeannie, and a bar of chocolate. I don't even want to sit down with them. It's enough to have them here.

"You *will* go, won't you, Daniel?" says Felicia. "To please me?"

It doesn't suit her to wheedle. I say straight out that she'll find me here the next time she comes. I tell Jeannie that I'll have something nice for her to eat then, but she only stares at me. I wish the dog was here for her to play with. I'm so tired that I could put my head down on the table and sleep.

"Is that the bed?" asks Felicia, looking behind her. *Where she died*, she means.

"You know it is."

"Were her things in the chest? Did you open it?"

"I didn't open it," I say, not expecting to be believed, although it's true.

"I wonder what she kept in there. Do you remember all the stories there were about her, when we were little? That she was a witch. Do you think I could open it?"

"Don't do that."

Is Frederick in the chest, or is the chest in Frederick? I know he won't come while Felicia's here. I hate the thought of him coming here again and again, all clagged with mud, as if for him the war hasn't ended. And yet I want him to come, because it's the only way I can see him.

"Do you remember the wigwam?" asks Felicia.

"The one we made?"

"You and Frederick wouldn't let me in. I tried to make my own wigwam but it was no good, just a heap of sticks with the rain coming in. And you said to Frederick, *Let her in*."

"Did I?" I speak as if I've clean forgotten.

"Yes. I think you must have been sorry for me."

"I was never sorry for you."

"Frederick wanted me to go away, but you moved up and made room for me. I sat as still as still. I don't think we did anything, we just all sat there, the three of us, and we could hear the rain falling on the gunnera.

You had a liquorice bootlace and we took bites at it in turn, until it was gone."

I don't remember the liquorice.

"They were calling for us," says Felicia, "but Frederick said, *Let 'em call. They'll never find us here. And they didn't.*"

"They winkled us out in the end, though."

That whole long train of us, boys and men, off the farms and out of the fishing boats and up from the mines. I can see us as clear as clear. Orange-peel teeth and talk about tarts. We'd never been out of Cornwall before. It's like a photograph. I can see it but I can't feel it. Maybe that's why there are so many things I can't remember. We didn't volunteer: they came to get us. Winkled us out of our shells, raw as we were.

"I wish Jeannie had a brother," says Felicia. "She needs company. She likes Dolly, though. They're always laughing — I hear them in the kitchen. You wouldn't think it, would you?"

I shake my head. She's a viper, Dolly Quick, if you want my opinion. Frederick told me once that the Ancient Greeks kept a house snake. Maybe Dolly Quick is Felicia's house snake.

"What are you smiling at?"

"Something Frederick said once."

Felicia looks down at Jeannie. "She's dropping off."

"We could lay her on the bed."

"She's not heavy. What was it he said?"

"It was about the Ancient Greeks."

"Oh *them*."

"What's the matter?"

"Girls can't learn Greek. They haven't the brains for it, and girls who try to be like boys only succeed in becoming unwomanly." Her eyes sparkle with temper. I hear the voice of Mr Dennis, round and pompous. She's a good mimic, Felicia.

"*Sing, O goddess,*" I say, "*the anger of Achilles son of Peleus, that brought countless ills upon the Achaeans. Many a brave soul did it send hurrying down to Hades, and many a hero did it yield a prey to dogs and vultures.*"

"What's that, Dan?"

"The beginning of the *Iliad*. Homer."

"You don't know Greek, do you?"

"It's Samuel Butler's translation, from your father's library. You'll like this, Felicia: Samuel Butler thought that a woman wrote the *Odyssey*."

"Did he?"

Many a brave soul did it send hurrying down to Hades . . . I haven't thought of those lines for years. They used to thrill me through, but now I'm not so sure. Hurrying down to Hades, as if they were running to catch a London omnibus.

"Did your father think mathematics weren't for girls as well?"

"I never asked him. You remember the tutor they got for Frederick, in the summer holidays?"

"Yes." I've never seen a vulture, outside the pictures in the Dennises' *National Geographic*. Only crows and buzzards, drifting lazily across the sky, with a wing-tilt here and there as they look down. And rats. "What about the tutor?"

238

"I saw him crying in the schoolroom one day, with his head on the desk. Just crying and crying."

"What did you do?"

"I crept away. I don't think he heard me. I was frightened."

"Did you tell anyone?"

"Only Frederick. He laughed, then he said it was probably because of something that had happened in the schoolroom."

"What?"

Felicia hesitates, looks down. "The tutor put his hand . . ."

I can see it. "And what did Frederick do?"

"Nothing. He said it happened all the time at school."

"I suppose the tutor was afraid he'd tell your father."

"I don't know."

Frederick would have forgotten about it by the next day. *It happened all the time at school.*

"The tutor was meant to be teaching Frederick Greek," says Felicia. "But we went out as much as we liked, after that."

I gave up staring at the pages of Frederick's Greek. I would never make it out. Instead, I read the *Iliad* through in English, and then the *Odyssey*. I was fifteen and didn't know how to pronounce the Greek names; I still don't. But inside your head, it doesn't matter. The words used to strike inside my head. I felt them go into my memory, like footsteps.

I watch the way Jeannie curls against Felicia, and let the lines unroll.

"The first ghost I saw was that of my comrade Elpenor, for he had not yet been laid beneath the earth. We had left his body unwaked and unburied in Circe's house, for we had had too much else to do. I was very sorry for him, and cried when I saw him: 'Elpenor,' said I, 'how did you come down here into this gloom and darkness? You have come here on foot quicker than I have with my ship.'"

"Did Elpenor die in battle?"

"No. He got drunk, fell off the roof of a house and broke his neck." Felicia snorts with laughter. "And then Odysseus meets the ghost of his mother and tries to embrace her, but he can't, because the dead aren't made of the same stuff as us. Every time he tries to catch hold of her, she turns to nothing. They put out bowls of blood to draw the dead."

"How do you know so much, Dan?"

"It's only bits and pieces. You have to have an education, to make it fit together."

"You could have an education."

"It's too late for that."

I want us to sit at this table for ever. Mary Pascoe is under the grass, where she wanted to be. It's as if the sun has come out on a small field, although there are such heavy clouds spreading over the rest of the sky that the wider landscape is blighted. Even here in the kitchen, the light shines. If I don't move, and Felicia doesn't move, and Jeannie stays in her mother's arms, then we're safe.

240

"I'll go to London," I say to her.

"Will you really?" Her thin face glows. "I'm so glad."

"But we'll have a day together first. Will you leave Jeannie with Dolly Quick tomorrow, and come up here? We'll go to Bass Head together."

"That's too far to walk."

"I'll borrow a pony for you, from Venton Awen. Don't tell Dolly you're coming with me."

"We'll be back before dark, won't we?"

I remember the bruise of rainclouds on the horizon, above the sea. We had to get home, I said. It was a long way back from Bass Head. We had to get ahead of the rain. Frederick didn't want to leave, but I made him. I remember glancing behind at the weather which seemed to be gaining on us, but held off and held off until Frederick said in disappointment: *We could have stayed*.

"We'll be back well before dark," I say to Felicia.

CHAPTER
SEVENTEEN

Officers and men selected to take part in the operation should, when possible, be volunteers. The men should be quartered together in a comfortable billet for the week preceding the operation. They should be taught the use of German phrases such as "hands up", "come out".

That night, I don't sleep. I lie down twice, but each time I have to get up again, because of the way my heart is beating. It makes no difference if I turn on my left side or on my right, if I count to a hundred or breathe deeply. It beats too hard, as if I've been running. I should get up, I tell myself, I've got so much to do, but once I'm out of bed there is nothing to do except wait for morning. I get my money out from the tobacco tin where I keep it, and count it. I move the tin from its usual place on the shelf over the fire, and then back again. I know I'm using up candles for nothing, but I can't sit in darkness. I ought to have bought more lamp oil.

I'm not afraid, though you might think so. My heart beating hasn't anything to do with fear. It's a new thing, that I don't know. Excitement, maybe. Exhilaration. Maybe I'll never sleep again. I seem to be going into a new life, which has nothing to do with the old one.

I want the day. I want Felicia to come. Already, I see her approaching. Her eyes will be wide and dark in her pale face. She's not very like Frederick, and yet she's entirely like him. At first light I'll go up to Venton Awen to get the pony. They won't deny me. I've got money and I'll make it worth their while. I'll walk, and she'll ride. A single day, that's all I want.

I might be afraid. Fear is a taste and smell more than a feeling, at least I've found it so. It doesn't have much to do with your thoughts. Some smells draw it up. The first time up the line, you don't even know what the smells are. They catch in your throat and you gag, but it's dark and what you have to do is follow the man ahead of you so that the man behind you can follow in his turn. Sometimes it's so dark that you'll feel a hand from behind coming on to your shoulder, like the hand of a blind man. And so you go on through the darkness, with mud sucking at your boots and clogging them so each foot weighs more than seven pounds. You get used to everything step by step, otherwise you wouldn't be able to bear it. Later on, you know what it is you're smelling. Chloride of lime, cordite, raw mud, latrines, petrol-tainted water, rotting flesh. You learn to put a face on it when fear swells up in you like a balloon. You sweat in your animal self, but being a man you hide it.

All night Frederick is close to me. I don't see him or hear him, and there isn't a moment when my hair crisps on my neck. He leaves me in peace, but he keeps alongside. He said to me once: "You know those cards people leave, when they go visiting? Hopeless system. I've a wider acquaintance among the dead than the living. I'd rather see them than anyone.

Except you, my dear BB." He said it so casually I didn't grasp it. Besides, how should I know about those cards? I didn't like to hear him say that. His company was cut to bits, and he was beyond finding new company in us. He had a way of staring into the darkness, very intently, which might have been only the sharpness of a good officer, but to me it seemed as if he was looking where he ought not to look, where the dead were.

We were billeted together before the trench raid, as Frederick said we would be. Forty-eight of us, Sergeant Morris and one officer in command: Frederick. Our purpose was to obtain maps, cut telephone wires and secure at least one prisoner for interrogation. The raiding party would be supported by three forty-five-second bursts of artillery fire at intervals, with the final burst being the signal for us to attack the enemy trench. Or so they said. We looked at each other. A ripple that you couldn't see or hear went round us.

We were told off for two days' training. It was a cushy billet, just as I'd hoped: a clean barn with clean farm rats that ran away into corners instead of looking at you bold as brass while they chirruped over bits of bodies that were blown out of the side of the trench. Frederick had a room in the farmhouse. We put on balaclavas, blacked our faces with cork and wriggled over a mocked-up no-man's-land. The ground was taped out to mark our route to the trench we were going to attack. They said the wire would be cut for us by the preliminary barrage, but no one trusted that. We had our wire-cutters. The way the German wire was staked in our sector, there was no chance of getting under it.

I was surprised how much care went into the preparation. Most trench raids, all you'd get was a tap on the shoulder the same day. This one was going to be a proper job, it seemed. Frederick was never still. He seemed fired up by it. We were issued with knobkerries, and we weren't to fire a shot until we'd gone through the first bay of the German trench, so as to keep "the element of surprise". Knobkerries, entrenching tools, knives and bayonets would do it, until the "strategic aims of the raid had been accomplished", and then it'd be time for the Mills bombs. That way we wouldn't draw fire until we had to. We'd be safe back in our trenches before Fritz had got our range.

"Mind you," said Blanco, too quiet for anyone else to hear, or so he thought, "by the time they've finished putting down that box barrage, every bastard from here to Balloo's going to know we're on our way."

Sergeant Morris heard that, though all he did was raise his eyebrows. He never said much. He had one of those long, doleful faces, and the cuttingest tongue. He didn't set much store by the plan of attack, you could see that. As for the knobkerries, his expression as he weighed one in his left hand, then swung it, was a thing of wonder. But he didn't say anything beyond "Very much favoured in Ireland as a weapon, I believe," and gave us extra bayonet drill. What he thought of Frederick, I had no idea. He rested his long, speculative gaze on him as he did on everyone.

The farm had a battered bit of an orchard, which might have been pretty in summer. But now, with the rain on it and the yellow-grey sky above, it was nothing much. The rain never stopped. *Send it down, David,* Blanco had yelled up at the sky that morning. Frederick was in the orchard, smoking.

"Why do the men say, *Send it down, David?*" he asked. I had no idea, even though I shouted it out myself when the rain fell in stair rods and we marched and marched under our waterproof capes, if we had them.

"It's for luck," I answered.

He offered me a cigarette from his case. They were Players. We smoked them silently, sheltering the cigarettes in our fists while rain dripped off the branches. The guns were sounding up the line.

"I wish I hadn't let you in for this," said Frederick.

I didn't answer. I'd volunteered, he knew that. I would have explained my idea about how you couldn't get out of your death by trying, but I was too tired. I felt flat, too, in spite of the tension. Nothing was going right, and Frederick hadn't got the knack of making us feel that it would. We weren't quick enough. We'd crawled over our makeshift "no-man's-land", following the tapes laid out for us. We'd captured the "German" trench over and over, but the rate we were going, Sergeant Morris said, Fritz'd have time to paint our portraits as we came over.

"I should think this was a nice place once," said Frederick, looking about.

"I shouldn't think so," I said. "It'd have been full of the Frogs, selling one another watered-down vin blanc and offering their sisters for jig-a-jig tray bong."

"They're only doing that for the duration, my dear BB."

"Roll on, duration."

The wind was from the east. Frederick listened, out of habit, as the firing became sporadic. It was a quiet day, or at least it seemed so from here. And we were here, where the loudest thing was the noise of rain on the few dead leaves that had clung on through winter. You couldn't join up the two things, *there* and *here:* they were so absolutely different. If one was real, then the other couldn't be.

Frederick looked around the orchard with disfavour. That muscle in his cheek was jumping again. "You're right, BB," he said. "It's a damned dismal spot."

"It's not so bad," I said. Suddenly, it was important that Frederick thought that. He seemed far away and sunk in gloom. We couldn't have him leading the raid in that state of mind. As if he caught my thoughts, he came to himself. Briskly, he said, "You ought to get into a sniper section."

"I'm better off as I am."

"Are you? Perhaps you are. You know that poem you were telling me in the garden? The one about the sea? Do you remember any more of it?"

"It's long," I said, although I knew every line.

"Is it? Tell me some of it, then. You don't know how lucky you are, you old blowviator, carrying a library around in your head the way you do."

"You never went near your father's library, if you could help it."

"Yes, but out here— You want different things, I suppose that's what it is. Can you believe that the harbour still looks the same? I try to picture it, but I can't get the colour of the water right. It goes as murky as the slop under the duckboards."

"I don't think about it."

"That's the best way, I suppose. But I can't help thinking of things." He pulls restlessly at a branch and a shower of drops comes down on us. I duck, and he laughs, but it's not a real laugh. His eyes don't change, and they are fixed on me. "Can you tell me those lines again?" he asks.

I know which one he means, and I don't pretend not to understand him.

"*Ah, love*," I say, and I have to stop because the lines are so strong in me. I look down at the wet grass, and then up at Frederick again.

"Ah, love, let us be true
To one another! for the world, which seems
To lie before us like a land of dreams,
So various, so beautiful, so new,
Hath really neither joy, nor love, nor light,
Nor certitude, nor peace, nor help for pain;
And we are here as on a darkling plain
Swept with confused alarms of struggle and flight,
Where ignorant armies clash by night."

248

When I've finished, we are both silent for a while. Then:

"That's us," says Frederick.

I wait. My heart thuds heavily.

"*Ignorant armies clash by night.*"

My whole body goes slack with disappointment. "Yes," I say.

Frederick looks around the orchard. Daylight is seeping away. Another raw dusk, another night. The raid. I need to be with the others. Sometimes it's lonelier just being with one other person than being alone. I'm tired of poems. Suddenly I'm sick of the whole crew of them: Matthew Arnold, Tennyson, Coleridge, Lord Byron, Christina Rossetti, the lot. The trenches of my mind are crammed with poets, squatting in their dugouts, not to be moved. I want Christina Rossetti up on the fire-step. And then I hear Frederick laughing, real laughter this time, warm and amused.

"What are you muttering about now, you old blowviator?"

"Christina Rossetti."

"You looked as if you wanted to shoot somebody. Who the hell's she? Sounds like a spy. Beats me, how you carry them all in your head."

"They were never in France."

"So much the better for them." He looks down at his watch. "I've got to get on. Shall we see each other? Of course we shall."

"We better bleddy well had, seeing as how you're leading this raid. Sir." As soon as I've said it, I wish I hadn't. He takes half a step backwards. I reach out, and get hold of his arm. "You picked the wrong line," I say. "You've got a terrible memory."

He's quite still, his eyes on me. In me, I want to say. I don't think anybody has ever looked into me like that. "You're the one who's got it wrong," he says. "I remember everything."

"Sir! Message from Captain Ferryman!"

We didn't see him coming. A runner all sopped with rain, panting as he crashes through the orchard gate. Young lad. Green.

"I'd best be off," I say. "The boys are in the Cat Fur."

"Have one for me."

I don't like leaving him. It's because of the rain, the dankness of the orchard, the gunfire that never knows when to stop. I half wish that he could come to the Cat Fur with me, but of course it's impossible. As if he knows what I was thinking, and doesn't want me to pity him, he says quickly, "More bumf come up from Battalion HQ. Think yourself lucky you don't have to read it."

I light the fire, mix oatmeal into water and add salt, then cook it carefully so it won't catch. The saucepan is thin, almost worn out. There's no change in the darkness yet, but I can tell that the dawn's coming. Out of habit, I glance down at my wrist to register the exact time. Maybe Felicia's awake. She doesn't sleep well, she said. It's because of waking in the night for Jeannie. And for Frederick too, I know that. You don't get as thin as Felicia's got because of a child. And then all of

250

a sudden I realise that the loneliness in Felicia is the same as the loneliness I saw that day in Frederick. You'd think that the baby would have anchored her, but she's adrift, just as he was. She wants to be with Harry and Frederick, even though she knows it's wrong and she ought not to want it. That's why the baby goes so often to Dolly Quick's.

I come to, and find myself standing stock-still, with Mary Pascoe's wooden spoon in my hand and porridge dropping off it into the fire. The smell is awful. I want to go to Felicia. I want to hold her. Frederick said, "I remember everything." I went away. The runner came but I could have waited. I hear my own voice saying: *The boys are in the Cat Fur*, as if that was what mattered. Then I'm outside the Cat Fur. The windows are steamy with the rain and I can't see in, but I open the door and the fug of heat grease boots smoke vin blanc and voices roaring *Mop it down* swallows me.

Only three minutes have passed. I'll eat my porridge and then scrub out the pot. Empty the latrine bucket, milk the goat, let the hens out into the run. I won't go up to Venton Awen, in case Felicia comes while I'm not here. We can walk up to the farm together, and take the pony.

Move the goat's tether-post, oil the spade that I should have oiled yesterday before I put it away. Sweep out the cottage. By then surely she'll be here.

CHAPTER
EIGHTEEN

And the coming wind did roar more loud,
And the sails did sigh like sedge,
And the rain poured down from one black cloud;
The Moon was at its edge.

As soon as we go into the yard at Venton Awen, the collie bitch runs to me and buffets her head into my leg. Felicia shrinks back, and I remember how dogs scare her, in spite of her talk about wanting to get one. The Dennises never kept any.

"She's all right. You're a soft old thing, aren't you?" I give the collie my hand to fondle with her tongue.

"Do you know her, then?"

"She was out on the coast path the other day, and she followed me home. She's a wanderer, not a guard dog. Here, give her your hand. She won't hurt you." Reluctantly, Felicia yields. I steady her hand, as the collie bitch sniffs but doesn't lick it. "Now she knows you," I say.

There are a couple of other dogs barking at us from the yard, chained up I should say, for they don't run out. The back door opens, and out bounces a red-faced girl in a blue apron. She has a scrubbing brush in her hand and it looks as if she's scrubbed her own face with it before she started on the floors. I don't know her. She looks at me and then at Felicia, and says something in a high, strange voice. I can't make out the words, but Felicia understands.

"She's asking if we want to see Mrs Paddick."

"Ask her if Geoff Paddick's at home."

"Why don't you ask her," says Felicia sharply, but the girl isn't looking at me. She's watching Felicia's face intently, and now I understand. She's trying to read her lips.

"Mr Paddick," says Felicia slowly, distinctly. "Is he at home?" The girl nods several times, very fast, and bounces back into the house. "She's deaf," says Felicia.

"I know."

We glance at each other. Felicia's wearing a shabby dark green riding habit which looks as if it came out of the Ark. Her hair is brushed smooth, and there are no red sparks in it today.

I hope it'll be Geoff who comes out, and not old Mrs Paddick or one of his sisters. They'll be bound to talk of my mother. The girl takes her time, and we look about us, at the well-kept yard, the rowan, the fine square shape of the farmhouse. I think of my mother scrubbing here, as this girl is scrubbing now. I kneel down by the collie, to hide my face in talking to her.

"Good morning, Mrs Fearne," says Geoff Paddick, crossing the yard from the dairy. I straighten myself.

"Felicia," she says, putting out her hand to him, and she smiles.

"How's Jeannie?"

The collie slinks behind me, pressing herself against the back of my knees.

"She's well, thank you."

"My mother wants you to bring her up here again one day, for tea. We've some new kittens."

Felicia smiles again, with a quick downward look. "She'd like that," she murmurs.

"That's settled, then."

He'd like it settled, I don't doubt it. All those Paddicks'd be pleased as Punch. Albert House and ten thousand pounds, maybe more besides. Harry Fearne might have had Felicia first, but that would be a small price to pay. What does Geoff Paddick know? He stayed on the farm, eating bacon and lording it over his sisters. Now he thinks he can put out his hand and pluck what he wants.

"Have you a pony we could hire for the day, Geoff?" I ask him. "For Felicia." He looks at me sharply. He doesn't like the thought of us going together, but equally he'd like to please Felicia.

"You could borrow my sister Judith's mare," he says, directly to Felicia. "You're about the same height. I'll get her saddled up for you."

And about half the weight. The Paddick girls are as square-built as their house. He doesn't want to take my money. That's something, from Geoff Paddick, who hasn't let a brass farthing slip past him since he was old enough to grasp it. He turns and hollers back into the house: "*Judith!*"

When Judith emerges from the dark innards of the house, she's big and raw-faced, her body hidden in a baggy tweed skirt and jacket. Grown into a woman since last I saw her. No, she tells us, the side-saddle's gone. They gave it to the church sale.

"We'd no more use for it. I'll lend you a pair of Anne's breeches, Felicia. You're smaller than her, but with a belt, they'll do." Her eyes size up Felicia quickly, as if she were livestock.

"I can't borrow your clothes," says Felicia.

"Anne won't care." She and Anne were always like twins; they did everything together. "You'd better come inside." Judith's high colour flares, and I see that she is shy of Felicia, while wanting to please her brother.

"We can put her up on Susan," says Geoff, and his sister nods, too quickly and emphatically, so that I guess she doesn't really want Felicia on the mare. And yet she does want to like Felicia. Geoff dominates here, with the heavy Paddick looks that have come out well in him, but not in the girls.

"Judith and Anne wanted to volunteer for a Remount Depot upcountry," says Geoff, with a bit of a laugh, once his sister and Felicia have gone.

"And did they?"

Geoff whistles softly through his teeth, shaking his head. "They're dead nuts on little Jeannie. Want to get a Shetland pony for her to ride."

"And shall you allow it?"

He looks at me, as if surprised. "They do as they like."

We keep on in silence. *Dead nuts on little Jeannie.* The child will be for all of them, until the others come, Geoff's children. His sisters won't marry. I can think all this, and stand apart from it, as if it has nothing to do with me, and yet as soon as Felicia comes back, awkward in Anne's breeches, my heart is hot for her. I could knock Geoff down for even thinking of her.

"Judith's awfully nice," says Felicia, once the brother and sister have gone off to saddle the mare.

"Is she? He's got her well trained, that's for sure."

Geoff Paddick's dad was a hard bugger, too. Felicia doesn't see it. It'd be all soft, until the ring was on her finger. And what's worse is that there'd be plenty who would reckon she'd done well for herself if she got Geoff Paddick, now there are so many girls without men to marry them.

I am glad when we are out of the yard. The morning is bright and sharp, and when we come off the farm track on to the high road the mare's hooves dance a little, as if she too is glad to stretch her legs. The high road unrolls, pale and quiet, although there are men working in the fields. On our right hand the land falls away westward, to the sea. I carry the canvas bag of food and drink that Felicia brought. Felicia reins the mare back to a walk, and I go at her side, like a groom, breathing in the smell of the mare, the open land, the catch of salt. There are violets and primroses along the stone hedges, and campion coming up among them. The mare slows to drop her dung, and Felicia peeps at me. That would have made us laugh, when we were little. I think how harmless the beast is, walking on the white road. A horse will walk anywhere you ask of it, or nearly. But when they smell death they can dig in their hooves.

There's Felicia's left leg, in the clumsy breeches. She rides easily, without thinking about it. Her thin hands gather the reins just as they should. I watch her muscles flex, and then relax. Her knee is just right, against the mare's flank, and her foot sits lightly in the stirrup. She told me once that she was put up on a pony before she was two years old, with the gardener holding the leading rein and taking her round and round.

We walk on as if in a dream, almost without speaking. If a cart passes, we rouse ourselves to call a greeting. The sky is still blue, but it is skeining over with mares' tails, and the sea has a dark, clear rim at its horizon.

"I used to think I could see the rain before it fell," says Felicia.

"How do you mean?"

"I'd screw up my eyes — like this — and I'd see it thickening in the air, sometimes hours before. At least, I thought I could. And we had that piece of seaweed hung up, do you remember? If it turned limp then there was sure to be rain coming."

All rain meant then was the hiss of it on roof and windows; the battering of a gale; the shine of the cobbles early next morning. It meant a heavy canvas sack over my shoulders at work. It meant, if we were lucky, an hour in the potting shed while the gutter chuckled with overflow. If we had mud on our boots we scraped them clean on the door-scraper at the back door, before going into the kitchen for our dinners. On bad days, we took off our boots and went to the table in our stockinged feet.

"I hate the noise of rain," I say.

"It won't fall before tonight," says Felicia. "We'll be back home safe."

We clip on. I've almost forgotten where we're going, and why. I went to Bass Head with Frederick. The day was so beautiful, but it's just as lovely now. Nothing cares a bit that he's dead. He doesn't take up an inch of soil. They ought to have put the graveyards of all the dead over here. They ought to have covered the farms and dug up the furze and foxgloves and had nothing but crosses as far as you could see. Miles and miles of them, going from town to town. Hasty wooden crosses like the ones we made, all leaning different ways from shell-blast. Bodies blown out of their graves.

I lean my head in, against Felicia's leg. The mare doesn't like it: she snorts and tries to dance aside, but Felicia holds her still.

"What are you doing, Daniel?"

But the landscape dances too. Men are rising lazily out of their beds. They stretch their limbs, and the soil falls off them. The uniforms are unmarked. Their faces are round, and tanned with living in the open air. They stare about them. I am afraid that one of them will catch my eye and so I lean my face right into Felicia and the flank of the mare, and I shut my eyes, but they are still there. Puzzled, looking about them. They don't know this place. I want them to go back. I want the earth to cover them. I want them to be blown to bits again if it only stops them coming on.

"Daniel," says Felicia. "Daniel!"

The mare has stopped. I pull myself away from her, and open my eyes. Everything is steady, and empty. There's only a distant cart, pulling slowly uphill.

"It's all right," I say to her. "I came over a bit queer, that's all."

"We can go back if you're not well. It doesn't matter about going to Bass Head."

Of course we can't go back. Felicia doesn't understand.

We leave the mare in a field at Bass Farm, then walk down the track until it narrows to a footpath. I carry the canvas bag, and a rolled-up blanket for us to sit on. It's easy to miss the turn in high summer because then the bracken grows up over it, but now, in March, it's obvious. Once it was a broad way, trodden by dozens of boots every morning and evening, before the mine closed. The tunnels ran out under the seabed. They say the men would stop for their croust and listen to the surge and drag of the tide far above them, but I don't know that it's true. Even with the pumps working day and night, the mine often flooded.

There's the engine-house, half ruined now. Crows fly up as we approach. The walls are thick with ivy.

"Could we go inside?" asks Felicia.

"It's not safe."

There are shafts, lipped with soft grass that quakes when the wind blows, so that you think you could walk on it. Frederick and I crawled on our stomachs, and dropped down stones to hear how they echoed.

259

The path skirts the cliff. We are above the cove, with its quay where the boats came to take off the ore from the mine. The cobbled slipway is as good as ever. How they got the loads down there, I don't know. They had winches, I suppose, I say to Felicia. All kinds of machinery that was taken away for use in other mines when this one closed.

No boats now. Only the tide, sighing its way in under the cliff. The white sand is all hidden. There are caves you can walk into at low tide, but they're covered too. I point out the way down across the rocks. It's a rough way, and not easily discovered until you've been shown. You have the cove to yourself then. If we didn't go down, we'd lie in the sun on the clifftops, while the seabirds wheeled above us, screaming out as the crows cawed in answer. All those cries, going up and up above us.

There's a broad, grassy shelf in the side of the cliff, above the cove. You can walk along it. The path must have gone right round once, but the rock has broken away. The shelf is wide enough for us to sit comfortably, with our backs against rock. Protected by the overhang, the grass is soft and dry, but I lay the blanket down all the same. The sunlight is hazy, but still has some warmth in it. Felicia unpacks the canvas bag, taking out bread, cheese, apples, chocolate and a bottle of cold tea stoppered with a cork. As we eat, a gull floats lazily, just below us, tipping its wings for balance and turning its yellow eye to watch us. A boat noses its way around the headland and we keep as still as still, but it's only a crabber. The sea is so flat we see the wrinkles on it spreading out long after the boat has passed.

"We could have made a fire. Are you cold?"

Felicia shakes her head. "Someone might see the smoke."

"What if they did?"

"I don't want anyone to know we're here. Did you come down here with Frederick, Dan?"

"You know I did."

"I wasn't sure. Did you sit just here?"

"Not just here."

"I'm glad."

"Why?"

"Because sometimes it seems as if whatever you do with me, it's because of Frederick. We don't do anything for its own sake. And because this is the last time, I wanted it not to be like that."

"It's not the last time."

"It has to be. You'll go to London, and I'll be here with Jeannie."

"You'll marry Geoff Paddick, won't you?"

She sits back on her heels and laughs. "You can't really think that."

"It's obvious. His sisters are dead nuts about Jeannie."

"Is that what he said?"

"And they're looking out for a Shetland pony, so she can learn to ride."

Felicia is no longer laughing. "They mean well," she says. "He's a good man. I like him."

I let this pass. "But marriage, Dan — it's got nothing to do with liking someone. I suppose you know that."

I have a faint but certain feeling that Felicia is daring to tell me about her own marriage. Harry Fearne wanted her. Jeannie was born out of that wanting. She must think that I don't know as much as she does; not really. Only in the way that boys and men think they know everything.

"Judith and Anne share a bed. They can't sleep apart," says Felicia. "And then there's old Mrs Paddick in her room. As Dolly Quick says, it'd be a braver woman than her who walked into that." She lifts the tea-bottle, takes a swig, wipes her mouth on her sleeve and smiles at me. "You don't like Dolly, I know that. But she was good to me, when Jeannie was born. I don't know what I'd have done without her. Harry was gone, and the doctor was away up in Truro. You know Jeannie was born three weeks before she was expected? And I was so frightened. You've no idea, Dan. I was sitting on the stairs, crying, and Dolly came back because she'd forgotten something — I can't remember what it was. Maybe it wasn't anything. She was so kind. She knew just what to do, and she got me upstairs and told me it didn't matter if the doctor came or not, we'd be all right. The thing I remember most is that she never took her hat off. I kept seeing that little jet bead on her hatpin. She was so good to me, but when the doctor came he ordered her about as if she knew nothing. His hands were cold when he touched me. When Jeannie was born he picked her up by her feet and shook her like a rabbit, and I couldn't stop him."

"Maybe that's what they always do."

"Do you think so? It seems a funny way of going about it to me. Jeannie screamed and screamed. She was all stretched out, flailing in the air. The doctor even slapped her, and she was only about this big — look!" Felicia holds her hands apart. "As if he were punishing her for being born. When he'd gone, Dolly said, "You pop her in alongside you," and so I had her in with me all night. Poor little thing, she was cold, but after a while she grew warm. Every so often she'd give a shudder, as if she was remembering. I told her nothing like that was ever going to happen to her again. But maybe it was too late, and that's why she's like she is."

I pick up a tiny, glistening pebble and spin it into the air. It goes down and down, catching the light, and vanishes almost without a sound. "Did you tell Harry about how it was?" I ask her. I'm jealous of all those things that have happened to Felicia while I wasn't there.

"I didn't want to write about it in a letter."

She'd have told him, I suppose, when he came home. But he never came home, or knew what happened when his child was born.

"I'm sorry," I say, and I am. My jealousy falls away. Harry Fearne, one of the unlucky buggers who thought they'd begun something, when it was all finishing for them. But that doesn't alter the fact that if he were here, I'd want to push him off the cliff.

The time glides on, and I let it, even though the sun is slipping down the sky, hazier than ever as the cloud gains on it. We ought to go back. The mare will be wanting her stable. The light in the cove is over-clear now, and the wind's rising. Below us, the swell heaves.

"Tide's on the turn."

"Is it?"

"Look at the rocks."

We swam here many times, me and Frederick, when the tide was down. There was only ourselves in the whole bowl of the bay. We shrieked and splashed and then we grew quiet, floating on our backs, letting the cross-current drag us from one side of the bay to the other. When we turned over and floated on our bellies we saw our own shadows on the sand below, quivering so that we looked like strange, forked fish. The sand was rippled up, like corrugated iron.

"Daniel, it's starting to rain."

Sure enough, the sky shakes a few drops out of itself, warning of downpours to come. We get up hastily, pack the bag and roll up the blanket.

"It'll hold off long enough for us to get to the farm. We can shelter there until it passes."

The sky darkens as we hurry up the footpath and then the track. The cows are coming in, jostling into all the space there is. We can't pass them, and have to stand while the herdsman gets them through the gate that leads to the dairy. It's raining hard now. I hold the blanket over Felicia's head, until the cows are through, leaving behind their churn of muck and mud.

When we knock at the kitchen door, a thin middle-aged woman with her hair scragged back opens it. She looks from one of us to the other, as Felicia explains and apologises and asks, all in one smooth breath and a voice no one could refuse. Even so I think the woman will be churlish, but no. She starts to excuse the mess, push things aside, sweep cats off chairs and get us to the table. You wouldn't believe that her raw face could lighten so. I've only ever seen her in the distance before, when Frederick and I dodged round the farm gates, avoiding her. In a minute the big blackened kettle is on the range. All Mrs Thomas's gestures are quick and nervous, as if she's half afraid of herself. But I remember her as a big, solid woman, with sons who put the fear of God into us the day they caught us trying to get milk out of one of their cows.

She doesn't know me. She doesn't even seem to know Felicia, which surprises me. The Fearnes and the Dennises are known all over. I keep quiet and drink my tea, while Felicia talks to her. She lost her son, the younger one. She will just fetch his photograph from the parlour. Here he is, look, in his uniform. The likeness was taken the day before he went off, at Harbin's. It's very like, only a bit solemn, and he was never solemn. His brother was the quiet one, and more so now. They can go a whole evening without a word spoken, him and his father. There are bright spots of colour on Mrs Thomas's cheeks now.

"They don't as much as notice the food that's put in front of them," she says. "These apricots." She points to a box of dried apricots on the table, half covered by a sheet of newspaper. "They were giving these away. Do you like apricot jam?"

"Very much," says Felicia.

"And your husband, I'm sure, if you made it, would be glad of it." She glances at me for confirmation, and I wait for Felicia to explain, but she says nothing beyond "You're always hungry, aren't you, Daniel?"

"That's the way a man ought to be!" exclaims the woman. "But I may as well tip these apricots on to the midden, for all the pleasure they'll give to anyone."

"It is very annoying," sympathises Felicia.

A squall spatters against the windows, and the woman laughs a high, nervy laugh and says, "I should think you'd better stay here tonight."

"Oh no, we couldn't do that. Your husband and your other son will be coming in shortly."

"They've gone to market. They'll stay out as late as they like, on market night. Maybe they won't come home at all," she says astonishingly, her eyes bright and wild. I wonder if she's all there.

"We'll go on, as soon as the rain stops," says Felicia. "Our mare is in one of your fields, you know."

"A horse won't die of a drop of rain. She can be brought in and stabled presently. I'll send Sammy down. You'd do much better to stop here."

She wants us here, I see that. She's on fire with the idea of it. Now I see that all the sewing on the table is for baby clothes. Maybe her son is married, and has a child coming. Felicia picks up a little vest, and admires the stitching on it.

"Is it for your grandchild?"

"Oh no! Oh no! Nothing like that." The woman folds and smooths the cloth with anxious fingers. Felicia's right, it is beautiful work. She must sit here stitching and stitching.

"I'm worried about Jeannie," says Felicia quietly, when the woman gets up to attend to a pot that's simmering on the range.

"She'll be all right. You said Dolly Quick often has her overnight."

"She does, but — they won't know where I am. They'll think something's happened to me."

"They won't think that. Listen to that rain: she'll know you had to take shelter."

She wants to believe me. My head is throbbing. The woman believes that we are man and wife. If we stay here, she'll put us into a room together. And Felicia's said nothing to contradict her.

CHAPTER
NINETEEN

The many men, so beautiful!
And they all dead did lie:
And a thousand thousand slimy things
Lived on; and so did I.

"Do you think that this was her son's room?" Felicia
puts the candle down on the washstand.

I look around. It's a narrow bedroom, very clean.
The walls are freshly distempered. "I shouldn't think
so. She'd leave his room as it was."

"I don't know." Felicia moves nervously around the
room. There's an iron bed, a rag rug, a washstand with
jug and ewer. A chamber pot under the bed. On the
wall there's an embroidered text:

And God saw every thing that He had made
And behold, it was very good.

"He wasn't looking very hard," I say.

Felicia is at the window, staring out at the darkness
and driving rain.

"We can't go back in this," I say.

"I know we can't."

"She wanted us to stay."

"Poor woman, she's half mad with loneliness."

"Maybe she'll keep us here."

"Don't say that."

"We can leave as soon as it's light. She's all right; at any rate, she's harmless enough. She was glad of the money."

The floor creaks as we move. We're up two flights of stairs, under the eaves, tucked away. That chamber pot. I push it a little farther under the bed with my foot. We shan't need it, I hope. We went out to the privy in turn, in spite of the rain, shielding the candle. The flame gulped and sizzled when a spot of rain fell on it, but didn't go out.

"Well," says Felicia briskly, "we'd better get ready." She pours water from the jug, splashes her face and hands, dries herself and then sits on the bed to unlace her boots. She arranges them tidily, clambers into bed in Anne Paddick's breeches and pulls the covers up to her chin. She even shuts her eyes tight, like a child pretending to be asleep. I nearly laugh out loud. Well, if that's the game . . . And then I think of what she said about Jeannie's birth. Felicia knows everything that a woman has to know.

I never went with the French tarts. I said I didn't want to catch a dose. I wasn't the only one. I thought of it more than I ought to have done. They used to light up the red lamp and there'd be so many shoving to get in that it was easy to slip aside. That red lamp. It was all organised for you. I knew I ought to want it, but I didn't. There were others who didn't as well, strong Bible Christians or married men with scruples. Some of them, like me, didn't give their reasons. Every night there were the tales afterwards, going on and on, but you could let them wash over you without listening.

I take off my own boots, and swill my face and hands as Felicia has done, before creaking round to the other side of the bed. The springs groan even more loudly than the floorboards. There we are, side by side, on our backs like effigies. I can hear Felicia breathing. That woman thought we were man and wife.

The rain spatters. It could have been like that, in another world. How Mr Dennis would have hated it. I don't know what Frederick would have thought. There's Felicia, breathing. No, it could never have happened.

This is a cushy billet all right. Out of the wind and rain and mud. Nothing to think of until morning, except sleep. But I can't stop my heart banging away as if morning's here already. Now I listen, I can hear the sound of the waves thudding in under the cliffs. It never stops. Like gunfire. Even in England you could hear it, they said. If you were in the southern parts, looking out towards France, you could hear the guns.

All at once I know he's going to come. The dead aren't tied to one place. He's as fearful as I am, more maybe. He knows what's coming to him, and he can't get away from it. Something's gone wrong. Things ought to stop, once they're finished, but this won't stop. They say the war's over, but they're wrong. It went too deep for that. It opened up a crack in time, a crater maybe. Once you fall into it, you can't get out again. The mud is too deep and it holds you. I've left him there. He thought I was coming back, and I never did.

270

"I'm sorry," I say, "I didn't mean it." I'm shaking all over and the bed is creaking too, banging off its springs. Felicia's hands are on me, touching my face, trying to wake me up, but I'm already wide awake and it still goes on. "I'm sorry, Frederick. I'm so sorry." I keep on saying it but he can't hear me, because there's nothing of him left. Now I want him to come. I must speak to him. I want him here, all clagged with mud, even if we both have to die for it.

"Frederick!" I say, and I'm bolt upright with my arms out, feeling for him. "Frederick!"

She has hold of me. She grips me and clings to me, saying my name. "It's all right, Daniel. I'm here. It's all right. It was a bad dream. I'm here."

She gets me down on the bed again and lies alongside me, holding me. I burrow my face into her neck and hair, hiding myself. Her hands are on the back of my neck, holding me in.

After a long time, I raise my head from her hair. She eases me into the softness of her. I can feel her bubble of laughter as she says, "You were making a terrible noise. We'll have Mrs Thomas up here if we're not careful." I am so light and empty that I could float away. "He isn't here, you know," she continues. "You think he is, but he isn't. He's gone. He's quite safe." Her words sink into me. I can feel her breath, coming and going. "We're alive, and he's not. We can't get away from that."

"How do you know?"

"I just do."

"It wasn't like I said in the letter."

I feel the deep, caught breath in her.

"I know. It's what they tell people, isn't it, to make them feel better? Everyone had a letter like that one we had. You can tell me the truth if you want."

"I was trying to get help for him."

Her hands grip into me. I don't think she knows how hard. "I know you were."

"But maybe I wasn't. Maybe I only told myself that was what I was doing. I ought to have stayed with him."

There, it's said. The words don't explode, they fall into silence like any other words. *I should have stayed with you.* You know that, just as much as I do. That's why you keep coming back. You can't find peace, any more than I can. We ought to have been together. I'd have been gone, like you, inside a second. With you. I've thought about it so much: how can a man be there, entire, one second, and the next there is nothing of him? It ought not to be possible. Even if you've seen it you can't believe it. It's the filthiest conjuring trick you can think of.

I can't live with it. I'm still trapped in it, going round and round. I never believed the stuff they taught us about hell, the burning and the imps running around with pitchforks. All that ran straight off me. But one year there was a Revival with a preacher in a field on the edge of the town. I didn't mean to go. We weren't even chapel. I didn't mean to listen, and as long as he was roaring out, I didn't. But then he dropped his voice and made it thrilling and silky, and began to talk to us about what hell really was. *You've all had a nightmare,* he said, *and you've struggled out of sleep and you've nearly cried with thankfulness that it was only a nightmare. There's your bed, and the chair beside it with your clothes on it. Soon you'll see dawn coming through the window. It was only a nightmare, and it's over. But in hell that nightmare goes on and on. You never wake up from it. Sometimes you think you're going to, but you never, ever do.*

It was about the simplest sermon I ever heard, and I never forgot it.

You reach out to touch all the familiar things: the blanket, the candle-holder on a box by the bed. But there's nothing there. No box, no blanket. Just thick emptiness that crowds into your lungs and sucks your breath out of you. You slap about with your hands, trying to find something to hold on to, but there's nothing. I left Frederick lying there and when I came back there was nothing. How can I tell Felicia that? When we came back from France the ship was overladen. She lay low in the water but it didn't matter. There was no wind, and the dirty grey sea was calm. We slunk over the Channel, going slow. Someone raised a cheer when we saw the cliffs. We'd laughed on our way out for the first time, and mucked about with orange peel. There wasn't any of that now.

I turn so that my face is in Felicia's hair. It smells of her, her body. And something else, a familiar scent that catches at me. I can't make out what it is. I breathe again, tasting the Felicia smell and then something else. Rosemary. That's why I knew it. My mother always steeped rosemary in a jug of hot water, and used it to rinse her hair. Felicia must do the same. I used to lie in bed and watch my mother, when I was little. She let me sleep in with her then. She would lean over the washstand, lift the jug, and pour a long stream of water over her bent head. Her hair would be swept forward, so that the water flowed and parted over her neck. I see, as clearly as I see the water flowing, that I should have died with Frederick.

"I ought to have stayed with him."

"No," says Felicia.

"You don't know how it was."

Water runs down the nape of a white neck. Frederick says: *I remember everything.*

"He'd want you to be alive," says Felicia. I feel the words go past my ear on her breath. I want so much to believe them, and yet inside me there's the part that's gone, seared, done for. I wish her words could touch that place.

"Move your head a little: that's right," she says. "Rest there." She takes a sharp, sighing breath. I feel her hesitation. "You think I don't understand. Perhaps I don't. Perhaps I can't. But all the same, we're alike. We don't want anyone else, now that they've gone."

"You've got Jeannie."

"That's different."

"It's enough," I say. I'm not envious. I'm glad for Felicia, that she has something to hold her.

I feel a shiver go through her.

"Think of that woman downstairs," she says, "making all those baby clothes, when there isn't going to be a baby."

"You should think of something else."

"What?"

I lie still, and let my mind float. "The cove," I say. "Us swimming there. I remember one day a seal came right up to Frederick. They're big creatures, up close. Powerful, too. They're in their element, and you're not. But he was only playful, wanting us to swim with him. I suppose we must have stayed in the water too long. We could barely put on our clothes by the time we came out, we were so cold. I can see Frederick now, hopping about to get warm. The seal was still there, lolloping in the shallows. He was waiting for us to come back in and play."

"I can just see him," says Felicia.

I can too. The whiskers and the glisten of him as he turns on the rise of a wave. But then, as quick as it has come to me, the water changes. I can't see through it any more. The waves slow to a crawl, thick as mud. It's a dark tide, eating up the sand, full of things that creep and struggle and clag. They push up through the slime and then they sink again and all the time the mud is moving, swallowing— If it touches me, I'm done for.

"Felicia!"

"What's wrong?"

I can't do more than whisper it. "*Hold me.*"

"I've got you. It's all right, Daniel, I've got you."

"I can't feel you."

"Don't be frightened. I've got you."

After a while I begin to feel her. She's hurting me with her grip. I'd never have thought her arms would have so much strength in them. I draw myself away from her, roll on my back and feel on the floor beside the bed for my packet of Woodbines. I strike a match, light a cigarette and draw in the smoke. The red tip glows in the darkness.

"Could you give me one?"

"No, Felicia, you'd never smoke a Woodbine."

"I could."

"It'd make you sick." She doesn't insist. I smoke. The red tip dims and brightens. "I don't know what to do. I'm not safe in my mind."

She doesn't say anything. She raises her hand, takes my cigarette delicately between her fingers and lifts it to her own lips. She puffs in a bit of smoke, like an expert, and blows it away.

"I used to steal Frederick's cigarettes, sometimes. You never knew that, did you?"

"No."

"I'll look after you, Dan."

She gives me back my cigarette. I finish smoking, get up, and throw the dog-end out of the window. It is cold and clear now. All the rain has been swept away. Above the barns there are stars knit across the sky. From behind me, Felicia says, "Maybe he's still there."

"Who?"

"The seal, down at the cove. They can live for thirty years, you know. We might see him, one day." She's silent for a while, and I follow her breathing until it breaks with another sigh. "I'm so tired, Daniel. Let's try to sleep."

"I don't think I can."

"Yes, you will. Come back to bed."

276

I lie down beside her, and close my eyes. Her fingers stroke my face, until I feel sleep coming at me like a wave out of a long smooth swell. Maybe she is a witch, as Frederick said. *My blessed Felicia*. As I go under I wish we could stay here for ever, not moving forward or backwards. Just the rainswept sky outside, the bed here, and never morning.

CHAPTER
TWENTY

Confusion is apt to occur in any assault.

Sergeant Morris pours out the rum ration religiously while the box barrage blows our ears off. One by one we take the shell protector and toss back the rum. Reach out, tip back, hand back again. Everyone does it. We're all blacked up and in our balaclavas. The noise of the barrage rips through every fibre of us.

One minute Sergeant Morris's hand, as steady as you like. The next we're on our bellies in the mud, crawling forward. I'd lost faith in the raid before we were ten yards beyond our wire. You might say that's hindsight, but it wasn't. Our wire had a way cut through it, and we'd brought our own wire-cutters for the German wire, not trusting to what we were told would have happened. Ahead I saw the outline that I knew was Frederick. He was counting the men through.

No-man's-land was as big as Africa, once you were in it. We knew that it was two hundred and fifty yards wide here, and how we had to cross it. We knew where the biggest shell-holes were. There'd be water in the bottom, but there was no deep, drowning mud in our sector. The ground heaved and rippled ahead of me. It was men moving, humping their way forward on their bellies. Frederick was in front, I do know that. Sergeant Morris was beside me, coming up to Coops, who was ahead of me on my left. Coops was one of the grenadiers. Sergeant Morris said something into his ear. Coops wriggled sideways and I did too, because I was meant to be following him. Sergeant Morris fell back. After the barrage it was so quiet my ears rang with it. According to the plan we'd crawl four hundred yards parallel to the German wire, to where the barrage ought to have cut it. There'd be a listening post there, forward of our front line, and we'd get a signal.

I'm not telling this right.

Start again. What went wrong, I learned afterwards, was our intelligence. That is, Fritz wasn't quietly waiting for our trench raid. There was no one in the trench we'd targeted. We'd been doing too many trench raids, signalled by too many box barrages, and they were sick of being brained by knobkerries, blown up by Mills bombs or taken prisoner. They wanted to put a stop to it, for a while anyway. At the first sign of our box barrage, the occupants of the nearest German trench fell back through their communications trenches.

We came on. This was the plan that had been taped out for us on the training ground. The earth clung to us, stinking of cordite and gas.

The flare went up just as we were going through the German wire. I remember being relieved that our barrage had cut it, more or less. Maybe the raid was going to be all right. I thought that, just as the flash came and we were sheathed in its light. They couldn't have caught us at a better place, crawling through the wire. All they had to do was get the range, which they quickly did. I threw myself down but the earth kicked under me like a horse, trying to throw me off. When I came to I was rolled up in a ball, choking out grit. I spat and ground my eyes with my fists because the earth had blown into them. I thought I'd been thrown a hundred yards. I didn't even know that it was a German shell.

It was Sergeant Morris who told me all this, the next day, or maybe it was the day after. His mouth sawed in his long face as he talked about machine-gun fire, and Minnies. He wanted it to sound as if what had happened was made from pieces that he could fit together, not the chaos it had been. My hearing was still bad. I watched him but I didn't say much. I was afraid of him. I ought to have been glad to see him, but I couldn't stand it. All he had was a minor wound to his right thumb.

The only thing that went wrong, from Fritz's point of view, was that our answering artillery fire did succeed in pinning them down, and so they couldn't counter-attack. It didn't matter. They knew that if any of us were still alive, they could mop us up.

I think that's what happened, but I can't be sure. The flare went up and there was all that light where there should have been darkness. I unrolled myself but I still didn't know what was happening. I swayed there on hands and knees, like a dog that doesn't know which way to go, looking for where Frederick had been. I was meant to be following Coops, but he'd disappeared.

The earth under my hands felt like plough. I was in my own world with no one to say what was happening. I didn't dare crawl any more: I went on like a worm, while the air was eaten up by the sound of crackling, like a furze fire above my head spurting and bursting out flame.

When I found Frederick it was his foot I felt first. It was a boot: his left boot on his uninjured leg. I patted it all over, not knowing what it was. Then I felt his leg and I moved up him, patting every inch, not sure if it was a dead man or a living one. He was lying on his stomach with his face turned to the side, or else he'd have choked. I crawled up alongside him, patting and whimpering, like a dog, feeling him all over to find out where he was hurt. There was a warm wet mess on his right leg. I could feel that blood was coming out of it, but it wasn't the fast pumping that kills a man in minutes. The mess was warm with blood but his hands were icy cold. I lay down and held him close, as close as I could. By then I knew it was him. I had to keep him low and get him into shelter. I was saying his name over and over and cursing but he didn't answer. Even so I was sure he was alive, and sure enough, when I tried to turn him a groan came out of him, right down in his belly where the sound will come even from an unconscious man.

Another flare went up and I lay as still as death, but I'd seen a crater only about ten feet away to my left, on lower ground. That was where we had to go. Suddenly I understood that the crackling of furze above my head was machine-gun fire. I had to get him to the lower ground, then I could get him down into the shell-hole.

It's dawn now. I look at my watch: six o'clock. The household will be up. I ease myself out of the bed, as silently as I can, go to the window and pull back the curtain, just a little. I don't want to wake Felicia before time. The yard is hidden by the bulge of the wall, but I hear the cattle lowing. A dog barks, and a churn clangs. Grey light clings to everything like mist. We've left the window open a little, and I catch the warm reek of the cows. The men will do the early work, then they'll come in for their breakfast. We'll wait until they've finished. I don't want them fastening their eyes on Felicia, and speculating about her.

I go back to the bed. Felicia sleeps, with her hair spread over the pillow. There's a glaze of dried spit at the side of her mouth. Her lips are parted, showing the edges of her top teeth. I see Frederick in her, and then she stirs under my gaze. Her face changes, wakes, and Frederick disappears. She opens her eyes and sees me watching her. I think she'll be confused, or even shocked, but she isn't. She seems to have held in her mind everything that's happened, even while she was asleep.

"There you are," she says, and she smiles at me.

CHAPTER
TWENTY-ONE

The other was a softer voice,
As soft as honey-dew:
Quoth he, "The man hath penance done,
And penance more will do."

Felicia doesn't come back to Venton Awen with me. We part on the high road, and I lead the mare down to the farm, to no very warm welcome from Geoff Paddick. I explain that we were caught by the rainstorm, and had to shelter. We sheltered until the worst of the weather passed, and by then it was very late. I took Felicia straight home, and kept the mare with me overnight rather than disturb them at Venton Awen. This is the story that Felicia and I have agreed. As long as Dolly Quick didn't wait up for her at Albert House, then no one will know that Felicia didn't slip in late at night, and sleep at home. I don't think Dolly will have gone up to the house, because she wouldn't have wanted to leave the baby. She'll have stayed at the cottage, waiting for Felicia, worrying, no doubt, but finding a good reason for her absence in the rain sluicing down and the rising wind. She believes I'm some kind of devil anyway, sent to lead Felicia on to the primrose way. It's me she'll blame.

Felicia is at home now. There's been no harm done. She trusted me enough to let me sleep beside her.

Something's over, but I don't yet know what it is. We synchronised our watches, the night of the raid, according to the time given by Frederick. I couldn't get beyond that time. Maybe now, time's been given back to me: my time, I mean. I don't know what to do with it yet. I'll have to work at it, like a blind man trying to put sight into his fingers.

After the wildness of the night, the day is still. The grey sky has thinned into blue, although the sea still heaves and surges, breaking white around the lighthouse. I've told Felicia that I will close up the cottage today, go over to Simonstown and sleep there, then catch the early train to London. She'll send Josh up later, to take the goat and chickens to Venton Awen. She'll persuade Geoff Paddick to give a good price for them.

I've agreed to take a hundred pounds from Felicia. Enough to travel to London, and live there until I can find work. She was as pleased as she was the day we let her into the wigwam with us. Felicia says she'll go to the bank this morning, as soon as it opens, and she'll come up later with the money. I've never seen a hundred pounds together in one place. I wonder if it'll be gold, or paper money.

The breeze floats around me, as if to say: Look how gentle I am. How can you think that I ever made a storm? But I don't believe a word of it. I can hear the sea pounding in under the cliffs.

Even though I'm leaving, I take my hoe and go up to the vegetable garden. Weeds are pushing up already, with the mild weather. The earth is soft with rain, and easy to hoe. I bend my back to it and work steadily. Sparrows come out of the furze in a cloud and peck over the soil. I have the feeling I get sometimes when I'm working, as if I'm balanced on the rim of the earth and can feel it turning under me. I know I'm not going to eat these crops and yet I still don't believe it. I thought I'd never go to London again. I thought that was all over. Felicia says she'll come. She'll take rooms for herself and Jeannie, and spend a week or two, once I'm settled. There's so much she wants to see.

There we differ. There's almost nothing I want to see, except these fields. Even then, it's not a warm feeling. I'm like the boy in the story, who had a splinter of ice in his heart. Felicia loved that story. She thought of herself as Gerda, going to the rescue of her brother Kay, pitting herself against the Snow Queen. I read all those coloured fairy-tale books Felicia had. I read anything.

I straighten my back, and turn. There's the lighthouse, and a line of white farther out, where the swell hits the reef. The grey roofs of the town. I haven't even asked who's living in our cottage now. I drop my hoe, and tread along the strip of turf I've left between the squares of my vegetable plots. I go up to the farthest part of Mary Pascoe's land, where she lies. The bright green ground betrays her. Maybe I should plant something here. A rose, maybe, a yellow one like my mother's. The granite boulder I rolled to her grave to mark it looks like an accident. I can't imagine what it's like, to be inside the earth as she is. We only talked about Blighty ones, not the dread of death that

285

jabbered inside our living bodies. But death came to her slow. I should think that if death seeds itself inside a person bit by bit over the years, it grows more familiar.

I remember that there's something I never did for her. I go back to my turned earth, with my eyes searching the ground for the finest patch. I stoop, and pick up a handful of soil, then crumble it even finer with my fingers. I ought to have cast it into the grave, but it's not too late. Maybe there are some seeds in the earth too, and they'll sprout into flowers. I tread back up to the grave, and sprinkle the earth on it.

Although the breeze is slight, the noise of the sea surges up in it. And behind the noise of the sea there are cries, like children playing. I brush my hands off. I'll finish the hoeing.

As I walk down the field, a movement catches my eye. Far away, on the coast path that runs up from the town, there are specks moving. I shade my eyes. I count five, ten, twenty of them. There must be a wreck, I tell myself, and they are going out to the cliffs to watch the lifeboat. That's the only reason for such a stream of people. But I know that there's no wreck. The sea is bare.

I have my hoe in my hand, clenched tight. They are coming up the coast path, disappearing into the dips of the land, and then suddenly they're much closer as the path rises. Soon they'll be at the point where the path to Mary Pascoe's cottage separates from the main path, and runs left between walls of furze.

I plunge my hoe into the earth. At the top of my land there is a broken-down wall, with a bramble entanglement over it. I've no wire-cutters but I can get through. I stand still, watching for them to come to the turn. I don't think they can see me yet, although I can see them. The doctor with his hat: no, he's not there. He's too old and fat to be in the advance party. There are men in uniform: well, of course. What else do you expect? They surge and swarm. Now the first ones are coming to the turn, and the others push and shove in behind them. If they go ahead, I'll still see them. If they disappear—

They are gone. I leap to the wall, and am on it and over it as stripes of blood spring out on my hands. The brambles pull at me to drag me down but I don't let them. I raise my boots high and trample them, kicking, wading, shoving myself forward through the stench of bracken. I'm making for the field path that runs off the downs to the sea. I duck into the dense mass of stalks and thorns. They tear me but I don't flinch. I'm on my belly now, wriggling through. Blood runs down my face into my mouth and I lick it away and shake my head to clear my eyes.

A narrow snaking path runs between the roots. I'm not sure if it's the right one but it's going downhill and I decide to risk it. Still crouching low, I run with fire in my back. But the cover is falling away now, to my hips, to my thighs, to my knees. I am exposed. I glance back and see that they have come to the top of the wall and are plunging after me. A cry rises behind me. They are baying as they pour over the wall and I know that I can't hide now, I must run. I pump my legs high so my feet won't catch in the roots and my boots pound the path. I am upright now, visible for miles. I run with my blood thundering in my head. My feet find their way blindly. The path won't run straight but I daren't leave it for fear of being tangled and caught. I run on, jinking stones, sending up the whirr and shriek of a pheasant. Even then I think: If I had my gun, I could have got him.

They are no nearer. I'm losing them. I'll outrun them and double back like a hare to my hiding place until dark, and then I'll walk over the moors and downs all the way to Simonstown. Or no. They'll be watching the station. I glance behind me again. They have fallen back for sure. But my eye catches another movement and I see that they're peeling away, left and right, to cut me off. They will block the coast path in both directions, and chase me down to where they can catch me. Whichever way I go, they'll be there. It's the advantage of numbers, I think to myself, and I laugh, or I would laugh, if I had breath, remembering Sergeant Morris and the German trench we were to walk into, cool as cucumbers.

If they'd taped out the ground, I couldn't know it better. Left here, behind this boulder. I stop, and peer round the side. They have stopped too, and are lagging, faltering at the loss of me. I might dig myself in here. But no. They'll surround me, and then they'll move forward, beating the ground, until they're so close they can join hands and have me.

They'll shut me up in a hole in Bodmin. I thought of hanging as if it was stepping free into the air, but it's a man in a dark hole dropped into a darker one. They'll

288

put quicklime on me and bury me in the prison yard. I shall never get out. A flash of panic goes over me, brighter than a flare. It sears me through but it lights up the ground I've got to cover.

I push away the boulder. Breath burns in my chest as I run on and I hear the cry come up behind me, ragged at first and then strengthening as it's taken up from all sides. They've occupied the paths, but ahead of me the sea shines. All at once confidence floods into me. I am sure that I can outrun them this time. I'm not a child now. I'll do what they don't expect: I'll double this way, and race back for the town. I know a hundred places to hide there. I reach wet granite where the stream runs down, and splash into the water, thinking to hide my traces. The furze grows high again and I duck down, going lightly, willing my back not to show above the furze. But again it tricks me, thinning out and showing me to them. I smell myself, the stink of fear that's drawing them.

They show baldly now. A party behind me, coming on, six or seven making inwards on my left, the coast path blocked to my right. I know them all. Mark Relubbus, the Sennen cousins. There's Quicky, with the rest of them, come up from the lodge. There's Dolly Quick, picking up her skirts and racing in the rear. Who'd have thought the old woman would have so much speed in her? Geoff Paddick is pounding down from Venton Awen, and his sisters in their breeches. Even Enoch's come out of his hole, with his tangled hair flapping in the breeze. Wherever I look, there they are.

I can't hide, so I go higher, up to the steep edge of the rock-strewn slope that slants seawards. I look towards the town. It's too far away, and there's no cover anywhere.

I can still outrun them. I push off from the rock and hurl myself down the path. I'm in no-man's-land, ahead of them all. They come in from the left and from the right but the path shines grey ahead of me. Now I'm out of the furze and on to close-bitten turf that bounces under my heels and makes me go faster. Boulders rise up to block my way but I swerve past them. It's steep now and I'm going down so fast that I am almost flying. Behind me the noise rises to a roar but the breeze carries it away. They won't get me now. I look up and ahead of me there's the coast path and beyond it the lip of turf. My feet touch the path and drag me to a stop. I can't go forward. The cliff edge stands in my way. Far below I hear the sea boiling. I look behind, and see them still coming. I look to my left and to my right, and they are closing in like cats from both directions. Mark and Tony Relubbus, the Sennen boys, Andrew Sennen lagging back, his sister screeching insults into the wind. Two policemen in greatcoats and helmets. There's the doctor's hat, bobbing down the furze. Dolly Quick and Ellen Tehidy. I even think I see Mr Dennis, dodging for a better viewpoint, but it can't be him. I see all their faces within a couple of seconds, as bright as if the flare had lit them. I am trapped. They've got me.

"You old blowviator," says a voice in my ear. I spin round. I can't believe I didn't see him before. There he is, standing on the edge of the cliff, easily balancing. We always dared each other to stand as close to the edge as we could. He's winning this time.

"Frederick!"

He's not in uniform. Of course he wouldn't be, not back here. The war's over. He's wearing a dark blue jersey, and there's not a speck of mud on him. He looks just as he always did.

"Come on," he says, and he stretches out his hand to me. I can't quite reach it. I go forward, one step and then another. Behind me I hear a groan of disappointment. They don't like it that Frederick's helping me. They want me hanging on the wire. But the sun's shining, the same old sunlight as ever. It shines on Frederick's hair and his clean skin, and on the wild sea behind him. I still hesitate. I'm not sure that I can reach him. He seems to understand this without my saying anything, because he says, "Come on, I'll give you a hand," and suddenly he is very close. I breathe his skin and his hair. He holds out his hand to me, and this time I take it easily. It's warm now. "That was a hell of a stunt, BB," he says, and we step out together.

Acknowledgements

The epigraphs to Chapters 1 to 17 and 20 are drawn from material produced by the Army Printing and Stationery Services during the period of the First World War, including *Notes for Infantry Officers on Trench Warfare*, March 1916, and *Notes on Minor Enterprises*, March 1916. *Notes on Minor Enterprises* is reproduced in a volume of First World War pamphlets and publications, *An Officer's Manual of the Western Front 1914–1918*, edited by Dr Stephen Bull.

I have also drawn on *Hand Grenades: A Handbook on Rifle and Hand Grenades*, compiled and illustrated by Major Graham M. Ainslie, 1917.

Other epigraphs are from *The Rime of the Ancient Mariner* by Samuel Taylor Coleridge.

The poem extracts, in order of appearance, are taken from:

The Rime of the Ancient Mariner, by Samuel Taylor Coleridge

"The West Country Damosel's Complaint", Anon., traditional (*When will you marry me, William . . .*)

"Invictus", by William Ernest Henley (*Out of the night that covers me, / Black as the Pit from pole to pole . . .*)

"When We Two Parted", by Lord George Gordon

Byron

"Peace", by Henry Vaughan (*My soul, there is a country / Far beyond the stars . . .*)

"The Destruction of Sennacherib", by Lord George Gordon Byron (*The Assyrian came down like the wolf on the fold . . .*)

"Dover Beach", by Matthew Arnold (*The sea is calm tonight . . .*)

"There Was an Old Man Called Michael Finnegan", Anon., traditional

Also available in ISIS Large Print:

The Greatcoat

Helen Dunmore

In 1945, newlywed Isabel Carey arrives in a Yorkshire town with her husband Philip. One cold winter night, Isabel finds an old RAF greatcoat in the back of a cupboard that she uses to keep warm. Once wrapped in the coat she is beset by dreams. And not long afterwards, while her husband is out, she is startled to hear a knock at her window, and to meet for the first time the intense gaze of a young Air Force pilot, staring in at her from outside.

His name is Alec, and his powerfully haunting presence both disturbs and excites Isabel. Her initial alarm soon fades, and they begin a delicious affair. But nothing could have prepared her for the truth about Alec's life, nor the impact it will have on her own marriage . . .

ISBN 978-0-7531-9060-9 (hb)
ISBN 978-0-7531-9061-6 (pb)

The Betrayal

Helen Dunmore

Leningrad in 1952: a city recovering from war, where Andrei, a young hospital doctor and Anna, a nursery school teacher, are forging a life together. Summers at the dacha, preparations for the hospital ball, work and the care of 16-year-old Kolya fill their minds. They try hard to avoid coming to the attention of the authorities, but even so their private happiness is precarious. Stalin is still in power, and the Ministry for State Security has new targets in its sights. When Andrei has to treat the seriously ill child of a senior secret police officer, Volkov, he finds himself and his family caught in an impossible game of life and death — for in a land ruled by whispers and watchfulness, betrayal can come from those closest to you.

ISBN 978-0-7531-8734-0 (hb)
ISBN 978-0-7531-8735-7 (pb)

Counting the Stars

Helen Dunmore

Living at the heart of sophisticated, brittle and brutal Roman society at the time of Pompey, Crassus and Julius Caesar, Catullus is obsessed with Clodia, the Lesbia of his most precious poems. He is jealous of her husband, of her maid, even of her pet sparrow. And Clodia? Catullus is "her dear poet", but possibly not her only interest . . .

Their Rome is a place of extremes. Tenants are packed into ramshackle apartment blocks while palatial villas house the magnificence of the families who control the city. Armed street gangs clash in struggles for political power. Slaves are the eyes and ears of everything that goes on. Civilisation and violence are equals, murder is the easy option and poison is the weapon of choice.

Catullus' relationship with Clodia is one of the most intense, passionate, tormented and candid in history. In love and in hate, their story exposes the beauty and terrors of Roman life in the late Republic.

ISBN 978-0-7531-8184-3 (hb)
ISBN 978-0-7531-8185-0 (pb)

Mourning Ruby

Helen Dunmore

Mourning Ruby is Helen Dunmore's most ambitious novel to date, hugely moving and strongly plotted.

More than 30 years ago, a mother laid her newborn baby in a shoebox and left it by the bins in the backyard of an Italian restaurant. Now the baby, Rebecca, is a mother herself and she and her husband Adam are about to experience the greatest tragedy that parents can face.

Like a Russian doll, this is a novel of interlocking stories, each one opening to reveal another. It tells not only the story of the loss of a child and its effect on three people, but an account of a young girl's life in a brothel during WWI, the magical story of a circus acrobat, and the history of Stalin's first wife and her mysterious fate.

ISBN 978-0-7531-7049-6 (hb)
ISBN 978-0-7531-7050-2 (pb)